If Not For This

If Not For This

a novel

Pete Fromm

ॐ   ॐ

🐓 RED HEN PRESS | *Pasadena, CA*

Book design and layout by Nicholas Smith

Library of Congress Cataloging-in-Publication Data
Fromm, Pete, 1958–
  If not for this : a novel / by Pete Fromm.—First edition.
    pages cm
  ISBN 978-1-59709-538-9 (tradepaper : alk. paper)
I. Title.
  PS3556.R5942I43 2014
  813'.54—dc23
                    2014007671

The National Endowment for the Arts, the Los Angeles County Arts Commission, the Los Angeles Department of Cultural Affairs, the Pasadena Arts & Culture Commission and the City of Pasadena Cultural Affairs Division, and Sony Pictures Entertainment, partially support Red Hen Press.

First Edition
Published by Red Hen Press
www.redhen.org

ACKNOWLEDGMENTS

Chapters in this novel were previously published in the following magazines:

Big Sky Journal, "Slap"; *The Idaho Review*, "Touron"; *Montana Quarterly*, "Morning After," "The Net"; *Narrative*, "Peas," "Bluff"; and *Whitefish Review*, "Trying."

Many thanks to their editors.

For early readings of some of these stories, I would like to thank my friend Jack Driscoll. For offering courageous readings of their own, giving me glimpses into the world of MS, both Tobi Cogswell and Kara Haugen, and for sharing his expertise, Doctor Arthur Ginsberg. For gifts more oblique, I'd like to thank Dorianne Laux and Joe Millar for their poetry and friendship. And for her earliest and latest and always sharp-eyed readings, the one and only Carly Zeller. I'd also like to thank Kate Gale, for believing in Maddy from the very first time they met.

For Nolan and Aidan

Everything, Always

ॐ ॐ

TABLE OF CONTENTS

So, my love, do you believe that we
Might last a thousand years or more
If not for this
Our flesh and blood
It ties you and me right up . . .
Tie me down

Celebrate we will
'cause life is short but sweet for certain
We climb on two by two
To be sure these days continue
Things we cannot change

from "Two Step" by Dave Matthews Band

If Not For This

Prologue

THE LOOKS. THE sideways glances. The open gapes. They drive Dalt toward the biblical. Smiting and rending. Relax, Bub, I tell him, they're not about me. Some hag in a wheelchair, arm quaking? They've all seen that before. Ho hum, ho hum. What snaps the heads around, drops jaws, is Dalt pushing the chair. I mean, Dalt, the original idea for Michelangelo's *David*, chained to this harpy? Of course we're going to draw stares, make people wonder. Hell, we make me wonder.

But, if it's a good day, the words shuttling down the frazzled synapses, I say to them, "This is nothing. You should see us in bed." That claps jaws shut.

I should be beyond that, but it's all I know how to do; dare this all to be nothing. Not anything that could ever get between us.

These strangers don't see beyond the twitching, the chair, that poor, hot, saddled man. But when I have to catch my breath, find something to convince me we'll always have enough to go on, I reel back to my anchor point: the morning after our first night ever. And the air I breathe gets all rarified even now, remembering how stunned I was, how hardly daring to believe. I can't quite swear

I believe it yet, believe we'll last through even this. But that first morning, the two of us so strong even Wyoming was nothing but our backdrop, we hardly had a thought beyond the rasp of the oars against our palms and the river's flow beneath us. Wheelchairs— any poor bastards caught up in them—were no closer to us than outer space.

Morning After

I EASE THE truck in against the willows and pop the door, but then just sit back a minute. The Tetons glow ruddy. The willows, their leaves fingering each other in some low curl of wind, hide the Snake, but I hear its whispery hustle. I step out into the dawn and breathe it in: the cold, the wet, the newness. My world. Shivering in the same shorts and sandals I wore yesterday, the dew-heavy grass soaking my naked legs, I can't stop a smile. I head for the water.

Last night, it'd been ninety something, the river a scorcher, the afternoon thunderstorms failing to materialize, the mountains and sky as washed out as my evening scenic float of wilted kids and parents, hardly a ripple among them even as I took them through the waves. No campfire talk in any of their futures. And then Dalt shows up at Deadman's to run the shuttle. Bribes Milt to let him take it. He doesn't even work for our company. Liability up the ass, my job on the line, I'd just grinned like a fool.

Now, four or five steps toward the river, I stop, look down at my empty hands. "Maddy," I say to the towering trees, the trembling willows. "Hello?" I turn around for my fly rod, my knees less like joints than simply looser spots in my rubbery bones. I'm kind of stupid with exhaustion, with luck, with, yes, sex.

Leaning into the truck bed for my rod, I picture Dalt this morning, rummaging for his clothes, his sunrise scenic probably already milling around the van by the gas station/boathouse. He wasn't having a lot of success in the clothes department, and finally just zipped up sans undies. I raised an eyebrow he smiled about, but, bent straight over at the waist, first light slatting through the blinds, I actually thought this was something a Frenchman should be painting. And, though we'd been over and over every inch of each other all night—"memorizing by Braille," Dalt called it—not once thinking to pause for sleep, or even leaving time for a shower this morning, thinking at all, the sight of him there, lifting up his shirt, turning to catch me staring, stopped me cold. I couldn't believe this was me, that I was here, that, well, now they were going to have to get Fabio for the cover of my life story. And, thinking of it now, heading out to fish my secret hole just because I couldn't face going home to sag into my dorm bed alone, my heart still kind of does this lurch and stagger.

I mean, there weren't lightning bolts all over the place, but there were definitely thunderheads. Huge, dark ones, stacked up horizon to horizon, miles high, coming on fast. Aunty Em screaming about the cellar.

"Maddy," I say, setting out again for the river, "what on earth have you gotten yourself into?"

Ohio to Oregon, to Wyoming, to, to a guy named Dalt? I was already getting to stare at the Tetons all day, watch the sun gold them every morning, turn them stark and flat through the day, leaving nothing but purpled cutouts against the evening. And I was getting to do it all from a raft, my hands on the sticks, a boat-load of admiring tourons in thrall to me. Even before Dalt had first mumbled about his moonlight float, I'd thought I was about the luckiest thing going. And Troy, too. I mean, a horse shoer? How much more western can you get? How much luckier? Troy, my older man in Wyoming, helping me curl my lip at all the college boys back in Corvallis. His own place in Wilson. His own horses, for crying out loud. My place to stay every summer till I graduated, and then, well, who knows? That's what he always said, Troy, nipping at the edges of plans. "Well, then, who knows?"

Which was plenty close enough for me. Who did know? Finish school, work the river, and then what? Life? Who wanted to think about that? Not me. Not ever. Not until now.

Winding my way through the willows, I let loose a total girl giggle, a sound I don't think I'd ever produced in my life. "Not until *now*?" I laugh. "Like what? You're making life plans now? *Maddy and Dalton, sitting in a tree, k, i, s, s, i, n, g.* Jesus, Mad, you've known him what? A month, two? Good god."

And, Troy. That, too, is not me. No multiples in my background. No stringing anybody along, playing the field. Serial monogamy. And when it's done, it's done. My whole ice queen side.

I make it to the river just as the sun slips through a gap in the trees, touching the Snake for the first time of the day. Like it was my master plan all along. See what I mean about luck? The flat just above the riffle shines, making me squint, pull up my shades. But in the shadows around me, everything's still and cool. I shiver and strip out a bit of line, lifting my arm no more than enough to cast, about all I can manage in my state. I drop the nymph in and let it sink, waiting.

Ravished. That's the only word I can think of that even comes close to coming close. I wish I knew some foreign language, some great compound verb I could conjugate all day long. *I ravished him. He ravished me. We ravished each other.*

"Ausgeravished," I growl, and strip in line, at least pretending to fish, tug after tug, a stone fly fighting to reach the surface, to break out of its hard case, find its wings. There's one tap, and I strike to nothing. Maybe just bottom. But, my head is about as far from this as it can be. Not something I'm used to. At all.

Last night? The two of us? It was just not ordinary.

I strip in again, and cast. And again. That smile. You want to talk about luck?

Okay. The dates, the whole history. First sight of him at that party, Troy, somehow—at a boaters' season-opener bash—finding another farrier, hunkering into a corner talking shop all night, me and Alissa just standing by the keg, her latest down in the canyon for an overnighter. We're suddenly two single chicks, scoping out the guys, laughing ourselves sick over some of them, hormone disaster zones barely disguised in human skin. All so young. So our age. So repulsively immature and desperate.

At the keg, we get every one of their lines run past us. We giggle. We roll our eyes. Alissa's all smiles, a wolverine in stilettos. Some guy finally says, "Hey, what do you think, yours is made of gold? Why don't you just kiss my ass?" and she smiles sweet and says, "Mark the spot, honey, you're all ass." I fight not to blow beer out my nose.

A while later she says, "Whoa. Now there is some real talent."

I follow her gaze, ready for the next beheading, but this guy is not coming over, not pulling on his rooster suit, sucking it in, puffing it out. He's just leaning against a wall, b.s.ing with some other guy. And, Allie's got an eye, she's not kidding about talent. But he's not some underwear model or anything. As a matter of fact, he's like Troy that way, totally put together, but not like they've spent their life in a gym, or in front of a mirror. Like they just happen to look that way, not their fault or anything.

We check him out a while, making up life histories, none of which, Alissa points out, contain a single horseshoe, and we get totally ignored in return, which, believe me, is not something that happens to Alissa with any regularity. Finally she shoves off, says, "What the hell? Did I get all hideous overnight, or what?"

I tail after her like a pilot fish, just to watch the feeding frenzy.

He's startled by Alissa's hand, stuck out at him like a knife. He smiles, though, shakes it, says his name is Dalton.

"Dustin?" Alissa says.

"Dalton."

"Boatman?"

"No, *Dal-ton*," he says, slow and loud, like maybe Alissa's deaf, or retarded.

I hide my face behind my plastic cup. Except for Troy and his fellow farrier, there isn't a person here who isn't a boatman.

"Signal Mountain," he says then, letting her off the hook.

It's a tiny lodge, one van, one raft, one boatman. Maybe two trips a day, tops. All those waitresses to run his shuttles.

"So, what are you guys discussing so seriously?" Alissa says.

"Moonlight floats."

Oh, please, I think, here it comes. *You babes want to come along?* Like no one in the history of moonlight has ever come up with that one before. Champagne or beer will be the next question.

Alissa waits, raising her eyebrow like a cobra its hood. But he doesn't say anything else. He was only answering her question. Alissa has to prompt, "So, when's the next full moon?"

He shrugs. His partner says something about werewolves, how we should pay closer attention. If they start talking about going feral, one word about animal instincts, I am not going to be able to keep it together.

But they don't. Dalton lifts a cup that looks like it's been empty a while. It occurs to me I've never seen him take a drink. It occurs to me that I've kind of been watching.

"Anything left in that keg?" he asks.

We don't answer, for no reason I could explain.

"I mean, I've been kind of afraid to check," he says, "with you two guarding it."

And that is as close as he ever comes to acknowledging any awareness of our existence. He kind of looks at us then, like, *Did you come over here for some reason?* and I look down at my cup, which is not empty.

"Well," he says, and shoves off toward the keg.

I don't even have an excuse to follow.

I glance at Alissa, who mouths, "Gay," and we laugh, but I am thinking, No way in hell.

The party swirls around us, and, a lot later, I say goodnight to Troy, who is heading home, but I'm on early tomorrow, so I'm staying in my room with Allie. It was the plan all along, but I admit I glance around once for the guy before leaning in and giving Troy a kiss.

It's not till I'm out the door that I see him again. Dalton. He actually moves my way this time, appearing out of the darkness beneath the ponderosas. "Your friend Alison never bothered with your name."

"It's Alissa," I say, then, "No, I mean, not me. Her. Her name's Alissa, not Alison." I can't believe myself.

"And, yours?" he asks.

"Maddy."

"Full moon is next Thursday."

"You said you didn't know."

He looks right at me. "I remembered."

I eye him a second. Eye to eye. He doesn't look away.

"If you're not doing anything, there's room for one more."

"How about two more?" I ask. Who knows what kind of gang he's got rounded up?

"Alison?"

"Alissa." A guy noticing me instead of Allie is not something that happens.

"Sure," he says.

So, next Thursday, we show up at Signal, half an hour before dark. Give ourselves time to see what we're getting into. I'm half expecting to see him with the lodge boat, fifteen people already half-tossed, a keg strapped in, but he's just got an old Avon rolled up in the back of a beater pickup, wooden oars thrown on top. Not even a frame.

Alissa says, "So, where's everybody else?"

"Nobody else," he says.

"You said you had room for one more," I say.

"Two," he says, and he smiles. "Hop in. Pacific to Deadman's all right?"

"Fine by me," Alissa says, and she leaps, straddling the stick, smooched up against him as soon as he climbs in. I get the door.

He's quiet, a pro with the boat, a hand on the oars. It goes dark around us on the river, the moon not yet up, and he rows more by feel, I guess, than anything else. Once, leaning forward and squinting low, trying to get some starlight reflection, he says, "Bar, or riffle?" and, man, that he asks instead of just bulling ahead blindly male is the highlight of my night.

"Bar," I say, and, like an echo, Alissa says, "Riffle."

She's making him choose, which he does in nothing flat, rows right into it until we ground out on the gravel. "Bar," he says, and smiles at me, says it's time for a pee break anyway, boys left, girls right, like he's just running one more trip.

Allie and I pop his beers while he's gone, Schmidt's, which cracks us up. "There's wooing on a budget," she says.

"Wooing my ass. We forced ourselves on him."

"Forced? Shit. All I know is I would not want to be Troy right now."

I take a quick swig, and Dalton steps back, gravel crunching under his feet. "Who's Troy?" he says. Who knows how long he's been lurking out there?

"Hello?" Allie says. "Helena of Troy, Greek gods and stuff. That guy they dipped in immortal juice or whatever, all but his heel?"

He smiles, gets his own beer, and says, "Oh, that Troy. I didn't know I was traveling with scholars."

Next thing we're trying to remember if Agamemnon was a guy or a city. Then Allie's onto the Trojan Horse, which leads to Trojans, the condoms, and horses, as in hung like, and he doesn't ask anything more about Troy. I think we're embarrassing him, which, well, there's more points for him in that.

Once the moon comes up, we risk a side-channel and at the root ball snag at the entrance we spook out a snoozing sandhill crane. It blasts the air with its wings, the night and us with its prehistoric hooting, pterodactyls coming down on our heads. Allie and I both jump, and Dalton gives out this, "Jesus Christ!" racking up a whole month's worth of points. Then we're all laughing, toasting our near-death experience at the hands of yet another of the park's wild and dangerous animals.

We take turns on the sticks. When I'm rowing, Dalton sits on the side tube up front. When Allie's rowing, he sits on the cross tube, right next to me. The moon is all over the place, the gravel silvered, the trees layers of light and shadow, the river pewter, daubed over with darting, glowing bits of sky.

At the take out at Deadman's, the only time I think I've ever seen it completely empty, except for the shuttle truck he'd left, Dalt just deflates the raft, and we pack up and hop in. This time, though, Allie lingers by the door until I have to get in first, pack in beside Dalton. We don't say much on the way back, but I'm aware of exactly where we touch, knee, elbow, hip. At Signal, where all he does is pull up beside my truck, not even letting us guess where he stays, he tells us thanks for coming along. Allie bails, but he touches my sleeve, says, "I've never moonlighted with anybody else. It was fun."

I say, "What?"

He nods. "Always went by myself. Never met anybody I figured might want to go. I mean, it's late, it's dark, gets cold." He lists each one of these like they're bad things.

"There's another full moon next month," he says.

"Yeah," I say, "they're weird that way."

"I have room for one more," he says.

"Two?" I say.

He shakes his head in the dark, holds up one finger.

"Meet here?" I whisper.

He nods.

On the way home, Allie is on me like stink. "God, I can't believe you just walked away. He's all over you, and you go Mrs. Paul's?"

"'All over me?' What? He must have sisters he misses."

She eyes me as I drive. "Watch for moose," I say. "The black bastards." But she keeps staring. I ignore her, until, finally, pulling back into the housing area, she says, "So, since this is all sisterly, you're going to drive down to Troy's now, right, spend the night, tell him all about your cool moonlight float?"

"It's two in the morning."

"Like that's stopped you before?"

"I've got a . . . Just quit, okay, Allie? Really. About Troy. Just for tonight. This doesn't have one thing to do with Troy."

She looks at me as I set the brake, opens her mouth, but then closes it. "So, I've got a roommate again?"

"Will that be a problem?"

She says it won't, and I don't tell her about the second moonlight, ever, before or after, just say I'm going to Troy's. There's the slightest chance he'll call, that decisions will be made that way, but I don't tell her either about the other float we take, daylight, down the Green, away from this valley and all its spying eyes. Or the day I skip work and Dalton drags me up the Grand, the view from up there before the lightning came in, the whole world before us.

And then, last night, his hijacking my shuttle, dumping off the tourons, diving straight into his truck, me lying down so nobody'd see, my face touching his leg, I mean, practically in his lap. Neither one of us could talk exactly right. My voice sounded like a pull-string doll, the words all that way, like I was trying to remember what I used to say. He said, "I was thinking we could float the Buffalo Fork." He actually had to clear his throat.

I sit up, say, "Is it safe?"

"The river?" he asks, and I'm glad to hear the shock in it.

"No, ass, the road. Spies." He knows, as far as I know, nothing about Troy, just that I'm keeping this all low profile so I don't take any grief from my boat crews.

So we floated the Buffalo, which I'd never done, and, it turns out, neither had he, which was kind of sweet, but it also turned out he lived up there, this little out-building behind the Heart Six, and, running the shuttle, we had to go right past there, and when I said I bet it beat dorm housing, he pulled in, said, "Not by all that much," and I said, "I bet," and the tour took us as far as the front step, where he turned to maybe say something, maybe to hug me, maybe just to get the door open, something I'm guessing we'll have opposing opinions on for a long time, and then we were kind of lip-to-lip, and I pushed my hips against his, kind of accidentally, just trying to stand on tiptoe to get properly mouth to mouth, and he pushed back just enough, and after that it was so bad Hollywood it's almost too embarrassing even to recall, but that mad movie rush is exactly what led him to going to work this morning without his undies. I hope he had the good sense to keep his knees together while he rowed.

And thinking of that, Dalton rubbing against the canvas of his shorts, I miss a vicious hit, the line snapped out of my hand before I even think about striking back, way, way off my game. The only thing I think is, I have got to bring him here. He would love this place. My secret spot. It's kind of all I think about anything anymore. How he'd like it.

Casting again, whispering, "Come on, Mad, pay attention," I shiver a little, and check the progress of the sun, still crawling around the lip of the last ridge. I start toward its warmth, away from the best fishing spot, but for now, I'll take the sun over the chance of a fish. A chance that's looking pretty slight anyway. Dalt'd be releasing them left and right, looking over his shoulder at me, smiling, making sure I was taking note. As if I'd be looking anywhere else. I'd still kick his ass though. If I was trying.

I only take a step or two toward the sun, still casting, dropping the nymph, stripping it back up high for a change, as if it'd just broken loose in the riffle, when the fish hits and I actually set the hook. I grin like an idiot, my luck just stupefying, and Troy steps out of my hidden trail right beside me.

I actually jump, yip, "Jesus!" Then, "You scared the shit out of me."

He doesn't crack a smile. Just looks at me.

"Troy," I say, but I have to swallow, feeling like big decisions may have been made without me thinking about a one of them. "What are you doing here?"

He says, "That's what I was going to ask you."

"Me?" I say, a total grade school stall. I lift up the rod, which bends double, dancing in my hand. "Fishing," I say. "I got one." And it's a good one, running deep, crossing the hole, maybe trying to go upstream, break me off in the shallows. I turn to Troy to smile, to welcome him, hoping I sound glad and happy to see him.

He nods.

"But, you, I thought, weren't you going to Kemmerer?" He's got a whole road show deal, a truck full of tools and enough gear to keep him out weeks at a stretch.

"Seems like that's what you were thinking," he says. He folds his arms across his chest, the muscles cording around bone. He's wearing his cowboy hat, black and filthy, salt-stained, his leather apron. At 6 a.m., none of this makes sense.

"But, it's what you told me." I turn back to the water, the fish. "Why wouldn't I be thinking it?"

"You told me things," he says. "Maybe they weren't what I should have been thinking."

"Troy," I say, "I don't know—" but the fish breaks out leaping, bursting into the sun just below the riffle, spray sparkling, and I say, "Check that out. A jumping cutthroat." As if he'd give a rip.

"Maddy," he says, and I turn to look over my shoulder, my stomach as knotted as that fish's, fighting for its life. He looks me in the eye and says, "I love you." It's the first time, actually, that anyone's ever said that to me.

The fish hits the shallows and rolls there, flopping, the big slab body finding purchase on the stones, slapping at the line, overloading it. I glance away from Troy, not because of any fish, but it's too late. It's gone. I feel the instant the line parts, the sudden deadness there, nothing but a slack line adrift in the current. I say, "How'd you know where I was?"

It's a few seconds before he says, "I followed you."

I crank in line, the ratcheting click all I hear. But before I've got half the empty line in, it just seems such a stupid thing to be doing. I mean, fishing. I sit down like my legs have been cut out from under me, my marionette's string sliced clean. The cobble is freezing against my bare legs, and I press them down into the rock. "You never told me that before," I say.

"You never asked."

I close my eyes. If he makes a move, either way, I'll hear him—the willows if he leaves, the rocks grinding and shifting if he comes toward me. "It's not something you ask a person," I say.

One rock clacks against another, but no more. "Well, I'm asking," he says.

Still clutching my fishing rod, I lift it, as if it's a shield, a weapon, a magic wand. I open my eyes, and turn to Troy, nothing but the silhouette of a big man, the sky day-bright behind him. My legs goose bump against the damp rock.

"Now?" I ask. "You're asking now?"

I can barely see him nod.

"Where'd you follow me from?" It's such a stilted, tiny whisper, I don't know if it will rise above the river rush or not, but he says, "From far enough."

He'd have had to have been off for Kemmerer when something came up, deciding to drive up to meet me after work. Followed us out to the Buffalo Fork, sat through the float, then, back to the Heart Six. He'd still be in his work clothes, his hat, his leather apron, would have had to have sat in them all night, parked out in the dark, beyond some stranger's place, waiting, and waiting, the night going frosty, coming up with no better plan than to say he loves me.

"Ah, shit, Troy," I say.

"I'm asking because I need to know. Whatever else, doesn't matter."

I lean to the river, scooping up a handful of the icy water, dashing it into my face. It is suddenly impossible to ignore that I never slept last night. "I don't know," I say. "I think, what you said, was maybe—I don't know, Troy—maybe something I needed to hear a long time ago." I pick up my rod, reel in a few cranks.

"Well, you're hearing it now."

But he isn't going to say it again. I can feel his own reeling in, pulling everything back, minimizing his exposure.

I keep cranking, circling around and around, the fly-line finally past the tip, snaking down through all the guides on its own weight, crumpling into my lap, the web thin bit of leader crossing my leg, the line, I see, snapped at the blood knot, my fly gone with the last section of tippet. Dalton and I'd tied these flies together, in my dorm room at the crack of dawn before the Green trip, his travel vise cranked down on the desk top, hair and thread and feathers sifting down across his legs. He handed me the first one, then palmed the second for himself. "One fly," he said. "Lose it, you're rowing the rest of the day. Most fish wins."

He'd never even asked if I could fish. I pounded him. Well, eked out a victory anyway. Same thing.

The sun reaches across the riffle, the glint on water almost blinding, Troy still waiting.

I put my elbows up on my knees, kind of hug myself. "I, Troy, it's . . ." I re-rig the rod, strip some line back out, leading it into the hole to watch it wave empty, circulating, diving out of sight.

"Who is he?" Troy asks.

I pull a stone out from under my hip, hold it a second in my hand. It's a skipper, a good one, and I remember the pullout on the Green, Dalton trying to talk me into a stone skipping contest to double or nothing the fishing prize. I watched him tail-walk one all the way across the river, skitter up on the opposite bank, still bounding. Fool. Like I was going to double down after that? No thanks. "He's a boatman," I say.

"How old?" he asks.

It's not as weird a question as it sounds. I've always told Troy I'd rather go lesbo than date a boatman, and that Troy's age, thirty-two, ten years older than me, is my rock-bottom limit for any man I'll have anything to do with. Too much growing up to see them through otherwise. "My age," I say.

"So, two strikes, and he's still in the game?"

I nod. "Where, exactly, did you follow me from?"

The wind rustles the willows, and for a moment I think he's left, but then the rocks crunch, and the next thing I know he's behind me, touching my shoulders. He smells of leather and horse, a smell I'm very much going to miss. "Into Heart Six," he says. "Away."

I reach forward, away from his hands, rolling the stone in the water, washing the dust off. It shines, flecked with darker bits, same as Troy's eyes. Dalt's are really kind of a run of the mill, everyday blue. I'll miss Troy's eyes, too, I realize. I tuck the stone under my leg, saving it for when Dalt's here.

"Maddy, three years. I always told you, every fall, you do what you want back at school, what you need."

"I did that. I didn't need anything."

"And now you do?"

I shrug, nod, both at the same time. "Troy, I don't know."

"But you have to find out."

I hold my hands in the water, the cold seeping into the knuckles, making me bite my lips, my eyes tear. "I do," I say. Only a minute or two more and the sun will reach me.

"And what if it turns out he is just a kid?"

"I guess I'll find that out."

Troy rocks me with his hands, one on top of each shoulder. "Our no planning," he says, "it was a lot easier, when," he clears his throat, "when you didn't have another plan." ✦

I nod again. "I never had another plan. I never had any plan, Troy. The last thing I'd ever put in a plan, ever, is hurting you."

The rocks shift and clack behind me. His hands leave my shoulders.

"Well, kid," he says, and in all our time together, nineteen years old until this instant, he has never once called me kid, "you go see how this works out, and, if it doesn't, well, then, who knows?"

I can't see him, he's standing behind me, but that *kid* rankles so bad, him so building up his story, his armor, that I can't help knock it down, say, "It's going to work out."

And that does stop him, his footsteps held just long enough I hear people talking, a little run of laughing, the way you can on a river, the water carrying everything. He says, "Well, good luck with that," and I hear the willows part, the slick whisk of them off his leather, and a moment later, I hear a new grind of rock, the slip and clack of a raft bumping through shallows, and I dart up, see Dalt with his dawn scenic, hauling them down this stretch no scenic ever goes, and I think I must have told him at least what section of river hid my secret spot, that I was going down here this morning to see if I could remember how to walk, and I can't help a smile, a little bit of a wave.

He grounds out, just like he did chasing Allie away under the moon. He has to jump out, start dragging, and I glance once at the empty willows, before starting upstream to help, the sun hitting me like a caress, the water biting my ankles as I splash out. I take the life line by his side and start to tug, jerking the people on the tubes, bouncing them maybe a little just for show.

Dalt says to his group, "Just a service we offer here, river nymphs stationed at problem areas to help us through."

Under his breath, he says, "Do I want to know who that was?"

I bite my lip, then shake my head. "I don't think you do," I say.

He glances at me once, sharp, surprised, then nods, and digs in, the two of us working side by side in the quiet, only the rush and slip of the river, the tourons too nervous for chatting. We're breathing hard, this really no place to bring a boat with a dozen people on it, and in between breaths, Dalt whispers, "Do I need to *worry* about who that was?"

"I don't think you do," I say again.

"Sweet," he says, just like a twenty-two-year-old boatman, and I turn to catch his smile, see that's exactly who he was trying to sound like. Last night, on the Buffalo, without going into details about any older men, I'd told him about my rules against the younger ones.

"I lost your fly," I say to him. "So, I guess you win."

"It's not a thing you ever win, Maddy."

"Well, it's definitely something you can lose."

"I'll make you more," he says. "We'll be okay."

And I believe him somehow, me, the ice queen, believing that the two of us will always be okay.

The boat bumps over the last of the gravel, and we have to hop onto the tube or be run over, and, taking the oars, Dalt asks, "Would the river nymph like a ride down to Pacific Creek?"

I start to say, "My truck, my rod," but it's my secret place. They'll be fine. I nod, say, "Okay, I'll go with you," and the whole crew of the boat, this mob of coffee-starved tourons, breaks into applause, cheers us like I've just said "I do." It's so ridiculous I'm still smiling like a clown when I leap off with the bowline, throw a clove hitch over the post at Pacific, and reach back to pull Dalton to shore.

The Net

WE GET MARRIED at dawn, outdoors of course, the Tetons all rosy, the knob of hill we stand on rising just above the thick white mist clotting the paths of the Buffalo and Snake, all exactly as perfect as we thought it would be, but, still, it's a time more rightfully reserved for executions. The September chill we somehow never considered, has everybody shrinking deep into their coats and fine clothes, rubbing sleep from their eyes. We all look pretty rumpled. Everybody except Dalton, who, I've learned in the last year, leaves the roosters blinking in surprise every morning. He'd spent hours and hours, weeks, composing our vows, pouring over every syllable, scratching away when I'd only wanted him to come to bed. And now, when it comes right down to it, I can only mumble my lines, my lips and tongue thick and slow with sleep and cold, Allie's going away bash.

All I really want to do is snatch Dalton by his collar and drag him off to some grizzly den and not come out again until spring. Maybe not then either. If I was awake, I couldn't be happier, but suddenly, every eye on me, my parents dragged all the way out here from Ohio, totally out of place amidst the frost-heaved bunch grass, the gloomy blue of the spruce, I feel less like a bride than a character from some old movie, blindfolded before the post, bull's-eye pinned over my heart.

Finally, Dalton's friend Jonna (a nurse and a preacher in some religion I know she invented herself) pronounces us a couple, and Dalton and I kiss—even his lips cold—and we walk alone down the hill, heading for the water. Instead of rings, which, besides being an archaic sign of ownership, Dalton says, are the source of countless open-pit cyanide-leach gold mines gutting the mountains and thrashing the rivers, we are going to dip our hands in the river, let it run around our wrapped together fingers, joining us on a journey as long as the water's, a cycle, Dalton says, bigger and more eternal than any ring. He can really get going on that kind of thing, but I couldn't keep from asking how something can be *more* eternal. He blinked, a bit lost, and I thought, *Nice, Mad*, but he smiled and said, "Just watch us."

As soon as we're on the flat, the frost sweeping my long dress, his black pants, my ridiculous heels glancing off river rock, negotiating wilderness instead of some church's red carpet, the fog closes down on us like a shroud, something so heavy it seems impossible to breathe under. I gasp, pant, turn to Dalt. Nobody in the crowd's followed us down the bank, and rather than starting on some journey together, I see we've taken a horribly wrong turn. We've not just tied our two lives together, we've cast off the rest of the world. But Dalt doesn't seem to notice, and though the cold has already turned me into one gigantic goose bump, I get a whole new run of them.

We do the ringless eternal cycle thing anyway, dipping our hands into water I swear is a hundred degrees colder than yesterday when Allie and the girls had my send-off float. Dalt's got his fingers entwined with mine and mine with his and we hold them in the river, lock eyes, fight to smile, until my knuckles feel like they've cracked. Then, standing, biting my lips, burying my hand between my legs, wiping that iced, crystal pure water all over Mom's wedding dress, Dalton turns to me and blows out this sigh like he hasn't been able to draw a breath all morning. "Holy shit," he says. "We did it."

My jaw, I hate to say, drops. His first married words? I say, "Holy shit, you don't know how close you are to starting your journey with a swim."

He stares, shakes his head, and I say, "You don't say that to . . . You don't . . . That should not be the first thing out of your mouth to your new . . ." But I give up. Watching him watching me, trying to figure me out, wondering what we've just done to each other, I wind up shrugging, then give him a hug. He's so warm it's downright lifesaving, and I whisper, "Holy shit, we did it all right."

We stay that way, holding each other beside the river, finally warming up. I keep my eyes closed, hope the fog will magically burn away, that when I open them again the Buffalo will stretch glinting before us, fall-scorched cottonwoods and alder burning in the first touch of sun. But somebody on the knob above us honks a car horn and clear as a bell somebody laughs and snorts, "You asshole." Our pals.

Dalton whispers, "They're probably freezing," and then he adds, and I love him for this, "I know I am."

I give a shiver and say, "Whose idea was this anyway?" only because it was both of ours. We turn, and I open my eyes, the fog as thick as ever, just like I knew it would be, a frosty dense mist clamped around us. But, crawling back up the hill, Dalt having to all but drag me and my stupid shoes, we break into sun, and the waterways below us are eye-burning bright, a cascade of cloud-filled paths just waiting for us.

Coffee and donuts sit stacked to the ceiling in one of the vans, and the silence breaks, and we all chat and chew, circling our fingers around our cups, greedy for the heat. Everybody is so glad for the sun they practically giggle. Allie huddles obviously tight to Dalton's pal from back in Montana, whose name right now I can't believe I can't remember. I raise an eyebrow and she gives me her swoon look, a quick dip of her knees. We had this big tear binge yesterday, her swearing she was losing me, me swearing that she wasn't. I said, "We'll always be here, all of us, right here in this valley," and she said, "God, you still believe in fairy tales, don't you?" Then she was off with Montana boy, changing forever his idea of luck.

Dalton and I take turns in another van, changing out of our wedding finery—more archaic tradition Dalton said, but, as soon as I saw that Mom had brought the dress, I'd insisted. When we come out, we look just like everybody else in the valley, bulky with layers of fleecy synthetic pile, neoprene waders, but for a few minutes there we'd been our parents, Mom's dress fitting so much like a skin it was spooky.

I walk straight to her and bury my face in her shoulder. I want to say something profound, deep, and as usual I cut right to the chase, choking out, "Well. Mom."

Under one of Dalton's spare rain jackets, she's wearing my favorite outfit, and she's done that for me, never before caught so behind the fashion. She holds me tight, and says, "Don't worry, honey." And she means, I know, the wedding dress, that she'll salvage it somehow, that dragging it through the wilderness here hasn't ruined it beyond her ability to repair anything, that though she doesn't understand anything about this, about anything Dalton and I will ever do, *our entire generation* I can hear her sigh, she will be a good sport and rise above it, always there to pick up the pieces. I can picture the what-can-you-do? shake of her head at bridge club, hear the rattle of her long earrings—*And, for their honeymoon, they've taken off on some river trip.* All sorts of old heads wagging in sympathy, someone saying, *Well in our day, there was still something left for the honeymoon.* Though I love her to pieces, I suddenly wonder how it had felt so comfortable to feel like I was becoming her. I sniffle once, and she lets go of me at the same time I let go of her.

Dad, I'm afraid, will stick out his hand, offer me a hearty handshake, but when I stand in front of him, he's the one with tears in his eyes, and he swallows me in a bear hug I can barely remember. "You take care, Maddy," he says. "You take care."

"I will, Dad," I say, wanting to add something reassuring, something like, *Jeez, Dad, we got married. It's not like we're jumping off a cliff or anything*, but I hear a scrape of gravel, a grunt of effort, and over Dad's shoulder I see Dalt and our buddies lift our raft off the ground, start heave-hoing it down the hill to the river, slipping and swearing and laughing, and it feels more like a cliff dive than anything.

Dalt leaps back up the hill, and then everybody makes the trip down to the water, Dad and Dalt on each side of Mom, and there are a lot of cheers and bon voyages as Dalton and I settle into our places on the raft; beside each other, one on each oar—more of Dalton's light-touch symbolism, but an impossible way to row a boat. Lots of hands push us off. As soon as we turn the first bend, one of us will have to really take the sticks and the other will unpack the rods and start to fish. We've side-stepped mentioning who will do which first.

But I know other symbolism—Vikings casting off the boat with their fallen hero, letting it drift out, an ocean-going bier. Or is it a pyre? We drift away, the people we leave behind, our family and friends, growing quiet, waving instead of shouting. Until the mist folds around the two of us in our boat, I keep my eyes peeled for any of our gang who might lob a funereal torch. Something any of them would do.

The quiet then. Just the two of us in the fog alone. I keep waiting for the gunning of engines, another har-har-har honking of horns. But they wait, letting us sneak off like we really are the only two people in the world. It must be my parents, standing there looking so serious, so old, that holds our crew in that kind of check.

But, at last, one of them breaks, no matter the look my mom must skewer him with. As Dalton and I ease alone down the silent river, as if even the water is holding its breath, their old war cry suddenly shakes out after us. "She's in the net!" The voice strangles on *net*, though, and I picture Allie vice-gripping that guy of hers by the nuts, doing that for me.

But I stiffen anyway, sitting beside Dalton at my useless single oar, peering downstream at the snaggle-tooth mess of snags and bars splitting the river. Only after the echo fades do we look at each other, Dalt trying to smile, but not quite making it. It's a shout from some old fishing show Dalt and his cronies grew up with, if you could say they ever really grew up. I've heard it bellowed over dozens of dropped eight-balls, hundreds of fish, a thousand crushed beer cans. Just too late, I realize I've married a child, a boy. What about my rules? Where's Troy?

"Mad?" Dalt says, and I say, "I am not in anybody's net. Not yours, not anybody's."

"I know," he says. "Why don't you start fishing?"

"Don't think I can handle the oars?" and before I can clap my hand over my mouth, stop the words, Dalt's a lot paler than he'd been an instant before, his summer-long tan bleached to a February pallor.

I gasp. "My god! An hour in that dress and I've become my mother."

"I, um, I didn't, I didn't sign up to marry your mom," Dalton says.

"Me either," I say. "To be her. I mean, I'm not her, Dalt."

"Why don't I start fishing?" he says.

He doesn't wait for whatever might come out of my mouth next. Just leaves his oar so fast I have to snag it before it slips through the lock. He has his back to me then, unscrewing the cap to his rod case. I spin us around to a decent ferry angle, relieved to have a hand on each oar after those few uncoordinated moments of holding only one, not knowing what the other might do.

We slip by a huge snag; hoary old root pad tapering down through its weather-beaten, spiral-grained trunk, speckled white with merganser shit. The hole it's dug is filled mostly with gravel this late and low, a hopeless place to fish, but Dalton works out just enough line to set down his fly. He's all quiet, waiting for me to say the first thing that will set my mother adrift, Captain Bligh her to the vast expanses without us. One little slip from me, and he's into a pout. Mr. Western Outdoorsman/Poet-at-Heart/Boatman Extraordinaire. The big cry-baby.

"Look," I say, "I'm sorry. It just popped out. The way you said that about fishing first. I can handle a raft fine."

"I was only asking if you wanted to fish. I was going to let you go first."

"Fine," I say. "Thank you. But as long as you are going first, the least you could do is try."

So, before we know it, we're into a cut-throat, down and dirty, who catches more/bigger/better/faster fishing competition. Like kids. *Nah, nah, my fish is bigger than your fish.* Unbelievable. Married forty, fifty minutes, we've come to this.

It's only a few more casts before I edge him by a pretty hole and he hooks into his first, and, as he crows, "it's a man-eater!" He does not say, "She's in the net!" It's a nice cutthroat he claims breaks twenty inches. Seventeen, maybe. At the outside.

We switch seats, and I tie on a humpy, just like him, and he rows like he would for a client, giving me every chance, but it isn't until we hit one of the rare, long, calm straightaways, where there isn't much hope of anything, that my fly disappears into this tiny dimple of a rise.

I strike back, something solid as a rock tied into my hook. Seems hardly to move, then, slowly, it sinks away and turns downstream. I tighten my fingers against the unwinding spool, take an instant to flash Dalton a look, but he just grins, not sulking about losing the first round so quick. We've been here before. I give him a quick one back, then turn to matters at hand.

The backing's showing when my monster, record shattering, contest clinching trout—it has to be a brown—just gives up the ghost. I start cranking in quick, then even faster, just to keep some tension on the line.

"Maybe its heart exploded," Dalton says.

I'm feeling a little sick, guessing that Dalton's guessing the same thing I'm guessing, even before I see the first scaly flash of dirty brown gold. Whitefish.

As I bring it close, Dalton says, "Snout-trout?"

I nod, working the tiny hook out of the blob of cartilage that serves as mouth and nose and bottom grubber all at once.

"Looks like a trophy one," Dalton says. It's a peace offering, but everybody knows whitefish don't count.

Leaning over the side of the raft, where Dalton can't see, I ease the ugly stepsister back to freedom as carefully as if it were a fabled trout. It sinks away, shaking its head, trying to figure out what just happened to it, and before he can know I've let it go, Dalt says, "She's in the net."

I turn and face him head on. "Look," I say, "did you even once consider telling me I made all your dreams come true today?"

His jaw works a second before any sound comes out. "What?"

"Even that I was the most beautiful bride in the world?"

"You? Tell *you* something like that?"

"Well, if I'm so hideous, why did you marry me?"

"Oh, I see," Dalton says, tugging on his chin this way he does. "We based this all on personal appearance."

"Hah!" I blurt. "If we'd done that, I'd have, I'd have, I'd have ditched you the first time you pulled that Sigmund Freud move of yours." I furrow my brows, pull on my chin.

Dalt's hand drops to his lap as if amputated.

I keep glaring only because I don't know what to say, don't know what's wrong with me, but then I can't keep in a chuckle, same way I never could as a kid, caught red-handed in something mean and nasty, all the wrong things sneaking out of me.

Dalton is too stunned to do anything but gape, not all that different looking, really, than that poor old, pooped-out whitefish.

"It's just that," I try to start. "I don't know. It's just that, you know, your wedding day." My voice sky rockets. I swallow, keep it down. "I'd always had this picture, you know? Cathedrals and all. The whole rice throwing, tin-can dragging, threshold carrying thing, the fear and surprise and waiting finally over."

"The fear and surprise?" Dalton says. "I wouldn't say they've quite played out of this one."

And that, for some reason, just cracks me up. I laugh too hard, holding my ribs, sucking air like a bank-tossed sucker.

The next thing I know, we're nudging the shore, Dalton petting my hair as I try to get my breath back, wipe away the tears. "You are you know," he says. "The most beautiful. I just thought if I ever said that, you'd brain me."

I think, *My god, this guy doesn't even know me,* but I say, "Probably. Any other day, probably. But this is different. We did something huge today, Dalt."

"You're telling me?"

I stare out at the roiling water, the straightaway breaking into a right hand bend, a gravel bar splitting off a skimpy side channel on the inside. "I wish there was a threshold out here someplace," I say.

I glance over at Dalton, his lips trembling on the verge of a smile.

"If there was, I'd carry you over it."

"Really?" I ask. I'm thinking of our vows, how I'd let Dalton have his say on every line. Instead of *I do,* which Dalton said was a ridiculous promise in the face of everything that could happen, every bit of it unknown, we answered our pseudo-preacher with, *It is my strongest desire.* "Is that your strongest desire?" I ask. "To carry me over something?"

He grins, slips an arm under my shoulders, starts to lift. "You bet it is. Over everything."

"*My strongest desire,*" I say, shaking my head. "How pathetic is that? My strongest desire two minutes ago was to tie into a fish that'd dwarf yours, that'd make me king of this boat. And now yours is to stumble me over some chunk of stale driftwood, 'Get that out of the way.'"

"That's not—"

"Dalton. We're going to desire just about everything before our run is through. We've got a pretty good jump on that already. What I want to know is do you really want to marry me? Right this instant. Mom and all. You want in on this freefall or not?"

Dalton swallows. His arm is still around me, but he isn't trying to lift me anywhere. The mist has left a little sparkly dew across the top of his shoulders.

"And I am not in anybody's net!" I insist, tears trickling down my cheeks, which only makes me furious. I take a swipe at them with my fist all balled up, just as Dalton bends low to kiss me, whispering, "I do." Nearly knock his block off.

He sits on the cobble, rubbing at his cheek.

I rub at my own, at my eyes. "Sorry," I say. "I didn't mean to hit you. That was an accident."

"Are you sure?" he asks.

"Of course I'm sure."

He tugs his chin. "Positive?"

"The idea's getting tempting, Dalton."

"Okay," he says. "Well then, *I do*."

"Not just the moment's strongest desire?"

"The moment's strongest desire is to be like we've always been. Not like this."

"This is part of it."

"Not the part I most strongly desire."

I can't help a smile. "No," I say. "Me neither."

"So what is?" Dalton asks. "What is your moment's strongest desire?" He sits beside me on the raft.

"To get back on the water, I guess. Start this journey of ours all over again."

"It's a long way to Wilson," Dalton says, which for him is agreeing and surrendering at the same time. I've booked us into a bed and breakfast there. It'll be a long float, not a lot of dawdling for fishing, but Dalton had originally, during the vow composing days, suggested we camp out, spend days on the river alone.

But I've drawn the line. I mean, I love all this, love that we can get married at the crack of dawn on some deserted riverside hilltop, that we can bundle into our waders and layers, spend the days fishing and floating, but just this once, for this occasion, we are going to sleep in beds, nice ones, that we don't have to make in the morning, and we are going to have breakfasts fixed for us, gourmet stuff, and we aren't going to wash the dishes, not squat scrubbing sand around some oatmeal bowl in water that'd freeze the tusks off a walrus. We've got the rest of our lives for that.

Dalton pushes off, and when we begin to just drift, neither of us at the oars, I think how much like marriage this is. Wondering who is steering, how we're ever going to get around all those wicked-ass snags, what's going to keep us from beaching on those long, gray, dry gravel bars.

I bite my lip till I think it's going to bleed, and Dalton says, "You caught the last one," leaving it up to me.

I stand, keeping low, and crawl back to the oars. We're all right for a second though, just starting into the top of the lazy turn, and I leave the oars shipped.

"Unless you want to say whitefish don't count," Dalton says. "Then it'd still be your turn."

"They count," I answer. "It's all going to count, Dalt. Snout trout and squaw fish. Even suckers. Not just the pretty cutthroats, the big bad browns."

He grins and says, "Well, we're even then. One species apiece." He starts working out line, his false casts cutting the hook back and forth just above our heads. "We'll start our life tallies right now. We've got decades ahead of us, Mad. You and me, head to head, side by side. Skin to skin. Whole life times."

He lets his flies down an inch or so from the bank, and peers after them, ready to strike. I watch with him, and drop my oars into that freezing water, lean into the first stroke toward happily ever after.

High Side

AT THE WILDNESS of the end, Dalt rushing to get there with me, his last thrusts go so spastic I grab onto him like he might fly off. The corrugations of his ribs beneath my arms are the last thing I know for certain before my nerves coil into my core, spool there, each synapse ablaze until nothing can contain them, and every neuron launches back out. My fingers, my toes, the top of my head all tingle as if these currents might just shoot free, pass right out of me. With no clue what I've done, how, I find myself curled up into Dalt, completely clear of our bed, clutching and gasping. We stay that way, still and tensed, holding on with a strength we hadn't guessed at, not daring to even close the surprised Os of our mouths. Then, blinking, I loosen my grip, feel the sheets against my back, and he comes over me like a quilt, something you'd spend your whole life making. I have to reach up and tug at my hair, rub my face, convince myself my head is still there, my hands.

"You okay?" he whispers, and all I can manage, one word per breath, is, "So, far, past, okay."

We huff and puff like wicked wolves, our lungs pink and perfect and young, but hardly up to the power of the two of us. Dalt braces his elbows along my sides, taking some of his weight off, trying to free me, but I pull him back hard. He's still inside me, still filling that void I never dreamed existed, and I am never letting go.

It's a minute before he can muster, "Feel anything?"

"What?" I say. "Only everything in the world."

He touches his forehead to mine and says, "Anything new?"

I hug him tighter, though I wouldn't have guessed such a thing possible. "Um, let me see."

"Concentrate," he says.

"Shh."

We listen and I hear the whisper of the willows outside, the alders, the quiet slip and fall of the Buffalo Fork. The breeze eddies through the window. I feel its chill on my knees, my forearms, tight across his shoulder blades. He feels it across the backs of his legs, I know, his bum, which is still flexed, keeping his hips as tight against mine as it is possible to get. In the history of time, no two people have ever been this close. I know this like I know gravity. Together we lie so perfectly joined, I swear we can hear the stars above this ancient, tiny building, the cascade of their light across the curled old shingles.

"There," I say.

"I missed it."

"No you didn't. Don't lie to me. He said, 'Daddy.'"

"A boy?"

"First. Then a girl. Haven't you been paying attention?"

"Then another boy, and another girl. I've been paying attention."

"Good boy," I say, and I can feel him smile, but he can't help it, he slips out, and I close my eyes so tight I can *see* the stars through the roof. Our first time ever without anything stupid. No sponges, or pills, or stupid fricking condoms. God, I hate those things.

He eases off, tilting to his side, still pressed against me shoulder to ankle. There's no weird untangling of limbs, jammed elbows— we glide around each other like fish in a school. He lifts up to one elbow. Looking down at me, he says, "Wow."

"You said it, Buster. Nine months now."

"You're pretty confident."

I open my eyes, can just barely make out the rise of a cheek, the line of his nose. "How could I not be confident? Name one thing about us that isn't ideal."

He laughs, something I feel rather than hear. "Ideally, I don't think it's a one shot thing, Mad. I mean, what's the sense of that? The fun's all in the trying, no?"

I shake my head, then sit up, kick my feet over the side of the bed. He moves with me and we sit there together, like we're on a dock, dabbling our toes in the water. Our arms touch shoulder to elbow, our legs hip to knee, as we marvel over this huge thing we've done.

I glance toward the window, no color yet, just a lessening of the darkness, but, still, it's dawn, something I'd completely failed to realize. We've been at it all night. I look all around, locking it in, something to tell this child, how he came in with the light, how Dalt and I sat here in wonder, like kids. I'll point to this loft, say, "Right up there." I bite my lip, the greatness of it just too much. I'll tell our boy how, when we pushed off into the mist that first day, he was right there with us, even then, our strongest desire.

Dalt nudges me, says, "Maddy? We can still keep trying, right?"

"We are going to try forever, don't you worry about that. Right here in our little Coop. But I've wanted this baby since I could walk, and I know what I know."

He puts his arm around my shoulder, says, "Okay," but he says it like there's bad news behind it, and I tilt my head until it touches his and say, "But?" knowing there really isn't a bad thing out there that can touch us. Let the wolves huff. And Dalt says, "But, not in the Coop."

"Hmm?"

"Bob talked to me. They're pulling the lease."

I feel a blow inside which is definitely not the kick of a baby. I think I even puff out a shot of breath. "What?"

Dalt goes into the details, all monotone, like the shock has not yet worn off. But, I'm a mother now, somebody who has to be responsible. "We'll find another Coop," I say.

I feel Dalt shake his head. "There's nothing. Not that we can afford. Not in this valley."

"'That we can afford?'" I say. "But we live here. This is where we live."

Dalt doesn't smile, just keeps wagging his head. He could be somebody's dog. "Even the Chicken Coop's not free," he says. "Not even cheap."

"We've got jobs," I say.

"Seasonal jobs. Poor paying seasonal jobs."

"But the winter, on the ski hill."

"Lift operators? Hardly 401(k) material."

"Four oh what? Hello? I'm sorry, to whom am I speaking?"

"Mad."

"Dalt."

We're still sweaty for Christ's sake, still trembly. All around us in the loft we'd christened our first night ever, had pretty much been rechristening every spare second since, things are coming into focus. I see everything. Everything we own, all we'll ever need.

Our first time without protection, a word I hate nearly as much as the stuff itself, and he chooses this second to tell me the lease is being yanked. Come fall, our one room outbuilding behind the Heart Six will be no more. They're tearing down our Chicken Coop, which, really, after starting everything off here, if I was like a real girl, would be just about enough to set off the waterworks.

"So, you think," I'm talking slow, like I'm out of breath, which, well, a minute ago I was, but I'm a chick in her prime, I should have my breath back by now, should be grabbing Dalt, saying, "Um, hello, twins, triplets?" But, instead, I plow on. "You think we need to leave the whole valley? Flee the state? That there's not some other Chicken Coop hiding out here somewhere, our names written all over it?"

He keeps shaking his head, a fighter on the ropes, knowing he just has to withstand the onslaught, let me punch myself out. "Maddy," he says, "I've looked. All over. Under every rock."

I shift under his arm, turn to look him eye to eye, almost too close to focus. "You looked?"

He nods.

"How long have you known?" I stare at him, my X-ray vision sizzling, but I feel something inside me cave, and I say, "Really? You've looked under every rock?"

He nods some more.

I take one shaky breath, then put my arm over his shoulders. "We could live under a rock," I say. "You and me? It'd be like no problemo."

He smiles. "I know."

"So?"

"Winter's coming on. Rock'd get pretty chilly."

"You spent a winter in a fricking teepee up here!"

"And got busted for it," he says. "It's not something I'd recommend."

That was with "the girl before," she who must not be named. I don't even want to think about how they stayed warm all winter. Dirty, rotten, lucky bitch. The ranger who finally found their camp, gave them the boot, the ticket—there's a guy I'd like to kiss. She who must not had had enough of her western romance by then, and was on the first plane back to the coast. The *east* coast. Please. I'd still like to whack him upside the head for that one. Some Boston chick?

"Maddy," Dalt says. "Where have you gone?"

"Boston strangling."

"Oh. I see. Maybe, when you're done, we could shoe some horses."

Ouch. "So, what? What's your grand plan now?"

"I don't have a plan. I've never had a plan. It's just, you know, you keep talking about Oregon. How hot the Rogue is, that other one, the K one."

"Klamath."

"We could guide out there. Probably a longer season."

"Definitely a longer season, if you move from river to river. Or get on with a company that does."

He nods, runs his hand down my bare thigh. "Or start your own company," he says.

I turn to look at him. "What? Us?"

He looks away from me. "I don't know. It'd beat working all day for somebody else."

"It'd be a shitload more work. Less time on the river ourselves."

"Only if we really got going. We could stop short of that."

I laugh, just a little, more out of nervousness than anything else, that light tumble inside when you realize you're rootless, that your next step could be in any direction whatsoever. Kind of like blowing out to Oregon in the first place, or following Alissa to Wyoming, packing my stuff into Troy's place, out again, setting sail with Dalt, leaving my parents and everybody else standing on the bank. Like the ceremony we'd had last night, dumping the pills and condoms into the trash. "'We could stop short of that,'" I say, forcing the laugh a second longer. "Your ambition. That's what sucked me in. Right from the start. Me and Mom."

"Your mom?"

"Well, you know what a catch she always thought you were."

"Past tense? She's softening?"

I give him a kiss. Not a short one. "She thinks you're hot. She told me so."

He pulls back far enough to say, "Your mom? She said, 'Oh, he's hot?'"

"Well, not in those words."

"What words then?"

"She said, 'He is very handsome,' and when I picked my face back up, she said, 'He has arms like steel.'"

Dalt flexes his forearm, twisting his fist this way and that, whistles the Popeye song. "Never thought of them as steel-like," he says. "Granite, sure. Something that should be done in marble, Michelangelo or somebody. Somebody with the talent to capture the true beauty."

"You," I say, "are such an ass."

We kind of laugh, but then go quiet. Moving, I think. Starting a business. Dumping the protection last night, I hadn't really thought much beyond that. Now I see myself as a partner in this fledgling business, not yet able to afford employees, this baby Snugglied against my chest as I take on the Class IVs, leave the Vs to Dalt until the baby's at least a year old, a sturdy swimmer, an absolute Tarzan. Afraid of jinxes, we haven't even talked about names. We haven't, really, talked about anything, thought any of this through. Responsibility incarnate. The parents from hell. From kindergarten.

I ease against Dalton's side. "When do we have to leave? Did they tell you that too?"

"They gave us till the end of the season."

"Another month? That was big of them."

But, really, I like the DeGroots. They've been kind to us, kind of into us, smiling these knowing smiles every time they see us coming home, like they know what we're getting up to out here, like maybe they had something like that back in the day themselves. We smiled at that, the very idea of anybody ever having anything like us. But maybe they came close, building this place together. They're still at it now, Dalt says, tearing down the Coop to put in some really nice cabins, places they can rent out at full touron prices, pack people into for a grand a week.

"*This* is a really nice place," I say.

"For us. But not the fly fishers."

"Orvis A-holes," I say, then, "Maybe the DeGroots would let us have the Coop. Trailer it up, drag it to Oregon."

He nods, says, "I bet they would."

"You really want to move to Oregon?"

He shrugs instead of nods, then starts listing off the names of people we've worked with who've moved on. Alissa off to Montana with Dalt's pal, straight after the wedding. Not that that will last. Others only over the pass into Idaho, the closest place they could afford, trying to hang on, but most just gone, off to be grown-ups. The Coop's all, I realize, that's stood between us and that ourselves, all of us priced out of the valley we worked so hard bringing people into. What on earth are we doing planning babies?

"And you think we could start up something on our own?" I ask. "Get loans? Buy gear? Rent property? Find insurance? Hire employees? Payroll and workman's comp and all that?" We're discussing this naked. Good lord.

He shrugs again. "It sounded easier a second ago."

"I thought we weren't ever going to grow up."

He leans back on the bed, on his elbows, runs a hand up through his hair. "What we just did, Mad. I think growing up might be a prereq."

I glance down at him and he blows out a long breath.

"Having kids?" I say. "Dalt, *not* growing up is the prereq. You have to stay a kid for them."

He looks at me, less than convinced, and he does look great, even my mom can see that, but, down there, he's not touching me anymore. So I roll over onto him, stretch myself out against him, thigh to thigh, belly to belly, chest to chest, nose to nose. "Peter Pan had his own gang, fought pirates, kept leading on poor Tinker Bell. All without coming close to growing up. He lived in a tree, for crying out loud."

"Good point," he says.

"We could run a river company from a tree."

"We might have to."

"Raise our kids there. It'll be perfect. Their friends will be green with envy. So will ours."

"You may be right," he says.

"May be? No maybes about it."

He nods, his nose still, literally, against mine.

I tilt back, peck him one on the nose. "Do you have a sunrise float today?"

I know he has a sunrise. He knows I know. I have one, too. "Be off by noon?" I ask. We both know the answer to this, too. "We could be in Ashland by midnight, two, three."

"Ashland?"

"Be a good base. Get Oregon and California. Won't be much cheaper than here, though. We might have to squat in Medford."

"How expensive can a tree be?"

I push up to my elbows. "Exactly," I say.

The alarm starts. Dalt hates that. He hasn't used one ever in his life. I reach over, smack it. "Time to hit the sunrisers."

"And you really want to take off right away?"

"No time like the present." We both have Monday off, our only day. "Just a scouting mission. Find a business. Employees. Clients. Bags of money. Our tree. Tear back here in time for the Tuesday dinner float."

He smiles up at me, says, "What planet did you come from?" He runs his hands along my back, over the rise of my bum, down onto my legs. Goosebumps follow his fingers.

I lower my forehead onto his, sigh. "Maybe," I whisper, "in Oregon, we'll bag the sunrise floats. I mean, I could kind of lie here all day."

"Me too," he says.

Then, together, we groan, drag up, haul into our clothes, and, eventually, look at each other, at the Coop. We go down the ladder from the loft, me first.

"Be nice to have stairs," he says. "Real ones."

It's such a lie. He has, before, just jumped from the loft, skipped the ladder all together. "There are not going to be stairs in my tree," I say, and when he takes the last step from the ladder I'm there waiting for him, wrap my arms around him, tip my head down so it's buried against his chest. "There are not going to be 401(k)s either.

We're not going to be old and stupid and boring, Dalt. Not ever. Never ever going to give ourselves up for a dollar."

He pats my head, running his hand down the length of my hair, which takes him halfway down my back. Mustering all the stupid he can, he says, "Duh."

"The only thing we'll be chasing, ever, are the kids. The little demons. Flying out of the tree house on the vines, though they know their little sister isn't old enough yet."

"How many times have we told them not to do that?"

"They're kids. What do you expect?"

Dalt smiles, and I say, "Pick me up after work?"

"I'll have the truck gassed."

"I'll give notice," I say.

"Really? Already?"

"It's all or nothing time, Dalt."

He drifts off for a second, and I know he's right with me, dumping the pills in the trash, glancing around, then at each other, finally tearing up that ladder, so ready to get after it. "I guess I missed that nothing part," he says.

"And you're going to miss it forever, Bub. No nothings for us."

He hugs me hard enough to crack bones. "Out in Oregon," he says. "Are we going to do scenics, or whitewater? Fishing?"

"All," I say. "We are so going to do it all."

Ambulance

THE VAN, IN person, is a greater heap of rust and loose bolts than we'd feared. Just walking around it sucks what little energy's left straight out of me. It had once been converted to an ambulance, still has that paint job, the lights, but the guy throws in what he claims are the original seats for nothing extra. It smokes, it stinks, the seats all leak stuffing. But Dalt says, "It's just burning oil. We'll get an air freshener," and, about the seats, only, "Duct tape." The riverman's cure-all. He smiles, which, for as long as it takes him to write the check, makes me forget, or ignore, the fact that he knows as much about auto mechanics as quantum mechanics, that I know less. Dalt hops behind the wheel and I collapse into the passenger seat. We leave the guy standing in front of his waferboard mansion, all his fingers crossed behind his back, praying the van gets us far enough down the rutted gravel that we won't bother hiking back up for our check.

Knecht's, in Medford, actually has a repair manual. I blow the dust off while Dalt works on getting the van started again. Flipping the pages, I say, "Know what a carburetor is?"

"It's where the gas burns, or is pumped to. Something." He looks at me. "Hell, Mad, it's a book, we'll have to read it." I stare and he adds, "Mechanics isn't exactly where they push the gifted kids."

"I wonder how those words will taste," I say. I wasn't born yet when this van was built. Wasn't even an idea.

He cranks the key again, the engine fires, farts, blue smoke wraps around us. "If you didn't want to get it, all you had to say was no."

I rest my head against the window glass. Close my eyes. "It's an ambulance, Dalt. How do you think that will make the customers feel?"

"Safe," he says. "We can promise them a quick trip home, lights and sirens."

"If it runs. If they're not afraid they're heading straight to the hospital."

"It'll run. We'll get Hondo to look at it. He's not bad around cars."

"Hondo." The name says it all. Though he can handle a raft, it remains to be seen how long he'll make it before rolling a post-whitewater number with clients on board, sneak off into the bushes with one of their teenaged daughters. This summer, with mono kicking my ass, we made him our lead guy, a foreman kind of, and so far, well, my fingers are as crossed as van-boy's.

"Hondo's okay," Dalt says, which, really, what else can we say? Our first real live employee, beyond the teen-aged shuttle drivers, after that first year going solo, driving ourselves right to the brink, but making a name for ourselves. He's the kind of guy who always drove Dalt wild in the Tetons, a stoner river dude/ski bum, forty years old without a real job, or wife, just some sort of live-in named, and I couldn't make this up, Morning Glory. But, we really aren't that far off ourselves, shave the years, and here Dalt seems to actually kind of like him. They even do stuff together now and then. Mess around in the shop. Check out used boats. And business? Well, just check us out. The clients swarming like locusts, business booming to the point we need another van just to cart the money around.

Dalt pulls out, the van chugging down the blocks to Costco. We wander the aisles with the big ass flatbed cart. Another bazillion lunches to get after. Since the mono set in, it's about all I'm good for, though we've sweated out the whole last month, afraid I'll be a Typhoid Mary, that our biz will get the mono quarantine. Mono. For crying out loud. The kissing disease. So high school, so beyond embarrassing. And if it's a kissing disease, how come Dalt just keeps sailing on? Not even close to fair.

Outside, the van smelling a little better with the bags of groceries, produce, Dalt drops a Christmas tree air freshener over the stick, grins, and it starts first time. "See," he says. "It just needed a new home. Love." It lurches and shimmies down the street, settling crookedly with the new weight, getting into something like its pace out on the highway. Almost cruising. I stare out the window, too tired to quite keep my head from rattling against the glass.

"Well, what?" Dalt says. "You want to have them walk to the river?"

God if he could just let it rest. "We're driving an ambulance, Dalt. It's a joke."

"I'd like new, too," he says. "But, for now, I guess we ride with the joke, okay? Unless you got any other ideas, any bags of cash you haven't told me about."

I pull my hair away from my face, let it fall back. "I've told you everything. You know that."

"I do," he says. "I also know we would have laughed our asses off over this once. Would have killed to own an ambulance. Would have spent nights making up names for our company. Cardiac Whitewater; First Aid for the Soul."

We go quiet after that, turn into the hills before Ashland, our spot up the Little Applegate, which, after renting the three years, we walked the plank and bought this spring, not ready to have another place yanked out from under us, but stretching ourselves so thin we're see-through.

Bounding up over our own ruts isn't as bad as getting away from van-boy, even with the suspension shot. I mean, it is our place, kind of, the bank's anyway. It will never be the Coop, but it really is pretty sweet, off all by itself, and the creek is what we fall asleep listening to every night, out on the paco pad on the deck until winter drives us in. "I'm sorry," I say to Dalt. "I'm just beat." I wonder if he's sick of hearing that yet, as sick as I am of saying it.

"Not much rest the rest of this season," he says. "I'll help with tomorrow's lunches, but then I've got to bolt for the evening gig."

He's teaching CPR. An extra nickel in the home base fund.

"Going to drive the ambulance?" I say. "Should get points with your students."

"I'll get Hondo to look at it first."

I've got the back doors open, a bag of groceries in each arm, one more pinched in between. Our first winter in, after closing up the last of the summer trips, Dalton and I put in the flagstone steps around the drive into the shop and then up to our front door, but now, my arms all full, the sun beating down on me, I can't remember where they start. I try looking around the bags, almost trip sideways, see them just as I hit them, avoid catastrophe by an eyelash. Behind me Dalt says, "Walk much?" but I'm still cartwheeling up the steps, just keeping my feet under me. He's funny like Ebola. None of the steps sit where I think they will, or my feet have suddenly sprouted an extra size. Something.

With the house sinking us low enough teaching CPR actually helps, I am not about to see another doctor about mono, but my internet research does not mention anything like this. It's exhaustion. I need a break. Need to quit worrying about every goddamn thing. I mean Dalton's right, years ago, hell, last year, last *month*, the idea of buying an ambulance for the shuttle runs would have absolutely cracked me up. Now I feel like I could cry.

Maybe I've got a migraine coming on. Mom used to get them to make crucifixion look like a blessing. Stocking the shop refrigerators with my first load, I beg off another trip up and down the stairs, just make for the house, a railing to hold onto, our bed room, the shades pulled.

Dalt, I can almost hear his impatient sigh, raises his voice to let me know he'll get the lunches as far as he can, but . . .

"I know," I shout back. "I'll get them."

ॐ   ॐ   ॐ

THAT NIGHT I wake up spinning, the whole room falling away, my breath rushing in. The old falling dream, but it doesn't quite stop. Spinning, dizzy, is not something I've ever been able to do. My dad tried, coaxing me onto the tilt-a-whirl, then stepping out, the ride emergency stopped, covered with everything I'd eaten since the day I was born, the only clean place on him my imprint, where I'd clung to him like a barnacle. Just driving by a state fair leaves my stomach churning.

I have to focus on the clock numbers, dimly aglow, before things line back up where they're supposed to. I'm gasping, biting back bile. Beside me, Dalt stirs. He couldn't drag me out to the porch when he got home, I remember that much, so we're in here, the curtains all fluttering in the breeze coming up off the creek.

"You okay?" he murmurs, his back to me, flopping an arm over, searching, patting my thigh.

"Shitty dream," I say.

He hums something, and is out.

The lunches. I actually focus on the clock, what the numbers say. Halfway between midnight and dawn. And now I'll worry about the damn lunches until they drive me down to the shop. Maybe Dalt put the coolers together after he got home from class. He and Hondo are bolting first thing in the morning. I'm shuttling, still too tired, too weak to take the sticks.

I drag out of bed, find a sweatshirt and grope my way down the stairs, out the door, the night cool on my bare legs, a thong maybe not the most sensible attire for 2 a.m. sandwich duty. I think what

Dalt would do if he came out looking for me, found me dressed like this. It makes me kind of smile, kind of hope he'll look. Maybe it's the cool, or the stars, or just that long pass out and sleep, but I almost feel like I can face things.

When I reach the top of the flagstones, I hesitate, then go down beside them, walking on what will one day be our flowers, if we ever get a chance to catch our breath. Right now I don't quite feel up to steps without a railing, which makes me shake my head. I mean, one stumble, one bad falling dream, and I'm tiptoeing around like I could break a hip with a glance in the wrong direction. "Save it for when you're eighty, Grandma," I say.

The fluorescents, which I hate, stab at my eyes and I stagger again, like this is my new thing. I hold an arm up against the glare, hold onto the workbench, and check the coolers. All the dry stuff is in already, and I honestly can't remember if I did that or not. In the fridge the big zip-locks are loaded, Dalt's meticulous butcher paper burrito fold evident around every sub, his draftsman's Sharpie label so precise compared to my scrawl. He did it all. After talking 15-2, 5-1, compressions and airways, all night with the glorious weekend warriors, the lifeguards and expectant mothers of Jackson county.

The expectant mothers. The bitches. I lift my sweatshirt, stare down at my stomach, flat and hard as ever, though layered now with a little baby fat, my month off the oars, of doing nothing. Still hot enough, I'll admit, though hot is not exactly what I'm looking for. My patience, to tell the truth, is wearing thin in the new mom department.

And that's where I'm standing, in front of the open fridge, sweatshirt pulled up to the girls, nothing but my thong down below, when Dalt says, "Everything okay down there?"

With no idea at all how I'll explain, I say, "Had to cool it down somehow. You know, before we lost the whole place to the flames."

He's smiling when I look at him. I let the sweatshirt fall. "You made all the lunches."

"You okay, Maddy?"

He means it. He's worried about finding his exhausted, jittery wife flashing a refrigerator in the middle of the night. "I got wondering if they were ready. The lunches. Couldn't sleep."

"Not some midnight craving? Pickles and ice cream?"

Another pregnancy feeler. That's what I need. At first he convinced himself the mono was pregnancy, even talked about getting those tests. EPT. Pee on a stick. But, um, no, I wasn't pregnant, and, somehow, that's not exactly how I envision finding out, sitting on the throne trying not to pee on my fingers.

And, the money again. After our second year out here, our second straight year of trying with no zygotes taking up residence, we talked about going the doctor route, doing the tests, finding out exactly what was going on. We balanced the check book the next night, and that settled that. Dalt said, "The fun's all in the trying anyway, right?" and I smiled a smile so brittle it could have cracked right off of my face.

"Go on back to bed," I tell him. "I'm awake now. I'll get started on Monday's."

"I'm awake, too."

"You've got to row in the morning, Bub." I close the fridge, pull stuff from the shelves, all the snacky crap you can get ready ahead of time. At the prep counter, I hook out a stool with my foot.

Dalt comes to sit beside me, I think, but as soon as I get things lined out, he starts picking them back up, one after the other, carting them back to the shelves.

"Dalt."

"It's three in the morning, Mad. You are not going to sit down here and pack coolers. Think that's going to make you feel better tomorrow?"

"You can't do it all, Dalt. I can't not do anything."

"I can do it all till you're back on your feet. And till then, you can do nothing. Remember? In sickness and in health?" While I try to remember if we even said that, he finishes reshelving everything I'd gotten out. He's got his back to me when he says, "3 a.m. I swear, you're the worst patient in the history of disease."

I decide not to tell him about the dizzies, the stumbling. "I don't do sick, Dalt. I told you. I never get sick. I can't stand being sick."

"Well, everything says ride it out, take it easy, avoid the relapse."

"It's supposed to be over by now."

"Maybe, if you'd take it easy, it would be."

I narrow my eyes. "What? This is my fault?"

He turns toward me, rubbing his face, his hair sticking up every which way. "Anyway," he says. "We should probably check out that fire danger you were so worried about. Can't be too careful about your place."

"Oh," I say. "That. Just a spot fire. Put it out myself."

"You did not," he says, and he's so serious I can't quite keep in a laugh.

I stand up and he kills the lights and we stand alone out there for a minute, letting our eyes adjust. I pull my sweatshirt over my head. It's white, and I know it'll be all he sees. I hold it way out to my side, as far as I can reach, and walk toward him. He falls for it like a mouse to the cheese. I wait until he reaches to wrap his arms around it, and pounce on him from behind. His ear in my teeth, I hiss, "There is going to be nothing left of you but ash, Buster."

He turns toward the house, those stairs, and starts to carry me off, me clinging to him, a second ago the aggressor. "What would you have done if Hondo showed up early?" he asks.

"Stopped his heart."

"Oh, you think so?

"You don't?"

We reach the back door, which he's left open, which we leave open again, and he takes me straight up the stairs. I'm not some miniature chick, but he does it without even breathing hard. As puny as I've been feeling, it actually kind of pisses me off. I slap at his rear, say, "Doesn't this thing have a high gear?"

"Oh, honey," he says, "high gear will only frighten you."

"Try me."

"I have every intention of doing just that."

"Oh, really. And just what are your intentions, sir?"

"Not stopping till you beg for mercy, ma'am."

"Well, I hope you've laid in provisions, because they'll be crying for blankets in hell before you get me begging for one single thing."

He drops down on the bed, doing this little spin move, leaving us landing side by side, the mattress bouncing beneath us. It's not a bad move, I mean, kind of slick actually, but, man, suddenly my head is where it was when I crawled up here this afternoon.

I have to take a few breaths to convince myself I haven't dreamt all this, haven't just woken up from another falling dream.

Dalt's flipped around, missed all that, and is kissing my neck, when, as suddenly as I fell through space he says, "We'll be all right, Mad. You know that, don't you?"

I can't think of a single way to answer.

"All this money shit. The loans. The debt. It's just starting out stuff. Growing pains."

"I know," I say. I thought he was talking about my exhaustion, my falling head, this mono that doesn't seem to be mono.

"This company's going places, even if we do drive an ambulance."

"Beats a hearse," I say.

"Exactly," he answers. "Float with us, the ambulance is for the ones we rescue on the way."

"Um, that could maybe use some work. How about, Triage Rafting? We hit the worst first."

"Better. Maybe. I still kind of like MD, The Thrill Doctors."

I laugh. We'd made up names for our company all the way out here, years ago, hour after hour in the truck, hurtling toward the unknown. MD. Maddy and Dalt. I'd forgotten that one. I was the one who pointed out that MD was also MadDog, the rotgut wino wine. Dalt wanted to know how I knew that. I punched him. We flipped it to DM, which Dalt said sounded too much like dim, like dumb, besides rhyming with BM. We wound up with Half Moon

Whitewater. I can't really say why. Dalt had something, each of us half of the whole, that kind of stuff he used to talk about. I might have punched him again, told him I was way more than half.

It's dawn before we realize that instead of going back to sleep, instead of him doing one thing to make me beg for mercy, me doing one thing to make him cave first, all we've done is talked and laughed, making up stupid names for stupid companies. We don't even know our time is up until we hear Hondo's tires crunching up the drive, the thrum of the bass on his stereo. We jump up, pull on shorts, hook up the trailer, load the cold food into the coolers. I drive them down to the river to set up, dash to town for the clients, haul them back to the boats.

I stick around for Hondo's safety talk, actually getting to be polished, even funny. They listen to him, instead of just glancing at Dalt, hoping they're going in his boat. Then, a total landlubber, I watch them go, heads bright in their helmets, arms eager on the paddles.

I wave goodbye from the put-in, promise I'll see them all alive at the take out, call, "Have fun," and before they're out of sight around the first bend, the first drop, I'm thinking maybe I'll work on getting the seats back into the ambulance so I can pick them up with it, lights and siren if they work, jump out fast, look all dumbfounded, say, "You mean you didn't lose *any*? Well, *this* calls for a celebration!"

I haven't felt this decent all summer. Just spending a night talking to Dalt, laughing, money hardly coming up. Mono, schmono. We'll get back on the baby thing. Tonight. It has to happen. I mean, it's part of our plan. What we most strongly desire.

Waves

DALT'S PACKAGE IS still there when I get home, torn open on the couch, Styrofoam ghost poop dribbled all across the cushions. I'd been drying my hair when the delivery guy rang—trying to spruce up for the doc's for Christ's sake—and it pissed me off, stairs a struggle I can do without. But I made it down, and there was this package from Dalt. Even over the dizzies, I went kind of breathless, stunned he'd actually think to send a care package all the way from Mongolia.

Mongolia. No lie. Before he left, I wasn't even sure it was a real country, or just some Bugs Bunny punch line. But the real punch line was inside the box, this humungous stuffed fish, the legendary taimen, at least as big as me, mouth a lion tamer could put his head into, teeth just like that, gills flared as red and swollen as sex itself. Funny, Dalt. Totally hysterical.

But, staring at it now, the room starts to sway, and I focus on the package, the Styrofoam pellets going double on me, triple. I close my eyes, run my hand up through my hair in the old finger-comb, like maybe one thing could still be normal, but the doc's electrode gel shit is everywhere, sticky, impossible to push through. Throw in some white streaks, push it all up with a good jolt of high voltage, and I'd pass anywhere as the bride of Frankenstein.

But man, I could use a jolt of that now, the waves surging from every which way, leaving me tossed out in Class V, blindfolded. I barely snag the banister before tipping over down the stairs. I work on breathing. "You and me, fish," I say. "We're swimming in the same sea."

I take a chance and set sail for the couch. It's like walking on a trampoline, the floor of suspect hardness, indeterminable altitude. "Well," I say to the fish, grabbing the recliner. "You're swimming days are over, aren't they?" He's nothing but a big block of Styrofoam, nicely airbrushed. But, me? My swimming days? I'm mid goddamn ocean. Shark-infested waters. I am fighting not to puke.

At the clinic, the lab tech spent half an hour sticking the electrodes or monitors or whatever all over my head. "Sorry about the hair," I said, but he said, "No, no. It holds them in place better." All chatty, he went on, "Once you try getting the gel out of your hair, that's when you might consider cutting it off."

Maybe once they have to saw off the top of my head, but, for just another test? I don't think so. Dalt has got a thing for my hair, which, girl or not, is something I'll hold on to.

Some of it, the TV's black and white squares sifting and shifting, brought on pretty intense badness, but I kept breakfast down, and thought I'd made it through. Then Dr. Wu slipped in, said a few things to tech boy, and flipped the eye patch to my other eye. Yeah, eye patch. Total Captain Hook. Wu stood back and watched for a second before starting out. Never even a word in my direction. So I asked what the squares were all about, more just to make him acknowledge my existence than out of any to-die-for curiosity. Wu didn't blink, just turned as he opened the door. "Visually Evoked Response," he said. I gave him a look, and he explained that, "VER is a test to back up MRI's MS indicators." He vanished in his cloud of acronyms, leaving tech boy waiting for me to stare at the screen again, which, after that, was pretty much all I could manage. Nobody'd ever said a single thing about MS.

Eventually, tech boy unstuck all the electrodes, told me they'd have results in only a few days, that I should make an appointment with Dr. Wu to review them.

I said, "MS? Like the multiple sclerosis kind of MS?"

He did this funny lip purse/sad-eyed nod/shrug thing, then was out of the room as fast as Wu, like he'd walked straight through the wall, leaving me anchored on the crinkly paper, wondering what I was supposed to do next, where I was supposed to go now, just trying to breathe, first out, then in—I remembered that much. But, I mean, I'm twenty seven years old. I run rivers. Blow right through the baddest they can throw at me. The picture of fricking health. Me, twitching in some wheelchair, head lolling, hands in my lap waving to their own invisible currents?

ॲ   ॲ   ॲ

The first real waves, the ones I couldn't ignore, coming out of nowhere, making me sway and grab for Dalt's arm, left us both wondering. Then the exhaustion. Holy shit. Suddenly I could sleep through whole days, which is not my style at all. I mean, give me back my mono.

Though maybe one symptom in ten had any chance at all of lining up with pregnancy, Dalt kept clutching at that straw, and when he brought it up again, a Sunday morning in bed, light streaming low through the window, birds singing, the whole nine yards, I finally grabbed at it too. God, finally. How fabulous would that be? A little pack of river rats tearing around the place? Exactly what we've wanted since day one. Dalt's face was, well, there's like no other word for it, sweet. All little boy at Christmas, barely able to wait to unwrap the biggest, best package he's ever received.

"Do you think?" he said. His voice shook, and, right then, I'd have been happy dying with him, that one instant being like the happiest of my life. And, goddamn it, I knew I wasn't pregnant, that there was no way it would feel like this. What pregnancy turns the ground liquid, steals your memory, pulls words off your tongue before you can open your mouth, swirls your balance into some kind of joke? But, his face, I kind of let it sweep me away, and when he bounced off the bed, whipped himself into jeans, banged into the doorway with a moldy old T-shirt stuck over his head, I held my tongue. I knew what he was doing, which drugstore he was headed to, and, well, I'll admit it, I let myself pretend right along with him. What's that bullshit they say, about how wanting something badly enough will make it come true? Well, yeah. I didn't really fall for it. But, I guess, really, I kind of did.

So, when he came back in, all out of breath, sweaty—he takes steps like four at a time—and flounced down on the bed, already tearing open the pretty little EPT box, I took the stick and disappeared into the bathroom.

I don't know why I bothered peeing on it. I mean, I knew it was only going to say what it always did. And, unlike now, I hadn't even missed a period yet. When I came back out, empty-handed, no little blue plus sign to show off, Dalt just hugged me and said, "The fun's all in the trying, let's not forget that," and I hugged him back, and, well, we spent the rest of the morning trying, and he was certainly right about the fun.

But what he did forget, if he didn't forget the fun, was what brought on the whole test kit rush in the first place. More waves hit right in the middle of the trying, and I tensed till they passed, which I could tell by the way he started going wild, made Dalt think I was close, right on the brink, that he'd try to meet me there, this place we, as ridiculous as it is to admit, sort of felt we were the only people ever to discover. Really though, I was just trying not to sink beneath the waves. My hand started to twitch, tapping against his back, a rhythm Dalt misunderstood, tried to fall into, and I closed my eyes and didn't tell him a thing. There was no way I could pretend I didn't have to go to the doc's.

But only days after the first MRI, still waiting on results, the whole Mongolia plan dropped into our lap. A friend quitting the biz, selling his permits, tired of the ups and downs, hawking for clients. We looked at maps, made plans, got talking about yurts, got laughing about living off yak yogurt. Came up with every y-word we could think of.

Dalt patted my tummy and said, "We can put the first one in the oven over there. We'll call him Attila. A good, sturdy Mongol name."

And we really kind of thought we would, maybe call him Atty or something, no matter how he'd hate us for it later.

We got everything lined out. Passports. Visas. Clients' checks piling up in the bank, which, well, do you have any idea how much an MRI costs, how many river runners have health plans? And the MRI results, they said, showed nothing more specific than possible points of concern. But the waves just kept getting worse, the tremors more frequent, and further tests sprawled a long way out ahead of me.

So Dalt left with Hondo instead. I mean, he had to. Cutting out on our first round of clients for Mongolia? Might as well have gone straight to McDonald's to fill out our apps.

We spent our last evening trying to count up the nights we'd been apart in the last five years and didn't get to a second hand. Then Dalt called from Russia, the last phone, some dilapidated field where they were going to catch what was supposed to be a helicopter, but he said was now a biplane. A fricking biplane? Completely off the planet for the next eight weeks, leaving on two wings, and he says he'll try to get a message out with the client exchanges. He didn't say anything about getting a message in. I was on my own.

"At least you're not pregnant," he said, the line all crackly, and though we're not newlyweds or anything, that's the first time I really meant it when I said, "You are such an ass."

ཉ   ཉ   ཉ

AT LEAST YOU'RE not pregnant echoing through me, I'd pushed myself to the edge of the doc's table, looked at the linoleum down there, reaching down a toe, finding the floor mostly where it should be. There wasn't so much as a Kleenex to wipe the crap out of my hair. I found the door next, the long hallway, and tottered down the stairs, white-knuckling the railing. I'd sat a while longer in the truck, waiting for my head to slow down enough to drive home, the parking lot every bit as sterile as their examination rooms, their bedside manners. I shouldn't be driving anymore, that's pretty obvious. But Dalt's in Mongolia, for Christ's sake. Fishing.

"Working," I'd said out loud. It's not like he's out there for fun. He's guiding the world's moguls, Outer Mongolian taimen fishing the soup du jour. The fun—that tramping through places like Mongolia is what Dalt and I live for—is all just part of the luck we've always known. That's us. The Luckies. We've actually called ourselves that. Like our own brand of superhero.

And, all superhero, I make it home. To nothing but Dalt's stupid fish. I push off from the recliner, embark for the last leg of my journey to the couch, make landfall on the cushions beside it. I touch the top of the fish's head, where you'd scratch between its ears if it were a dog, some trusting, clueless Lab. I tell it, "That was the last thing I called him—Ass," but it couldn't care less. It's got a fly the size of a softball stuck in its jaw. As a matter of fact, it's a mouse, all deer hair and rabbit fur. Hook the size of a pirate's claw. Jesus. Rodent eating fish. I look him in his cold glass eye and say, "Well, *at least* I'm not pregnant." I swallow hard, let a wave pass through me, then pet the fish, run my hand along its flank. "I mean, thank god for MS, you know?"

And then, talking to a goddamn fish, I'm suddenly crying all over the place. No little misty-eyed shit for me. Nope. Full on blubber sesh. Like chicks on TV. I yank the Kleenex box off the coffee table and before long it looks like I've lived through a blizzard, the floor littered with crumpled white tissue. I'm a streaming ball of tears and snot and drool and I start to laugh, say, "Hey, Dalt, how about we *try* right now? I mean, how hot is this?"

The fucking fish just stares at me, not giving a rat's ass, wanting nothing in the world but to close his predator jaws around that hapless mouse, and finally it just gets to be too much. I punch him one right in the kisser. His barracuda teeth rake my knuckles, and I break the jaw and the paint pops and cracks and the Styrofoam core splits back to the gills. His glass eye angles out of its scooped dish in total shock. He just can't believe I did that. I shrug at him, say, "Sucks for you, Sugar Ray."

But I've knocked him completely out of the box, and his face is ruined and I'm already thinking about how I'll blame the shipper, when I see Dalt's note underneath. I have to use the rest of the Kleenex to get myself cleaned up enough to read that it's not a present for me, but belongs to somebody in the first round of clients, how he'd found a screaming deal from some Mongolian taxidermist. The client's only over in Grant's Pass, and Dalt was hoping I could deliver it.

"Ah, shit," I say to the fish. "Sorry about your face."

My knuckles are bleeding. I stick a ghost poop pellet on each cut, staunch the flow. "That was a cheap shot," I admit. "Total sucker punch." But the fish, with his jaw like that, doesn't say a word.

I look around, pluck one of his teeth off the couch cushions. These goddamn fish must have been what gave them the idea for sharks. "But, god," I say. "That's life. Get over it, would you? They'll just cut in some new foam, dash off a few squirts with the airbrush, superglue the old eye back down. You, my friend, you will be as good as new."

I lean over the back of the couch to the desk, and snag the phone book. "T" for taxidermy. I punch in the numbers without having to stop once. I'm on a roll. Queen of the Luckies.

He says he'll have to see the damage. That it might be easier just building a new one. "No doubt," I say, then "Hey, how are you with people? You ever patch up MS?"

He gets off pretty quick after that, and now I've got a fish to deliver to the dead animal vet. Yay for me. I'm not even sure I can get him down the stairs.

Reaching back again to the desk, having to stop till the world realigns its orbit, I snag the laptop. No internet connex in Mongolia that's for sure. But I google "M.S." and "pregnancy," and check this out, no complications except that being pregnant may *reduce* the attacks, especially in the second and third tris. Of course, whoever's up there running this shit having his hysterical sense of humor and all, other studies show the attacks coming back harder than ever in the months after delivery. Isn't that just perf? You finally have this baby, finally get to try breast feeding—something I've wanted to do since before I grew boobs—and all of a sudden just crossing the room to the crib becomes a carnival ride. You can't even pretend God's a woman.

But, nowhere in everything I click through is there any mention of what I was really looking for, MS affecting menstrual cycles, and once I get up the nerve, I shove off for the bathroom, that other stick saved so hopefully in the torn open box. I mean, maybe that's all that's happening, some weird reaction to the hormone changes. Dizziness alone won't make you miss a period, will it? And, Dalt and I, well, the send-off, waves or not, was kind of all about trying. I've never been the most regular girl, my periods I mean, and pregnancy hitting me this way is never something I even thought to hope for.

I sit, I think, for hours on that toilet, my ass going numb, opening my eyes as every wave passes, only to see the little blue plus sign still staring up at me, Dalt all the way to hell and gone, no way at all to reach him.

This is not the way to find this out, and I can't believe I didn't use this stupid test the first late day. I mean, who knows what all these tests have done, me never telling any of the docs about *my condition*, because, duh, I didn't know myself. I mean, what the fuck is an MRI anyway? Do they shoot you full of X-rays in that fricking tube? Fry all those tiny cells trying their hardest to divide and separate, making lungs and fingers, brain and heart? I wave the little stick like an old thermometer, trying to change the reading, and say, "Oh, Attila, honey. I am so sorry."

I make it to the couch, push taimen boy onto the floor and curl up with the laptop, start trying to study this now. But, even trying to find what I've done, this MS or whatever the hell I have, drags my ass so hard I don't last long.

౭   ౭   ౭

IT'S JUST CLEARING dawn when the phone blasts me awake. I almost don't go for it, but creep up over the back of the couch, the laptop hitting the floor, my head starting its nasties, stomach rolling. I close my eyes, try breathing like a normal person, and still manage to snag the phone just in time, and thank god, it's Dalt, the joker upstairs relenting just this once.

One guy in the newest round of client's has a satellite phone. Dalt's laughing all over the place, saying he loves me, saying how are you? saying "God it's good to hear your voice," when all I've managed is one slurred, "Hello?" And the phone must be bouncing its waves off of Sputnik. I can barely hear him, but I press my ear flat with the phone, grip it so hard the scabs on my knuckles crack, start seeping watery blood, taimen stigmata. As soon as there's a gap, I cry, "Dalton, I can't hear you. Is it really you?"

Then it goes crystal for a second, so clear I'm sure I've lost him, and into the void, he says, all unsure, "Maddy? Are you there?"

"God, yes. I am. I am here."

He takes a breath, and I know he's doing the same thing I am, trying to breathe me in through the satellite waves. "Dalt," I say. But then don't know what I could possibly tell him. I kind of laugh, sob, blurt, "I got your fucking fish."

And then we're both laughing, the world so normal for that one second it's hard to remember ever having it tilt on me.

"It's all busted to shit," I say. "I already called about getting it fixed."

Then we're crackly again. I mean, what is the deal? Do satellites go behind clouds, or what? "God, you bastard," I shout. "Don't leave me now!"

Dalton shouts, "You don't have to call me God, Mad. We've been over this."

I try to laugh, but my hand starts its thing and I pinch it between my legs. With absolutely no idea what's going to slip out of my mouth, I say, "Dalt, I'm, I, they say maybe, I don't know, that I might have MS."

There's an empty patch then, so filled with space buzzing and droning I think maybe Dalt's found a way to transport himself through the ether to me. It's totally something he would do. I'm waiting for him to materialize right in front of me when I hear, "What? What? Goddamn this thing. I can't hear a single thing." It sounds like he's talking to somebody else.

I close my eyes, a wave hitting hard. This is not something you can do over the phone, no matter the technology. "I said," I shout, "that, that there's a little blue plus."

Even in the grip of the wave, I smile saying it. Not alone in the fricking bathroom, but to Dalt, no matter how far away he is. I'd double all this nasty shit in a heartbeat if it'd bring us Attila, and, really, the coming months of clear-headedness seem right now like a total Luckies thing, a bonus undreamed of. I just won't let myself think of what's in store down the line. I mean, isn't that kind of a prereq for having a kid in the first place? *Not* thinking? Not of extra chromosomes, or missing parts, even just colic, terrible twos, adolescent rage—shit, international terrorism, global warming. You think too hard about anything, and, poof, gone, your whole life wasted cowering in a corner, afraid to so much as open your eyes.

Dalt is saying something. The waves recede, a calm after the rapids. "What?" I say. "What?"

"A blue plus? You're not telling me the trying is over?"

"Oh, no," I say. I'm squeezing the phone in half. "We'll still try all over my place, Dalt. I promise."

"Man, Maddy," he starts. "I'm, I just, you wouldn't kid about this?"

"Ah, Dalt, no. Never. Not this."

He screams something then, a huge halleluiah ringing down some wild Mongolian river valley I'll never set foot in. Then he's back, saying, "Shit, Mad, and I was just calling about the test stuff. The VIP. To see how that went."

I listen to the vacuum of space hum over the connection. "They don't know anything, Dalt. I mean, I don't, they're not . . ." Jesus, just as articulate as ever. But what's he been doing, keeping a calendar, painting out days on the yurt wall in yak blood? I smile so wide it hurts. I say, "They don't have any results yet."

"So, no idea?"

"Not really," I say. "But, Dalt, I . . ."

The line crackles, and he says, "I'm the happiest person on the planet, Mad, I—"

The connection fades bad, and he shouts my name, and I'm shouting his, and then he's gone. I haven't even told him I love him.

I lower the phone to my lap, staring at it there until it starts its off the hook wail, which hits me just like the shifting squares on the TV, and I have to hunker over it, put my hands out to the cushions, hold myself up, fight the urge to take the big spit right there. I fumble for the phone with my eyes closed, shut it off, then sit still, every muscle clenched.

When I do open my eyes, I find the fish on the floor, where he's been lying all night, scoping me out with his crazy eye. I had a biology teacher in high school with an eye like that, always looking off over my shoulder. I say, "That was pretty chicken-shit, wasn't it? Only telling him the good part."

I start pushing him back into his box. "There's things you can't tell anybody, though," I say. "Things it's best not to know." I'm talking to a fish again, a dead one, and I wonder, really, how great a loss my brain would be. But I go on. "Who wants to know everything anyway? How could you ever make a move if you knew what was out there waiting for you? That how-long-you-have-left shit? Who the hell would want to know that? Hmm? Answer me that."

The fish keeps his eye on me, pretty skeptical looking. "I mean, what good is it going to do Dalt right now, worrying about this crap? Man, ignorance is bliss. Give me more of that. Make mine a double."

But, shit. I'm whistling past the graveyard. Attila. I open the computer, but there's nothing there, or too much to find anything, and I wind up calling the clinic, try to make a Wu appointment. They tell me four weeks. Is he the only doctor on this planet, or what?

Grabbing the phone book, I make myself this big mission plan. Drop the fish off for repairs, then just show up at Wu's and make him lay down some answers. *To back up the MS indicators.* That is just not the way one human being informs another about something like this. Only in cartoons is it funny to drop an anvil on a person's head. One more bonehead line like that and Wu will be up the same creek as taimen boy. With the paddle shoved up his fricking ass.

I stand up with Dalton's fish, take a second to get my feet under me, my sea legs, and we make it down the steps together. I set off in the truck, hardly spinning at all, supercharged by an actual mission, by my news, by Dalt's call. I watch the traffic, the other cars staying in their lanes right where they belong, the lanes staying on the ground. I am Supergirl.

It isn't until I get taimen boy out of the truck, slam the door behind me, that I realize I'm at the clinic, that I never even looked at the taxidermist's address, that I hadn't brought the phone book like I'd planned, that it never once crossed my mind I had no idea where I was going. And I wind up here? Like this hideous place is some sort of destination?

This is the baddest shit, the very worst, making the dizziness and hurling something to hope for, this idea that I may actually, truly, be losing my mind. Couldn't they just tear off a leg or something, some non-vital organ, call it good, quit fucking with me? The brain, the ovaries, they're all I need, though Dalt would throw my heart in in a second. It's the way he is.

Instead of turning around, going back home, starting over—facing the whole trip, the roads, from the beginning—I stop only long enough to stuff taimen boy back into the truck, promising I'll be right back. I even crack a window. Jesus. I'll be picking out a car seat for him next.

I straighten up and face the building, start wading toward the smoked glass doors of the entrance. Some Class IV, but I plow on, run a hand up for the finger comb, trying my hardest. And that's when I realize I never took a shower, never stepped out of my clothes, never did anything yesterday, last night, today, but fight off waves, find out about MS, about Attila, talk to Dalt. Kind of a swirling vortex with me at its center. My life.

I mean, I take one glance at my reflection in the glass doors, and can't help shaking my head. The bride of Frankenstein? Totally something to strive for now, to ever look that hot again.

The receptionist recognizes me, but is kind of flustered, kind of speechless, when I say, "I forgot my phone book." I mean, I have to ask, "Um, could I use yours?"

She fumbles for it, sticks it out as far as she can, like whatever I have might be catching.

"I forgot the taxidermist's address," I say, which leaves her more speechless. Can you even be *more* speechless? God, I miss my brain.

I flip through the pages, thinking T, T. Q, R, S, T. I know I'll find it. But receptionist chick is staring at me like I might go off. "You see," I say, "my husband? Dalt? If this doesn't all work out? If it comes down to death sentence time and shit? He wants to have me stuffed." I smile at her. "Is that sweet, or what?"

Her eyes bug, and it's all just so stupid I shove the book back at her, and say, "I have to see Wu. Now. No kidding. No excuses. It's an emergency." I'm in the elevator before she's said a single word.

The elevator, of course, takes me straight to my knees, but literally this time. I slide down the wall, afraid I'm going to pass out. Even MS. I mean, what the hell is happening to me?

The doors swoosh open, and there's somebody starting in, then stopping. I'm looking at his shoes, moving left, then right, swirling, shiny black leather with all these tiny, tiny holes punched through. When he says, "Miss?" just from the accent, I know it's Wu, and I say, "I'm pregnant."

He says, "Miss? Can you stand? Do you need help?"

Jesus. I'm on all fours in a fricking elevator, my hand twitching like I'm waving a beggar's cup. *Do I need help?* "No," I say. "Totally golden here."

I pull myself into the corner, buffeted by Muzak, trying to keep my head above the waves, feet pointed downstream. I look up at Dr. Wu, surprised to see him looking right at me, no crazy eye staring off into space. The waves pound me toward the bottom. I can't catch any air. "It's Attila," I say. "I need to know if he'll be all right."

I hear Dr. Wu suck in a breath.

"Is it that bad?" I say. "Tell me. You've got to tell me everything. I need to know it all."

Flip

HONDO CAME BY before I was awake. Before dawn probably, if Dalton got his way, trying to get this over with before I had to witness any more. By the time I make it down my path beside the flagstones, the shop is cleaned out. Empty. Not a boat, not a frame, not a cooler. Not a single loose quick-release. Even the rafters stand empty above the swept concrete floor. Where the refrigerators hummed there's nothing but a dusty blank gap in the counter space. Dalton's got Hondo's Ryder backed right up to the shop doors.

I set Atty down at the base of the steps, let him hold my finger, swaying, taking a few steps with me before dropping onto his seat, gawping at it all, this wild commotion, the only world he's ever known being packed into boxes and carried, by his own father, into the gaping black maw of this monstrous truck. Even the ambulance, what he came home from the hospital in, his very first ride, is already gone forever. We've only been on one float, the three of us together. We own a single raft now, the one so badly beat up we wouldn't take clients in it.

I want to drop down on my knees, sag onto my side, some Meryl Streep move—"I had a hill above the Little Applegate, a house beside a creek." All I'd have to do is let my mind slip for one second, drop the defenses, and I'd be down and sobbing.

We tried so hard, the whole year after Mongolia only a blur, filling trip after trip, me back on the sticks whenever I could manage, the drops and the dips having me fighting back vomit, fighting just to hang on, the Typhoid Mary mono days a promised land of liability issues, the guilt of leaving At with Morning Glory's daughter all but gutting me. But every month, Dalt and I surrounded ourselves with paperwork, building income towers the medical bills toppled as fast as we could stack them up. Twice as fast. Ten times. So Dalt, without a word, goes to a friend of a friend, gets himself hired on to a carpenter crew, only after making sure he can sneak my preexistings through the hoops at Kaiser.

And now this. As if losing the Coop had only been a warm up. Our own house. Atty's creek. Half Moon Whitewater in Hondo's hands. Maybe a month, I figure, before we're buying back one of our good rafts at the bankruptcy sale.

But he's gotten Morning Glory to take the whole Oregon/California side of it, which might just save his ass. I'm sure she put up the buyout money. Hondo's back to Mongolia as soon as it ices out. More money there, he says, than fish. Twice as easy to reel in. But Dalt's told me he's got some native girl over there too. Someone we've argued over telling Glory about. Someone half his age, their own yurt. I can see Hondo trussed to a spit, an angry father, all drooping Mongol horde moustaches and arcing scimitars, rotating him slowly over the coals, Hondo saying, "Dude, like, what?"

Hondo waves at me as he comes out of the dark of the truck, jumps down grabbing the webbing handle, the door thundering shut behind him. He swings the latch around, double pumping it to make sure. He dusts his hands against each other, says, "So, that's like it?"

Dalt looks away. "It is," he says. "It's exactly like it."

"Sell the place already?"

Dalt can only nod. I bend down, rock Atty into my side. He squirms.

"Sucks," Hondo said. "I could have lived here for sure."

"It's a great spot," Dalt says.

"You need some help moving stuff over to town?"

Dalt points out the other truck, backed up beside the one Hondo's taking. "That's the last of it right there. We'll get it."

"Yeah, well, okay," Hondo says, and then, almost as if he's launching an attack, he thrusts his hand out toward Dalton, and I realize he's having trouble with this too. "Thanks man," he says. "For the chance. For, like, everything." Then he chuckles his stoner chuckle, and shakes his head. "Thanks for making me a business owner and all. Should probably hate you for that."

"You may still," Dalt says.

Hondo shakes his head. "No man, lot of bad karma in hate." Then before I have a chance to suspect a thing, he bounds over to me, his legs tanned near black, roped with muscle, his feet gnarly as a toad's in his battered flip flops. "You," he says, hauling me to my feet, wrapping me up in a bear hug. I reel slightly, fight not to have to hold on to him, breathe his patchouli and garlic reek. Those Mongol girls must be tough as hammered steel. "We would have been perfect together," he says to me. "You're right. But, like, thanks for not making a scene."

I blurt, "What?" but he's already hopping away, jumping into the cab, gunning the engine, honking the horn for Atty, who whoops in delight and waves.

Then he's gone, and a moment later so is the crunching of the gravel, the grinding of the gears. Nothing left at all but the breeze in the long needles of the pines, the rustle of the creek, the perfect quiet we're leaving.

Dalt looks to the ground, his guard dropping for just that instant, his eyes wandering the gravel and the grass, as if he might find his old life there, sigh in relief and pick it up, slip it back on, wonder how he'd ever fallen out of it. "I guess," he says, and clears his throat. "I guess I'll go in. Make one last sweep."

"Just the bedding," I say, our paco pad, Atty's collapsible crib. "I stacked it by the door."

Dalt goes by me up the steps without saying a word, just reaching out at the last second to touch his hand to my wrist. "You doing okay?" he says.

"Golden," I say, "just had my hands full." But I've got a new numbness, in my ankles and wrists, like they're asleep, barely attached, joints as solid as Pinocchio's. They still work, but they don't feel like they should, and I've learned to trust nothing. I was great till Atty was born, but since, it's been like falling off a cliff. Just carrying him anymore gives me the spooks, like we could go down in a jumble together, all sorts of bones snapping. My last few river trips were beyond hair-raising.

I hear the sweep of the paco against the floor, a sound that used to mean we were making our bed out on the porch, a memory that, if I let it, might still get some action started down below. The nights we had out there? The stars on our skin? There'll be none of that outside our little bungalow in Ashland. God, no. Wouldn't be right. Decent. We're moving into a town. A city, for god's sake. Neighbors.

Dalt walks past me, eases our stuff into the back of the truck, slides the rolltop door down much more quietly than Hondo did. You can hear sorry and sad all down its long, creaky unwinding. He holds the latch in both hands, trying to lock it some way that won't sound so deadly permanent.

He turns and looks at me. "Want to walk down to the creek?"

Atty's up in a flash, but I shake my head. "I don't think I can, Dalt. I really don't."

"Bad?" he asks.

I shake my head. "Only my heart this time."

He walks up the stairs to me, stands one step below me, the two of us eye to eye, and he takes me in his arms, gently, the way he does when he knows the nasties lurk. "Town'll be okay," he whispers. "It's a great house. There's work everywhere."

I nod into him, our foreheads touching. "I don't want you to work everywhere. Only where you want. Only ever on the rivers." Back in the Coop, between the sheets, where we'd talk for hours and hours, days, weeks, never enough time, he'd told me about his high school carpentry apprenticeship, sticking with his dad after the divorce. "Mom was taking off. It wasn't some big decision. But, man, I didn't know I was hiring on." He laughed. "Wasn't quite slavery. What's that other one, where you can't leave till you've served your time?" I ran my hand along his side, down his forearm, the corded ridges of muscle and sinew making more sense now. "Indenture," I said, and he said, "That's it. Fourteen years old." We lay quiet a while, so played out and content, before he said, "Really, I was lucky. Got that whole trade thing over and done before I found the rivers, knew right away I could work them instead, not be one of those poor bastards I'd grown up with, swinging a hammer just to live for the days off." He kissed me, said, "And I didn't even know the rivers were flowing to you, didn't know the first thing about luck yet."

We were in bed the day too, only months before we got married, Dalt got the call, his dad keeling over at work, right off the saw horse he was using as a step. I pictured a tool falling, hammer or saw, fingers just like Dalt's clawed to a chest, a look of surprise and awe, maybe not all that unlike the one on Dalt's face only a little while earlier as he strove to the end deep inside me. But Dalt only dropped the phone and sat up, swung his legs over the side of the bed, plucked up clothes from the scramble of them on the floor. "No wonder," he said. "Never took a day off in his life. Never set foot on a river." He shook his head as he slid down the ladder in the Coop, a move he'd told me his father taught him, insteps clamped along the outside of the rails, hands too. I'd laughed, but Dalt shook his head, said, "It wasn't for fun. Just to save time. To hurry." He hid out beneath the loft while I lay in bed, hardly daring to breath, move a muscle, rustle the sheets, the phone like a grenade on the pillow beside me.

From below, a voice detached from anyone I ever knew, called, "Do you know who that was on the phone? Karl. His fucking foreman. Jesus. He never even had a friend."

I stayed up there for an hour or more before sliding out, reeking of sex, which, for the first time ever, seemed completely wrong. I found a T-shirt to slip into, and tiptoed down to him in the dusk, thinking the dark might be easier for him. Under the loft it was almost black, but I could just make him out in the corner by the wood stove, hunched into his beat to shit old barber's chair, staring out at the river, our Buffalo Fork, the willows and dogwoods and alder barely a lighter line against the glimmering black slide of the water. "Dalt?" I said. I came up behind him in the chair, putting my hands on his head, petting down his tousled hair, gliding my fingers across his face, down his jaw and neck, to rest on his shoulders. Finding his cheeks as papery dry as my fingers was the only time ever I wondered about marrying him, a man who didn't cry after learning his father died. I had this shuddering thought: *Do I really know anything about this guy?*

Now I know everything, and I hold him tight and hate what he's giving up for me, for us, what he has to, what we do. Atty starts tugging at his hand. I feel the jerk through his shoulder. Atty would live in the creek if he could. We've named it for him. We've checked for gills. Dalt turns his forehead against mine, rolling it, bone to bone, nose to nose. "I love you," he says, and though we say it all the time, it surprises a smile out of me still.

"Me too," I say, "I do," and he says, "We'll be okay, Mad. No difference where we land. Under a rock even, right?"

"In a tree."

I watch him take Atty on his shoulders down to his creek, slipping between the trees, disappearing, Atty reaching for the needles, pulling them off when he can, and I reach the truck, brace my hand along its side and try not to leave any telltale fingertracks in the grime and dust. To tell the truth, I can barely stand, feel like puking right this instant. But that's the last thing Dalt needs on his plate now, more of his fucked-up wife. And maybe it's only the move, the hollowing of it, rather than more dished up MS goodness.

In the cab, I lean back, the sun already baking, which, this time, actually feels good. I close my eyes, will the world to still, even just for a moment, and I hear Atty's laugh float up above the creek, and I can't not smile.

I've drifted off by the time they get back, the squeaking swing of the driver's door jerking me forward, my head swimming. I grab the dash, breathe, then help strap Atty into the car seat between us, avoid Dalt's eyes. He works the giant stick, bumps it against the car seat as he bangs it out of reverse. I say, "Should I switch places with At?" and he says, "No. I got it."

Dalt says, "Goodbye house, goodbye creek," and Atty, recognizing some echo of *Goodnight Moon*, babbles the same, over and over, and I squeeze my eyes shut as hard as I can, don't dare a look back in the huge mirrors.

I'm still nearly hyperventilating when Dalt eases us up Granite in Ashland. I mean, we've taken truckloads of stuff here, me mostly having to just sit and watch, unpack boxes while anchored on the floor beside them, Atty's toys first, to keep him occupied. But this time, knowing we're not going back up to his creek, well, it's like I see it all for the first time.

Dalt picked out this house on his own. Pretending he was going to work. It's old, needs work, a ton of it, but how he found a bungalow like this I have no idea, how some realtor hadn't snapped it up, poured fifty grand into it to turn a hundred. He must have looked for years. The back yard looks down on Lithia, the park—we can even hear the creek down there—but the very first time he walked me through, rattling off his grand renovation plans in such a jumbling rush it was plain it was only to keep me from speaking, I spotted every single real reason he picked it, and wondered how many others he'd looked through, all without a word to me. Single story.

No stairs. Well except for the basement, the laundry room, but there was a clothes chute, I wouldn't have to have anything in my hands. He even tugged at the railing there, demonstrating its sturdiness, while in the same breath telling me he was going to rebuild the steps anyway, that they were too steep, not even close to code.

The claw-foot tub, too, he said, would have to go. "What?" I said, nearly the first word he'd allowed in. "Why?"

He stammered, admitted it was nice, would be with a new porcelain job anyway, but that he'd always wanted a walk in shower, which was such utter bullshit I actually laughed. That stopped him, at last, and I said, "Dalt, I'm not blind you know. Maybe that'll be next, but not yet."

"What?"

"Two stories," I said. "You told me you loved them, looking out over the lay of the land. Remember garrets? Your widow walks? Our loft?"

"That's all a little out of our price range here," he said. "Light years out."

"Uh-huh." I stared him down, said, "I've got a brain. Half of one anyway. You found me a handicap house, Dalt." I waved around the bathroom. The only way you'd fit a walk-in shower in here was with a shoehorn. "You're already making it wheelchair accessible. Christ, the only thing you've left out is the fricking ramp."

He looked at the floor, the tiny white hex tiles.

"Do you see a wheelchair anywhere? Do you, Dalt?"

He shook his head, but I knew he saw it clear as day, had been walking one through house after house, rebuilding, tearing down obstacles, shaking his head again and again until he found this place. The very idea was so effing scary I could hardly make my legs hold me up. I reached out, held onto his arm. "Don't push me into one of those yet, okay, Dalt? Not yet."

"I'd carry you first," he whispered back, and we signed the papers.

Now, pulling up with our last truck load of stuff, he does just that, carries me. Atty's dozed off in the car seat, any ride like some sort of narcotic for him, and we go up the walk, Dalt with the seat in one hand, my elbow in the other. He eases the seat down on the peeled and splitting porch decking, then, saying "Easy does it," he lifts me into the air as if he's lifting glass, nitro.

He carries me across the threshold, same as he did up at our creek place, same as our first night back at the Coop after the wedding. I bury my face in his neck, fight not to let him see how his move, no matter how careful, leaves bits of my balance scattering like leaves every step of the way.

When he sets me down on the dingy gold carpet, I hold on for dear life. "Dalt," I say, and I want to say something profound, something that will put all this in some better light, but all that comes out is, "How did we get here?"

"Mad," he starts, but I say, "No, not the house. Just here. Where we aren't talking anymore? Where we walk all around the obvious, like if we ignore it, maybe it'll get tired of us and go away."

"What?"

"We talk about everything, Dalt. But you found a job without me. A house. One you can make fit whatever happens."

"It's just—" he starts.

"That we're scared," I say.

He leans back to look at me, study me, and maybe shrugs. You'd have to be quick to see it.

"Let's not get so scared we quit talking, okay, Dalt? That'd suck. Letting some stupid disease do that to us."

"To us?" he says. "The Luckies? Impossible."

"Impossible," I say, "but already started."

He reaches back out onto the porch, swings Atty up and in, his tiny hands jerking up, fingers wide, startled into his grab reflex even in sleep. "We've got the good stuff started, Maddy, that's all."

Dalt, my king of denial. And he's the one sketching out the blueprints for my disintegration, nailing together the boards of our ark.

Maybe At really wasn't so asleep. He starts to crank a bit, and Dalt waits for me to find my spot in the recliner, unbuckles At, talking nonsense to him. When I'm ready, he lays him into my lap, and I look down at that shock of black hair, those wide blue eyes of Dalt's. My hand's tremoring too bad to stroke his back, so I start whispering stories to him, the wild adventures we're bound for, and Dalt says, "I'll get to unloading."

"Moving in," I say, a correction he may not even feel.

In the days that follow, weeks, it feels like I've never left that chair, that Dalt has hardly stopped moving back and forth through that door, somehow pulling the carpet out from under my feet, running the floor sander around, brushing down the polyurethane, tiling the kitchen floor, building new cabinets, rewiring, insulating. He never even thinks of stopping until the day we get another phone call. The fucking phone. I hate it.

I hear Dalt say, "It's all right. Calm down, Glory. What is it?"

I look up from, and I hate to admit this, knitting. The physical therapist's idea. With my right hand doing the bob and weave, I'm inventing never before thought of knots, turning out another Maddy original. I raise my eyebrows. Dalt shrugs. He says, "What news, Glory? No, we haven't heard anything. What's happened?"

The business, I think, Hondo, Half Moon flushed away already, just like I warned Dalt. But I see Dalt's face go slack, see him hook out a chair from the kitchen table, sit down hard.

"The biplane," he says, like he's been punched, but a punch he saw coming, was just waiting for.

He says, eventually, "Okay. Okay, Glor'. Get your clients home. Get up here quick as you can. You'll stay here. Of course. Long as you want."

She's just off the Klamath, Dalt tells me. She just got the word. "She kept apologizing for not letting us know in person."

"Dalt," I interrupt. "Know what?"

"Mongolia. Hondo."

His little Mongol trollop, I think. That fucker. Glory putting up with his shit for how many years now? And then I hear Dalt again, the way he said biplane.

"Is he all right?" I say.

Dalt shakes his head. "Remember how scary that thing was?" He's always talking like I was there, like he's forgotten I missed that trip. "We kept fighting the Russians, trying to get the helicopter they promised."

"And?"

"They got it. It went down. Hondo, the pilot, half a group of clients."

"All of them?"

Dalt swings the twisted and knotted phone cord back and forth. "No survivors."

I watch the noose of the cord, the shadow of it on our floor. "How's Glory?"

"About like you'd expect."

But I haven't expected anything. Don't ever want to expect anything like that. Dalt? My god. I don't think I could hang on even for Atty.

Dalt sucks in this huge breath, blows it out. "I'm going to set up the other room. I don't know when she'll get here."

"What about . . ."

"Half Moon? The call she got was from a lawyer. Representing one of the clients. They were on it before she even knew. The insurance will help, but she's through."

"Ah, Dalt."

He's already down the hall, pulling sheets and pillow cases out of the linen closet he lined with cedar. He's a nester and a half.

The Luckies, I think. Never ever greater. That call to me, from the lawyers? They would never have risked a second, would know in that one instant that they would never get anything from that screaming, keening banshee, her mind snapped like a wishbone.

I can't help a chuckle verging on madness. The only reason Dalt wasn't included in that casualty report, the only reason at all, was my MS. Hauled him straight off that helicopter's skid, straight out of Mongolia, out of the whole business of rivers, landed him here instead, a carpenter, a husband, a father, this man in the back room, making a bed for a friend, who has already put his son to bed, singing "The Big Rock Candy Mountains" to him, his voice whispering down the hallway, "I'm a gonna stay, where you sleep all day, where they hung the jerk, that invented work, in those Big Rock Candy Mountains."

I look down at my lap, my hand twitching over the tangle of moss-colored yarn, my joke of a project—a scarf for the crooked man, I'd told Atty—and quiet enough Dalt won't hear, I whisper to my hand, "Thank you," and I send another thanks, guiltily, out to Hondo too, let him know I'm sorry I ever dreamt of him being spitted by an enraged Mongol father.

When Dalt comes back down the hallway, I've made it to the fridge, have two cans of Caldera in my good hand, starting the wake I know has to happen. I'm trying to use my claw to open them, but it just clacks around the rim. Dalt smiles, shakes his head, whispers, "Maddy. What would I ever do without you?" and takes the beers and follows me out to the porch.

And we sit there in the late dusk like every night, our unknown neighbors locked away around us, and Dalt cracks our beers, handing mine to me, and we click the cans against each other.

"To Hondo," I say, because Dalt knows I never really liked him, and Dalt says, "Hondo," and we sip, and the next thing he says is, "I can't believe our luck didn't protect him."

I look up and down our safe block, no traffic edging along. "Too busy here."

"I suppose," he says, almost a sigh, and I look over to him, find that I can't quite make him out in the dark, can't quite see even where he might be looking, at me or away, down the block someplace, or just out at all those rivers he could have been on.

Bracing for a night of Hondo stories, but knowing they need to come out, I say, "What are you thinking about?"

"Us," he says.

I manage to get my beer up to my lips, hold it there a moment, catch my breath. He takes my hand, my bad hand, stills it by wrapping it up in his, and for once I don't mind him touching it, making it something impossible to ignore.

"Us," I say. "You were thinking about us. Of course you were." I take a tiny drink. "You," I say, "are so predictable."

Bluff

THE DOORBELL, SOMETHING Atty discovered with a glee completely out of proportion to the thrill, bongs twice, high/low, and Atty's startled grin just slays me. I'm telling you, the magic of the big city. "Somebody's here," I say, surprise enough itself.

"I see," Atty says, as if announcing some major policy decision.

"Okay," I say, just as serious, having weighed all options before moving forward.

I get back after my onions, trying to chop with my left hand, my jittery right ready to dodge. When Atty says, "Mommy," I turn to find a woman standing in my kitchen, some adult who would follow a toddler's invitation into a strange house, and I dip my hand behind my back and stammer out, "Um, hello?" without a thought beyond wondering when I last washed my hair. It's not the most gracious welcome ever delivered, but it beats, "What the fuck?" which feels more appropriate.

"Hi," she says, a woman maybe a few years older than me, a hell of a lot fitter. She could be a Patagonia ad: *My name is Winter and I love running triathlons in chill mountain air.* But she says, "I'm Janice, from across the street."

"Hi, Janice from across the street," I say. "I'm Maddy, from the pig-sty kitchen." Half our stuff is still in boxes.

She blinks, and it occurs to me I'm holding an eight-inch knife. The kitchen reeks of onions. I set the knife down.

We look at each other until she remembers she's holding a big aluminum pan, a towel, no lie, draped over it. "I brought a dinner, knowing how hard it can be, settling in, the kids, Dad off to work. It's nothing. Just lasagna. I didn't even get a salad together for it."

Settling in? We've been here weeks. Should be way past the box stage. "No salad?" I say.

I'd take the dish from her, set it down, but my hand is thrumming behind my back, and, well, that's the last thing I want to show off. In fact, the one thing I thought this place had to offer, after the loss of our house, our creek, the business, clients, was anonymity, isolation. I saw it as my den, my cocoon, lair, whatever, where it could just be us, me, no one to ever have to explain MS to ever again.

"I'm making meatloaf," I say. *Look at us,* I want to trill, *we're both fifties housewives.*

"Smells great," she says, her smile wilting.

I laugh. "It smells like raw onion."

Her smile flares again, however briefly, and having waited long enough, she sets her pan on the counter. "Well, I'll get out of your way. I just wanted to say hello, introduce myself." Her hands empty, she sticks one out to me, the dreaded handshake there in the offing.

I look at it maybe a tick too long, right/left, right/left, then decide before it gets any more awkward, reach out with my left, give her that half-assed, backward clasp, and say, "Thanks, Janet, really. It's like, hugely considerate. I'm so far behind on this meatloaf already."

She looks straight at my wrong hand, and says, "Janice."

"Janice. Of course. I'm sorry. I'm hell on names." I let go of her hand, edge the towel off her lasagna like a sheet from a corpse. "It's beautiful," I say, but, god, it's just lasagna.

"375," she says. "Forty-five minutes should do it."

"Yeah," I say. "I've made lasagna before."

That's too much, even for Janice. She says, "Well, sorry to interrupt. I've got my own two to look after. I better go before the fire department shows up."

She turns and almost runs over Atty who hasn't moved since following her in. "Oh," she says, "I'm sorry. It was very nice meeting you."

Atty starts toward me, slides in under my arm like we lived in a cave before this move, have always slaughtered foreigners straying into our territory. It is so tempting to let her go, let her spread the word to the whole neighborhood about the feral family across the street, do that dirty work for me—it'll save so much work digging the moat, sharpening the stakes—that Janice is out of the kitchen before I call her name, take a step to chase her down.

She's stopped in the living room, her hand on the knob.

"Look," I say, "I'm sorry."

She shakes her head. "No. Don't. I know, it gets overwhelming," and I can't help but think, *You don't know. You don't know shit about it, about us, about anything. I mean, look at you, a shot out of* Housewife Magazine *or something,* but I agree, play along, say, "It has been wild, and I, I can't remember the last time I slept, or sat down, took a break." The real answers to those unrememberables is, an hour ago, in the recliner, dropping straight out while Atty built a tower out of the castle blocks Dalt made for him. Woke up to him crying, staring straight at me, ignored, saying, "No sleeping!" It's why the fricking meat loaf is so late. Tail ends of afternoons leave me tilted past collapse. "I appreciate the lasagna, really. And I have friends, who, believe it or not, will swear I'm not a bitch. At least not always. Used to anyway."

She doesn't flinch at the "bitch," instead actually smiles, and it's the first ray of hope I've seen in Janice. I push my hair away from my face, touch an old wooden oar we're passing off as decor. "Have you ever been rafting?" I ask out of nowhere, but it beats, I figure, *What's your major?* or *What does your husband do?* "We used to own a whitewater company. At least then we knew what the end of the day was for." She doesn't quite pick up on it. I have to ask. "Would you like a beer?"

I want to bang my head against the wall. Wine, you dope, she's a chardonnay sipper from the word go. But she says, "If I'd only listened to myself, had an ounce of faith, I would have brought the six-pack, not the stupid lasagna."

My sigh of relief is more a gasp, and I say, "Well, hello, Janice," and wave her back to the kitchen, and when Dalt comes home the lasagna is still on the counter, the onions drying on the cutting board, the oven not preheating. Janice has just admitted she picked up the lasagna at Wiley's World, knows Wiley herself, and we're howling. Dalt stutter steps, stares—this is not what he's grown used to coming home to—then grabs himself a beer, sits down, gets introduced. Later he puts the lasagna in the oven, and walks up the block to intro himself to Jared, Janice's other half. He brings him down to our place to eat her dinner. Her kids, not the fire-starters she made them out to be, are already into their teens. They play with Atty, and the girl, I swear she called her Seabring, is all over him, like he's a doll, which, for her, he is. Dalton catches my eye once and mouths the word "babysitter," and I give him a secret fist pump in the air. Janice catches me red-handed, thinking who knows what—that we're just jazzed to meet anyone?—and raises her bottle, tilting its neck toward me in a toast.

?   ?   ?

IT'S WEEKS LATER, a month, before Janice asks about my arm, that lefty handshake simmering that long. She just appears in the yard the way she does, the first thing I hear her call of, "Atty, my boy!"

I'm having myself a day, the nasties nowhere to be found, like I've never been off balance a day in my life. At's right beside me, hammering away at the dirt. I'm actually digging, like with a real shovel, flexing muscles that barely remember the word, starting in on the terraces above the creek, gardening what I've settled on for my hermit phase. What I know about gardening wouldn't fill a pea pod. But, I can't just sit around and twitch and tremor for At. He's got to see a mom in action, a chick on the go, a babe unfazed by the world and any of its hijinks. At's got to learn women rock, and Izzy, our daughter to be, when she finally shows up, will know that *she* is the king of the jungle, that it's Tarzan's who'll be asking her permission to come up into her tree.

I swipe my hair away from my face, lean into my shovel. "Jan," I say, "did you bring a pick ax?"

She pats down her pockets, shakes her head. "Sorry."

My hand, forgotten atop the shovel, twitches away. I must be getting tired. Jan tilts her head toward it. Nothing more.

"Oh," I say. Brilliant. I grab the handle tight, dig it into the soft, damp soil.

"What are you doing?"

"China," I say. "Making my break."

She walks down to me, looks across the hill in both directions, down to the few hikers in Lithia. "Are you even on your property?"

I shrug. "This is the lowest one. I'm terracing."

"Like the Incas?"

"Exactly."

"But why so far down the hill?"

"Maximizing harvest."

She looks at me.

I plant my shovel deep. "Did you see those railroad ties?" I ask. "Dalt said he'd do the heavy lifting when I was ready for it, but I bet the two of us, we could get them."

She nods, and I tell her I've got a spare pair of gloves.

"You're not wearing any," she says.

"Rowing? My hands are thrashed."

"Teenagers? So are mine."

She's got beautiful hands, long-fingered piano players, perfectly steady. We climb the hill together, and, keeping my twitching hand occupied, working, I grab onto the top tie in the stack Dalton's been bringing in from some job, one or two at a time. "Ready?" I say.

We grunt and stumble, then settle into it, carrying it down below our waists. We're good till we're going down the hill, me stepping over ground I've torn up. I lean right, get just a hair dizzy, swing my left hand out for what I remember of balance, and find my right's not been doing its share all along. The tie tumbles free, me just dodging clear, and Janice saying, "Good lord," behind me, tripping over it, falling into me, the two of us pulling up just short of a cartoon snowball trip down the hill.

Her hand's on my shoulder. My hand is on my thigh, not grabbing, just sitting there, pointer and middle hooking back toward my palm, my thumb twitching over them like an anxious mother hen.

Behind me, almost in my ear, Janice says, "Are you ever going to tell me?"

"Nope," I say, and stick my hand between my legs. "Funny what a conversation stopper MS gets to be."

All she says is, "How long now?"

"What? Do I have left?"

"Have you known?"

"Since," I start, but my supply of one-liners goes Gobi on me. "Since before Atty was born," I say. "There's no genetic link. As far as they know. Nothing direct. Nothing confirmed anyway."

"Dalt knows?"

I laugh. "Yes, Dalt knows. What . . . how . . . I mean, it'd be kind of hard to hide something like that."

"Not for some couples I know."

"Well," I say, "we are not some couple, believe me."

"I've seen you in action, Maddy. I know."

"Oh, honey," I say, then stop myself.

Janice bursts out laughing, says, "Must be hot," and I blush, say, "You have no idea," and after that we just kick the railroad tie into place, start building in the deadman just like the gardening book said to.

We carry down six more ties, and get them mostly in, but I'm augering in myself, can't come close to hitting the spikes with the maul, even hold it up, have to let Janice take over. While she drives in the last, laughing over how heavy the hammer is, how poor her aim, I feel the nasties in full charge, thundering down after the exertion, the Pinocchios claiming my joints, the puppeteer out on strike.

We can both hear Atty pounding away at the tie pile with his hammer. I left a handful of nails started for him. Roofing nails, just like Dalt said. Their big wide heads. I sit down on top of the first wall we've built, the lowest course of my terrace and tell Janice I've got to rest before facing the climb back up. It's not something I like admitting, but she sits beside me without a word.

Down below, in the park, there's a kindergarten class playing Ring Around the Rosie, circling the adults, holding hands. The creosote stench of the ties makes my eyes water. My whole arm is twitching, shoulder on down. *Ashes, ashes, we all fall down.* I wipe the sweat away, leaving, if Jan is any indication, a streak of mud in its place.

"Does Atty know?" she says.

The whole circle of kids collapse. A moment later I hear their laughter. "He knows I have bad days. That I get sick. We haven't thought it necessary to hit him with acronyms just yet."

She nods, picks up a handful of the black loamy soil, tosses it inside my terrace box. "How much do you know about it?" she says.

"Way, way more than I ever wanted to." I look over at her. "Don't worry. We're not head-in-the-sanders. Not by a long shot."

"My brother's wife's," she starts, but I hold up my hand.

"Everybody knows somebody who knows somebody, but, I'm sorry, this one is all mine. I'm not your brother's wife, it's not . . ." I trail off. I'm grabbing the tie under my ass like it's the only thing holding me to the planet.

Janice says, "Maddy? Are you all right?"

"Overdid today."

"Do you want me to help you back up?"

I shake my head. "Dalt will be home soon."

"And, you're just going to wait for him down here? Maddy, we carried half a railroad down here. I think that qualifies me to help you up."

"I just have to catch my breath. I don't need help. Not yours. Not anybody's."

She doesn't point out that I just said I'd wait for Dalt's. She doesn't say anything. I reach over, pat her thigh with my good hand, and, bless her, she doesn't reach to hold it or anything. What she does is say, "What if the city comes up here, tells you you can't extend your garden into their park?"

I laugh. "What, Janice? They're going to take me to court? Drag my staggering, twitching ass before a judge?"

"But, why so far down? Why risk it? Why all the extra work?"

I blow out a breath it feels like I've held for days, weeks, since we moved in. "Because I can now. I'll start blackberries down here. Raspberries. Things that will go wild."

"And?"

"The kids can." I shake my head. "I'll work my way up the hill, Jan. This will be for them, when I can't get down this far. All the way down here, I've got a longer run back to the house, you know? Years worth."

Ah shit, I can feel tears, and I swipe at them with my forearm, same way I did the sweat.

Janice puts her arm around my shoulders. My arm twitches against her side. "Please don't," I say.

Her arm eases off instead of jerking away. "There are all kinds of treatments, Maddy, new—"

"Oh, god," I say. "Please. Not that. I'm already supporting the entire pharmaceutical industry. Not to mention the physical therapists of Southern Oregon. Now, here, the naturopaths want a piece of me, the homeopaths, who knows who else, the druids."

Dalt, as usual, saves the day, calling, "Maddy?" from above. I turn slowly, keeping my head attached, and see him up top, Atty at his side, hammer still in his hand. He's got the attention span of a rock, the patience.

He spots us, says hello to Jan, then turns back toward the house, disappearing. I wipe more at my eyes, and Janice reaches out, rubs at my cheek with her thumb, says only, "Dirt."

I brush some off her forehead.

She helps me up the hill, just a hand on my arm, grabbing hard only the one time the ground fails to be where I expect it. I tense, and she says, "Wow, you have got some guns."

"Thank you," I say.

"You want more help on this bluff restoration project of yours?" she says.

"I can do it."

"Of course you can. And I can help. It'll give me something to do."

I glance at her, do not detect a trace of pity. "Okay," I say. "But, tomorrow's a day off."

"We can just have coffee, bitch about our lives."

"I don't do that," I say.

"Drink coffee?"

"You," I say. "Are an ass."

☙   ☙   ☙

ONE GLANCE AT the clock, and Jan streaks off across the street, saying, "Cripes, mac and cheese again tonight."

We'll be lucky to eat that well. I can barely stand up.

Dalt walks me into the living room, sits me in the recliner. He says he's glad to see Janice over again, how he was afraid I was going to clam up here, hide out, pretend the fam was enough for me forever.

"It is," I say.

"You know what I mean. How you need to get out. Make friends. Have a life besides just us."

"Keep it up and it's your life you'll need to be worrying about."

He looks at me a second, his lips tightening a way I don't like, but then he gives a little shake of his head, a little smile. "Looks like you slaved all day."

I nod.

"I told you I'd get the ties down there for you."

It takes all my strength just to nod again. "Dinner," I say. "We'll do a strir fly." Seriously, that's what comes out. *Strir fly*. Dalt does a double take. I try again, but it takes three times to get out stir fry.

"Maddy?" Dalt says.

I can hardly breathe. He steps toward me but I wave him off. "Just tired," I say, and it comes out right, which is a huge relief, but still, strir fly? Not my words. Please. Not that.

"I'll cook tonight," he says, and he's off, retreating to the kitchen.

But, god, I will not be helpless. Even if I can't talk. This day started out so strong. I collect myself and then work the lever on the side of the chair, propel myself up onto my feet, find my balance, teeter out to the kitchen.

Dalt's mixing up some soy marinade, dropping chicken bits into it. I find the peppers on the counter, one orange, one red, Dalt all about color coordination. He says, "Mad."

"I'm fine," I say, and get the other cutting board, my eight-inch knife, start out.

But, my knife travels with a mind of its own, bits of pepper scattering to the floor. I'm afraid to look, afraid I'll see bits of my fingers down there as well. Dalt says, "Mad," once more, and comes up behind me, tries to ease the knife away. It's nearly a hug, gentle as foreplay, but I hold up my knife, say, "Don't make me use this," and he backs off, says, "I can cook dinner once in a while."

"So can I."

It's quiet for a few ticks before he says, "Well, they want me to do a bid. I'm going to go out to the shop. Give a shout when it's ready."

"You got it," I say, but a bid's big news. He'll be a foreman in days, be talking about starting out on his own soon. So I say, "That's great, Dalt. Really," but as soon as he's out the door, I grab a stool and collapse, drop the knife before I hurt myself.

I get it together eventually. The dinner, I mean. Getting myself together is not a project I'm up for at the moment. Atty comes in and I get him up into his booster, then, just to prove I can, set off for the shop, the ground everywhere but where it should be. It's a job At would kill for, retrieving Dad from the shop.

It's dusk now, dinner late, Dalt probably starving, but half way there—what, maybe ten yards?—the deck I'm walking, pitching and swaying to some hideous gale, feels as if it's going all the way over and I have to sit before I go down with the ship. I drop just the way At does, legs folding up, plop, down hard on his rump. But he has a diaper, a little padding, which is not to say I don't have my own padding issues, but, still, I'm surprised to find myself on my ass in my backyard. I rest a second, and then another, whisper, "Mad, what the hell?" and push myself up. I am not going to crawl. Not now. Not ever. I hold my arms out to my sides like a tight rope walker and make the building, grabbing the window sill, not the doorknob, because, well, I get to listing there at the end.

I catch my breath, or begin to, until I see Dalt in there. He's only got the gooseneck on, and he sits in the cone of light, leaning forward over the drawing board I got for him years ago, before he went pro in the carpentry field, some joke about finally drawing out all the presents he'd make for me. It's tilted up, the paper bunched a little under his elbows, but I can still see it, see our house sketched in, but our house without stairs, a ramp angling down from the porch instead, switchbacking at the corner, returning to meet the existing walk in from the street, the old paving stones gone, a smooth plane of concrete in their place. A fucking wheelchair ramp. Into our house.

I push back, ready to stomp in there and tear his plan to shreds, beat him to death with the stupid easel board, but I make the mistake of pulling my eyes away from that hideous drawing to Dalt himself, and I see that he is not even holding a pencil, that it's lying there on the crumpled paper before him, that his hands instead are wrapped around each side of his face, that he's rocking just the slightest bit.

All I'd have to do is look at his back, his ribs, see if his breath is stuttering in, to know if he is crying, but I close my eyes before I can see anything like that, and without taking time to gather my sea legs, or my wits, or anything else, I let go of his shop and set sail for the house, my child, and when the deck sways beneath me I sway with it. A ramp. He has seen so far into the future, so far past anywhere I ever want to go, I don't even know if I want to go there with him. But I grab the walnut tree beside the deck like it's a life line, and I have a hollow feeling that his vision is as open-eyed and as long distance as ever.

I make the back door, turn the knob, slip inside, glad for hallway walls, counter tops and chair backs, even for Atty's little whimper, so long waiting for his dinner, for some attention. He's glum until the second I reach the table, pull back his chair and help him slide down to the floor and say, "Atty, sweet pea, would you go get Daddy out of his shop? Tell him it's time for dinner." He's off like I touched the fuse to a cannon.

The stir fry is congealing in the wok, and I wonder, really, how long my trek out into the future took me. I goose the burner to full high, lean back away from the flame, and begin to stir.

I whisper, "Bubble, bubble, toil and trouble," a line Atty loves for the rhyme, and brace myself against the waves and wait for Dalt, my seer, my prophet, my love of my life. But I can't stand. Only just remembering to kill the heat, I grope my way to my seat, get down where I'll look less like a person with a handicap tag dangling from her neck.

Dalt, one word about his plans, and it is all over between us. I can't believe he's drawn those up. He's got to get out more. Make some friends. Think of something else.

Second Run

THE SUPERHERO NIGHTLIGHT gave up last week, even Batman too tired to go on. But At never really needed it anyway. As hard as his nights are, it's never been darkness chasing after him. The light's more for us. So we can look for his sucky, find his bear, tuck him in, just see that we're really still connected to the planet. But tonight, I'll admit, there is comfort in the dark when Dalt slips under the sheets, runs a hand up from my knee, and whispers, "We always said there'd be two. At least."

It's been three days since my I'm-off-the-pill meltdown. Exactly.

I came apart in the doctor's office. For nothing more than a new drug regimen, another stack of prescrips clenched in my fist. Daily injections now, instead of once a week. And, like an idiot, I came straight home to Dalt with it, told him I was a walking toxic waste dump, that there was at least one drug I could cut. Dashing my birth control wheel into the trash—nothing like the ceremony we made over starting to try for Atty, absolutely nothing like that at all—was the wrong thing to let Dalt see. I was not at the height of my powers. Told him I was going IUD. Then realized that would take another appointment and lost it again. I used to hate doctors, but now? Where do you go from there? What lives so far beyond hate?

Nearly nose to nose, Dalt and I are invisible to each other. "Dalt," I say. "I wanted a hundred babies. You know that."

"Ditto."

"But now?"

"Atty's out like a light. The timing is perfect."

I wonder if Dalt just unscrewed Batman's bulb. "Dalt," I say. "Perfect? There hasn't been a whole lot of perfect in the way things have turned out."

"You're right," he says, and I nearly sigh in relief, but he follows it up with, "Perfect doesn't do us justice."

I reach to touch his face, bump into his nose. "You know," I say, "that relentlessly sunny nature of yours? Well, it can get to seem pretty relentless."

"So he's not the world's best sleeper. Even if Izzy sleeps just the same, really, how much more tired can we get?"

He has no idea how tired it's possible to get. I'm an expert witness for exhaustion. "I'm not talking about sleeping," I say. "You know that."

"What then?"

I wonder about punching him. I know right where his nose is. "It's not fair, Dalt. Not to any kid. We've been over this."

"To be born into this family? It's not fair to the *other* kids."

I count to three. His obtuse act. Maybe he thinks it's cute, somehow endearing. It makes me want to rend and gnash. "We didn't know with Atty," I say. "We know now. We can't pretend we don't."

"Maddy?"

"Goddamn it, Dalt. MS. There. Happy? You made me say it. M fucking S."

Now he sighs, like, oh boy, here we go again. "There's no tie," he says. "Your having it doesn't mean our kids will."

"There's a risk." The one stat I cling to.

I feel him get up on an elbow, peer down at me, all intimidation. "The one percent increase?"

"You want to tell her one in a hundred was good enough for you? When she's twitching and crying, asking why?"

"No. I want to tell her, 'Look at your mom, how could we not have you?'"

Easy for him to say.

He says, "Every single thing we've read, every doctor we've seen, they tell us the same thing, that this is no reason not to have a baby."

Facts. Figures. Statistical projections. Useless. "I know all that," I whisper.

"So?"

"Shit, Dalt. That's not even it. Have you given up listening?"

"What is it then?"

I try to touch his face again, forget he's lifted up. I end up with his forearm instead. "Dalt," I say. "There are days I wouldn't make it back to the house if Jan wasn't here."

"You only push that hard when she is."

"There are days I can't stay awake even to watch At play. To watch him play, Dalt. All I've ever wanted."

"He's fine. If something happened, he'd let you know. He's—"

I slap my hand down on the bed. "God! Would you quit? Do you always need to have a rebuttal? To every single thing I say? I'm trying to talk here, Dalt, not debate."

He lets that settle. "I think you're scared. It makes you mad." I can almost feel him cringe, waiting. Then, into the darkness between us, he says, "I want another baby, and, you're going to kill me for this, but I know you do too."

I could kill him. He's right. About all of it. "Izzy," I say, nearly choking on the name, like she's already the child we lost. But, I try. He is not doing this to hurt me. I say, "What if she's a boy?"

"Couldn't happen. That's not our plan."

I smile there in the dark. Beats crying. You couldn't dent him and his plans with a hammer. "What if?" I say, only because I know the answer.

"Genghis. We've been over this."

"You'd do it to him, too. I know you would."

"Of course. You've got to admit. It'd be a cool name."

"Oh, totally."

He goes quiet. Touches my hip.

"Dalt. What if, if, you know, I can't do it."

"Maddy, it doesn't affect that. How long it took before doesn't mean—"

"Not that."

"What?"

"If I can't handle it?"

"You're the greatest mom in the history of—"

"Don't," I say. "Please don't do that. Please. What if I have this baby and I can't take care of it? You say I'm scared. Well hell yes. I don't even know if I can take care of Atty. Want to talk about scary? What if it's you trying to do it all, taking care of all of us, all the time."

"That's not going to happen."

"You can't know that!" I say, and it's way too loud. We both freeze, wait for Atty to start up, but he holds off for us just this once. I want to kiss him. Hug him. Hold him forever.

"What if it does?" I say, "and please, for my sake, don't just pretend bad things can't happen to us."

"They can't. Not us."

"I will kill you," I say. "Without a second thought."

"Name one thing that hasn't gone according to plan?"

I can't even laugh. "That's it," I say. "She's reaching for the ax."

"Okay. Wait. Don't chop."

"You have two seconds."

"Remember how it was with At? When you were pregnant? You were Supergirl."

"Remember afterward?"

I can almost feel him take that punch. Fall into the ropes. "Okay. *If* it goes that way, *if* it gets harder, too hard, and I don't think it will, well, then, you're right. I'll take care of us."

"Dalt."

"I can do it."

"I know you can. But, Dalt. That's not a life. Not for you. A care-taker? That's not a life for any of us. It's not what superheroes do."

"Exactly," he says. "They rise above, crash through a wall, jump out a window, fly. We'll fly, Mad. It's what we do."

"Dalt," I say. His hand travels up to my boob. I close my eyes, but can see no less. "You know me better than I ever thought anyone ever would, or could. But, but . . ."

"But what, Mad?"

I can feel him against my leg. "Dalt, you can't know, even if you say you do, you can't have any idea how scared I am. Hitchcock would be a fricking clown here."

"Mad, it's all scary. But look at us. We're doing great."

"We gave away Half Moon. You're a carpenter. I'm, I'm," I'm one breath from a sob. "I'm, *gardening.*"

"Atty's with us."

Shit. The chink in my armor. He does know me. Atty. Every breath he takes makes it worthwhile. Anything. Everything.

I reach down, touch him. Men. Like this conversation has been pure pornography.

"Izzy will only make it better," he says.

"Dalt. Remember how long it took with At?" Like he could for-get. "What if, if Izzy's—or Genghis—what if they're the same way? What if it takes years? Who knows what shape I'll be in?"

He isn't kidding then, when he says, "I don't think we should wait any longer."

I'm holding him there in my hand. Shouldn't wait any longer. Like I better pop this one out while I still can, get the most out of my womb while the getting's good. "It's not even a good time right now, in my cycle. And the pill. How long to get those drugs out of my system? The odds won't be with us."

"The odds," Dalt says, "are always with us."

My hand, on him, begins to tremor. I bite my lip. Want so badly to believe him. "I'm not ready, Dalt."

His hand zeroes in like a heat seeker. "I have ways," he promises.

Like that's what I meant.

But he does have ways, and I do love him as much as ever, more, and I want this baby as much as he does, and, as hard as I've tried to convince myself otherwise, I've been ready since the day Atty was born. It could take years. There's no time to waste. We need to get on the job. I need not to cry right now. I need to find a place to hide from my fear. There is just so much I need, and as he comes into me, blowing out my breath the way he does, as if he could take over even that, become my own lungs, my own heart, I cling to Dalt like he's everything I will ever need, something I once thought could never be anything but true.

Earlier, while he sang Atty to sleep, I closed myself off in the bathroom, sneaking, tearing open the sponge's package, wetting it down, slipping it in. I have not lost all my superhero powers. I have seen this coming long before he slipped into bed, before he slipped into me. Doing this to foil our perfect plans, I thought I could never sink lower, but now it's all I can do not to break apart, knowing he will not feel the sponge, will never know, and I shut my eyes so hard I finally see; stars, lights and colors, entire auroras, all things Izzy will never see, never know, because I love her too much, cannot bring her here, not into this, not to a mother who cannot hold her, who cannot lift her out of the crib when she cries, who will never be able to walk her down the hill to the park to play with the other kids.

Dalt is only trying for what he thinks is best, and I bite my lip, make it sting, and move up against him. Izzy, I am so sorry. Though nothing has ever felt so wrong, I know I am doing the right thing.

❧ ❧ ❧

BETWEEN ME AND At in his infancy, throwing up became something of a spectator sport. He's growing out of it, but in his day he had me cold for distance, though unpredictability was always a dead heat. Atty can do the whole deed without so much as a single apparent muscle contraction, but sometimes my balance goes, the world spins, and I get that old state fair hurl out the side of the tilt-a-whirl thing, end up puking without taking a step toward the bathroom.

But this time, it's not out of nowhere. I've felt like shit all morning. I'm down in front of the toilet when it comes up, but it's the timing Dalt's all over. He's got the bathroom door popped before I'm even off my knees.

"Mad?"

"A little privacy?" I say. "That'd be nice." I flush.

I hear Atty in the hallway. "Mommy, okay?"

I actually do feel a lot better.

Dalt says, "She might be way better than okay, champ."

And, honest, that's my first clue. I mean, I am the woman in this house, right? I grab on tight to the bowl, close my eyes. I am not dizzy. The room is not spinning. Throwing up actually helped. I feel like I should eat a cracker.

It's not possible. It just isn't. Every night, soaking those horrible sponges, pushing them into me, lying to Dalt in ways he'll never know. It could not come to this.

Dalt steps in. Opens up the cabinet under the sink. He's got the EPT box stashed behind the waste basket. His hands are trembling as he tears open the cardboard. "We are superheroes, Mad. We are."

He holds the stick out to me.

"Privacy," I say again, and he's so hopeful he backs out the door without a word, calls, for some reason, to Atty. What kind of father-son chat they're going to have, I don't even want to imagine.

To tell the truth, I don't need any stick. As soon as Dalt said, "Way better than okay," the way his voice shook, I knew. Knew what can't be true. After all that. I should sue the sponge company. How dare the bastards give me what I want so badly it's split me to my core.

I hold the stick, still hermetically sealed in its wrapper, and tap it against my leg. Why waste it? I know.

Outside the door, Dalt says, "Maddy?"

He's never guessed. Weeks of the sponges, whole boxes. Each sneak tattering at my heart. I don't even have an appointment with the gyno yet. Could not make that call, not to have the IUD put in, five years' worth of no pregnancies stopping my finger above the dial like Kryptonite.

Five years? Might as well be the rest of my life.

But, trying to slip around Dalton's plans? I don't know why I bothered. Might as well try to row back up Lava for a second run, some sort of do over. It is not going to happen.

"Maddy?" he says through the door. "Plus?"

Izzy. Izzy. "Plus," I say, though you'd have to have CIA listening devices to hear it. I clear my throat. "It's, Dalt, it's your plan. Iz is on her way."

Dalt eases the door open. I'd have guessed he'd blow it straight off its hinges. Wrong again. Instead of any echoing halleluiahs, he says, "Maddy, are you okay?"

He sees me sitting on the throne, my jeans still up, the wrapped test untouched in my fingers. He hitches and I can see him trying to realign the last minute of his life. "I thought," he starts, shakes his head. "I thought you said, plus."

"I don't need no stinking stick," I say, but just that effort hurts, and isn't right, at all. "I know, Dalt. I can tell. It's my body. She's in there."

"Really?" he says. He seems to have no idea who he is talking to.

I nod, all I can manage.

He kneels in front of me. "You're sure?"

"Your plan," I say, and my breath surprises me, stuttering in. "God, Dalt. What have we done?"

He holds me, pulls me off the toilet into his arms, rocks me there, the two of us on the bathroom floor. It needs to be mopped. Which, for some reason makes me laugh, just the whole patheticness of me.

"It's ours," he says. "It's always only been ours."

"What is?"

"Our plan."

I nod. Shrug. Whatever.

"It's not something we can escape," he says.

"Sounds like a sentence, not a plan."

"Best sentence in the history," he starts, but this time he stops himself, just holds me, asks again if I'm going to be okay.

"I don't know," I say. "I don't think I'll ever know that again."

He looks away, then back at me. "But, why," he says, "why did you . . . Why, Mad?"

He can't finish, but I know. Behind the waste basket, under the sink. His EPT box. He never goes under there. Why, with all my sneaking, would I have been any more careful? He must have had to push aside my next box of sponges. I see him sitting on the throne, just like me, pants up, head in his hand, reading the label on that box, feeling, maybe for the first time, how much, every night, I was trying to try, how I kept fighting to remember how we'd always done it before. I actually thought I could fool him.

What chance did I ever have of imitating abandon?

"Dalt," I say.

He shakes his head. "Don't."

"I'm sorry."

"Don't."

"I wasn't—"

"Maddy. Please don't."

"Ready," I finish.

He rocks me. "Are you now?"

I think of the next months, MS dropping out of my life, being able to play with Atty like a real mom.

"I am so ready for it I might die," I say, and I have to remind myself to ease up, stop hugging him like this before bones start to break.

Chisel

I LEAN IN against the wall, still jittery, hollowed. The door's open, Dalt back and forth to the shop, working fast while Izzy's conked out, finally settled into the bassinet on the kitchen table. The breeze flutters Atty's hair, just enough nip to make me tuck the blanket up under Izzy's chin. Atty's helping, keeping his hands tight around the end of the new railing Dalt's installing in the hallway. Railings. Down a hallway. Not a stair in sight. I tell him again I don't need it. "Really, Dalt. It's lame. A railing down a hallway?" After this morning, it's not what the first words out of my mouth should be, but I can't stop myself.

He nods, but he's got his head down, screwing the brass mounts into the wall, his string line pulled Z-rig tight, everything flat and level as an ocean horizon. Classic Dalt. Can't just truck up to Home Depot and buy some closet pole, screw it into some studs. Not for me. No way. Not Dalt. He had to tear open the walls, both sides, lath and plaster flying, squeeze 2x backing between all the studs, patch all that broken plaster—learn how to plaster, for Christ's sake—then anchor the railing every single foot, the railing he had to, of course, make by hand to match eighty year old moldings. You could anchor sailing ships to these. What does he think, that I'll be reeling down this hallway, clutching his handrails as if the house were caught up in Dorothy's twister, Miss Gulch cackling?

"Dalt?" I say.

He looks up, his face as frazzled as his hair. "What?"

"Really, it's too much. I mean, this, today, that was practically the first bad time all summer."

He blows out a breath. "And now she's born."

Atty bobs his end of the railing up and down. He's wearing the tool bags I got him for Christmas, so he could be like Dalt, a present he shrieked over, but which flattened Dalt's face like I'd taken a steam roller to him. "What?" I'd said.

"How about a boat or something? A tiny pair of oars?" He was already showing Atty how to buckle the bags, where to slip in the little hammer, the measuring tape, but over his shoulder, to me, he said, "Last thing in the world I would've ever let him play at."

"Well, thank you very much," I answered. "Ho ho ho to you too."

Atty glanced between us, said nothing. Not even two and as finely tuned as a Geiger counter.

Our first Christmas in our new house. Our in-town house Atty still called it, like we had two now, our place up on Little Applegate, in the hills and trees, and this place with the neighbors and sidewalks, the streets and cars.

Come to think of it, their first project out in the shop that spring, Atty sporting his bags, Dalt as nervous as I'd ever seen him, trying to childproof a shop for crying out loud, was a pair of oars, Dalt clamping some old pallet wood onto his bench and working it with a draw knife, then a spoke shave, the long curls of shavings piling up on the floor. Atty tugged at my hand as Dalt worked, till I had to let go, say, "Dalt, incoming." Dalt lifted his plane out of reach, and started to explain the mechanics of the oar, the lever, how the blade grips something as ungrippable as water, but Atty bent straight over and gathered up the shavings, delighted with how light they were, wooden feathers. He put them on his head, like hair, Harpo's wig. Dalt bit his lip, tried to look bummed out, but couldn't hold it in. Neither of us could. Delighted with himself, At made us both bend down, put wood curls on our heads too, more and more, getting them just right. "Um, boatman extraordinaire, or fashion designer?" I said, and Dalt nearly strangled. The oars stayed on the workbench.

Iz, then, was well past the zygote stage, but not yet showing. We hadn't told Atty yet, figured we'd wait for my belly to give us away. And those months? Good god, paradise. Just like with At, just like the books said, me throwing the fricking MS for a loop for a change, the hormones or whatever knocking it down, me almost totally my old self, Dalt getting right there with me. And this time there was Atty. Me finally an actual mom. I chased him through the park. Me, running. His mom. He could barely believe his eyes, screeched with delight, sprawled headlong into the grass, me rolling in after him, my head staying right where it belonged. We wrestled. We threw handfuls of grass at each other. I held him and held him.

All the drugs, Dalt slipping the needle under my skin every night, like some kind of twisted quiet time thing we do? God, why can't they just bottle the pregnancy stuff? I'd drink it like a tonic, a total brown bag alky. Or why can't I just stay pregnant? *I know it's crowded*, I'd tell the seventeenth, the twentieth—we'd be down to numbers by then—*but, well, you're really just medicine for Mommy*. I'd shrug it off, say, "Thanks," and grab Dalton for twenty-one.

Dalt says, "Hello? Maddy."

I look up, see he's got the last railing anchor in, all these brass teeth studding the walls.

"Where on earth have you been?" he says.

"I don't know," I say, my knee jerk. How could I tell him? What? Who could possibly follow along?

They lift the railing to show how it will look. I run my hand along it, think how I'll grow to learn its feel, the warm smooth hardness of it. The pieces for the other side still lie on the floor, useless yet, two of them, the break for the bathroom door. I'd said at the very least he could only put it on one side, and he'd glanced down at my bad hand, not saying, *How long do you expect to be able to hold anything with that?* I said, "I'll walk backwards."

Now he says, "Like it?"

Atty holds the other end, resting it on the anchors, waiting for my answer as much as Dalt. I don't know what to say. I whisper, "I have been pretty good."

He nods, like he's considering it, or maybe acknowledging that. But he says, "Remember At?"

Atty perks straight up. "What about me?"

"Not you," Dalt says, which, really, why don't you just step on him? "Mom," Dalt explains, "got pretty sick after you were born."

"Like this morning?"

I narrow my eyes at Dalt. Scooping Atty onto his side that way, it's like hiring mercenaries. "Yes," I say, "But that doesn't mean it's going to keep happening."

"Of course not," Dalt says. "The doctors. The books. The web. History. What do they know? Why prepare for that? Even think about it?"

"That's right, there's got to be a dark cloud somewhere around this silver lining. We just have to look hard enough."

Atty looks at the floor, and Dalt shoots a screw into the railing's bracket. He can't look at me that way, and the driver's whine makes talking impossible.

As he reloads, I get in, "Fighting this thing, Dalt. That's still my plan. Total capitulation doesn't seem that hot an option."

"Being reasonable doesn't seem completely stupid either," he says, eyeballing the railing. He tells At to shift his end some imperceptible amount, and as soon as he does, Dalt spies a snag at the light switch across from the bathroom, some Dalt-worry nobody else on the planet would ever notice. The gap's not equal or something. Oddly enough, it requires him to head for the shop. What a coincidence. The perfect time to bail out. I know he's got his ramp plans squirreled away out there somewhere, too. He asks me to watch At while he runs for a chisel.

"I'll get it," At offers, but Dalt says, no, it's sharp, you wouldn't know where to look, there's too much dangerous stuff out there. He has no idea how these kind of answers cut Atty. *Well, show him*, I want to say, but Dalt's close to finishing now, and he gets blindered then, the end the only thing in sight, same as when he used to pick his line going into some particularly heinous stretch of water. You could set off a bomb in his boat and he wouldn't notice unless it broke one of his oars. And even then he'd just dive for the spare, like a robot, never questioning what had broken it in the first place, chalking it up to the river banshee or some such thing, flashing in the spare, keeping his line, his run.

So it's me and Atty, and Iz, if snoozing on a table counts. Atty runs his hand down the railing, varnished so many times it's like glass. Clear, vertical grain, Douglas fir, Dalt told me. "It's a nice railing," Atty says, serious as a pope.

I smile. "A very nice railing." I hate it, hate every single fucking thing about it, except, maybe, that Dalt made it for me. I love when he makes me stuff. But this? This huge, perfect, gorgeous reminder? "And you helped," I say to Atty, who shakes his head, no room for exaggeration in him. "I'm very proud of you," I say. He hooks a thumb under his tool belt, fights back his smile.

This morning I'd told him he was my hero, and he hadn't even been able to muster a smile to fight back. I'd been feeding Izzy, which Atty loves to watch. He held her hand, smiling at her grasp on his finger, and I eased back in the recliner, switching her to my left, holding her in my right arm, that perfect tug and pull, the milk letting down, making me close my eyes, drawing a smile straight from my core. And then the tremor hit, jerking me up straight, popping my eyes open, as if I thought they'd never be back. Izzy's eyes popped open in a surprise as great, the back of her head cradled in my hand, my hand twitching again, first time in months, rocking her head.

It was that, seeing her surprise, then the furrow of her brow as the shaking finally pulled her mouth from my nipple, that made my world tilt, go cyclone on me. It was just so wrong. My stomach lurched. I had to lean forward, which only tilted Izzy farther away, which started her screaming, which sent the first ice pick into my temple, watering my eyes, making my breathing go haywire. I dug my fingers into the arm of the recliner, hanging on for dear life, hunched over Izzy, but then had to let go, had to grab her with my good hand, had to close my eyes, whisper, "Please," as I fought not to throw up, not over my baby.

Then Atty, with more lung than I could have given him credit for, and, I'm afraid, more fear, bellowed, "Daddy! Mommy's sick!"

Dalt streaked in from somewhere, superhero cape fluttering, and pulled, all but yanked, Izzy away from me, and I said, "No," and she screamed and screamed, only wanting what was hers. And I did everything I could to stay in my chair, to bite back the bile, not comprehending, for an instant, that it wasn't the centrifugal force of the room spinning that was pulling me out of the chair, but Dalt, tugging at me, saying, "Come on, Mad, come on."

He was trying to get me to the bathroom. Trying to save at least that much, Atty having to see me hurling across the carpet, send him running for the rag drawer again.

I batted Dalt's hand away. Hit at his arm. "No," I said. "I won't. I'm all right."

Izzy wailed like a siren. I said, "Give her back. She's hungry."

But Dalt wouldn't. He stood there, holding her, gaping at me. We locked eyes, and I didn't say, *Remember who was so hot to get after this baby?* but the words smoked out in the air between us, some dark power at work. We had never talked about that again, me packing sponges into one side of the cabinet, him pregnancy tests into the other. We didn't have to.

I turned to Atty, swallowed, said, "You saved the day. You're my hero," but he stood locked in place, staring at me just like his father,

as if the two of them would go off and discuss the demonic posses-
sion of this woman in their house.

Now, watching Atty steadfast, holding his railing, I say it again,
"You are, Atty, you know, my hero," and Dalt returns with a pair of
chisels, the tiny-bladed coping saw. He sets to work, and I'm proud
of him now too, the way he explains what he's doing to Atty, the
way he lets Atty move in close to look, doesn't bitch about the way
he blocks his light. He peels a curl of wood off a piece of scrap, just
to show Atty how sharp the tools are.

Maybe it's because I'm watching them like that, close, a total
mom, that I see what's going to happen before they do. Finishing
his saw work, Dalt hooks the saw around his last two fingers instead
of taking the second he'd need to set it on the floor. Maybe he's
only trying to keep anything sharp physically attached to himself.
I don't know. He nudges Atty's fingers back a little farther, safety
first all the way. He takes his quarter inch chisel—these tools he
hones with the same deadly patience he'd applied to rope splices,
shows me, not without his own pride, how they'll curl slices of his
own fingernail into the same pigtails his spoke shave peels away
from pine and fir—and explaining every step to Atty, how he's going to just push it toward the saw line, which will stop the chisel's
cut, though the knot there, which can't be helped, which shouldn't
even be in clear wood, will make it just a little trickier, make him
have to push just a little harder.

And as he says *push* he reverses the chisel, points it away from
Atty, toward himself. He is a dad, after all, as sure as I'm a mom.
But as he nicks the blade into his starting point, leans into it, then
harder, I see how his two-fingered grip with his other hand leaves
the fat part of his palm, the base of his thumb really, tensed and
wide open, a bull's-eye for the chisel's path.

I want to say, "Dalt, be careful, look out." I don't know what
stops me. Same thing as when I do these things to myself, I suppose. Back in the Tetons, our oar blades attached to their shafts
with spring-loaded push buttons. No problem putting a blade on,

just punch down the button long enough to get it started into the shaft, but breaking them down, you had to push the button in, stiffened and stuck with sand and grit, spring as stiff as hardened steel, and rotate the blade to get it started. Even though my fingers still worked then, I don't think I ever did it without leaving a half moon of skin hanging from my thumb, a nasty burning blood blister at the very least, and every time, I'd look at it, think, Mad, this is going to catch the shit out of your finger, and twist, shit! yep.

I get as far as saying, "Dalt," when the piece of fir breaks out along the knot's fault line, springing the chisel free, Dalt still driving it ahead. The blade he's worked so carefully to take beyond razor slides into the muscled pad of his thumb as if it weren't really there, butter, or cotton candy, smoke, something as substantial as that. The blade sinks in deep, the bevel vanishing. He stares at it for a second, shakes his head. But then, instead of pinching down around it, easing it out, Dalt rips the chisel straight back, banging his elbow into the wall behind him.

Maybe it's the dam of his patience caving under the pressure of me so deadset against the whole project, or Atty trying so hard to help, always just an inch too close. More likely, my collapse, Izzy's hour of enraged screaming afterward, me finally getting her down. But, instead of a muttered damn, about all he's ever cut loose with around At, Dalt blurts out "Motherfu—" somehow stopping himself there, superhuman, really, considering our river rat trash mouths. And maybe that takes the last shred of control he has left, because what he does next is not something I've ever even come close to imagining him do. His right arm still reared back after yanking the chisel out of his hand, he, while in mid swear, suddenly drives forward and flings that chisel as hard as he can possibly throw anything, straight down the hallway away from me, but still, it's only another eight or nine feet to the kids' room, where it hits the casing of their door, and, that much force behind it, has no recourse but to come sailing straight back at us, all Newtonian, equal and opposite reactions.

I stand there like a manikin, thinking of Newton of all things, but in what must have been all one movement; "Motherfu," blowing out, the chisel hurled, the realization that he is not out on some river bank where he can throw any offending bit of gear across the water, he has followed the path of the chisel and sweeps Atty under his arms, grabs him to his chest even as he spins, his back offered to whatever is going to come flying back down that hallway, his head ducking over At's like a turtle locking its shell.

This is, of course, all in one second, less. I think I get so far as to blink, close my eyes, like my lids will deflect Dalt's chisel, his stunning moment of loosed rage. Maybe even before he has At covered up, the chisel has struck butt first into the door casing, leaving a perfectly circular dish there that for years I will dip my thumb into, filling its void with my own flesh. On the rebound it hits the oak of the floor point first, digging in a gouge Dalt will fill that very afternoon, so we don't shred our socks on it, he'll lie. But it's going too fast to be drawn to a stop, even on Dalt's vicious blade, cartwheeling instead over its own point, pulling itself out of the wood, but robbed now of momentum, merely clattering along the floor, spinning. I lift my foot as if the entire maneuver has been choreographed, and the chisel slides underneath. I drop my foot down on top. Safe.

Dalton is just beginning to lift his head, just beginning to relax his arms from around Atty, when Atty says, "Blood. Bleeding."

Dalt's voice shakes when he says, "It's okay. I just cut myself."

Atty says, "Mommy, we need a band-aid."

Dalt pinches the wound, applying pressure, and there is enough blood I'm sure we're heading for the hospital, something that will cause confusion to reign. They'll have me trussed into the MRI before we can convince anyone that I'm bringing him in, not, for once, the other way around.

But Dalt shakes me off, says, "It's just deep, not long. Nothing for them to stitch. I'll have to clean it though." He shrugs.

"Blood's good actually. Flushing out whatever might've been on the end of the blade."

He steps past me into the kitchen, his steps every bit as shaky as his voice, something I know has nothing to do with his hand, only the idea of what he'd just done still ricocheting through him. He holds his hand under the cold so long I think any blood left would be frozen out, retreating to his heart.

I bring in one of the old raft first-aid kits and he sinks onto the benchseat and lets me butterfly it for him. My hand tremors enough it's really more of a collaboration, and, watching the band-aid wrapper fluttering in my fingers like a banner, I realize I'm looking straight into the nasties heading my way, the pregnancy hormones flushing away. Izzy sucking them straight out of me.

I catch Dalt staring at exactly the same thing, as if his hand, his chisel stab, never happened.

I swallow, say, "Do you even know what you did?"

He looks away from my hand. "I saw it coming. Knew it was going to happen."

"No. After. I mean, I know what you mean, but, after."

"Threw that thing. I can't believe it."

"After that, I mean."

"Ducked."

He won't look up, meet my eye. "Ducked over Atty," I say. "Total secret service move, ready to take one for the commander-in-chief."

He does look up then, just this teeny, crooked smile wavering there. "Let it hit our chief? I'd take a hundred of them myself."

I pet his cheek, his jaw. My good hand. "I know," I say.

"You would too," he says, and I can't say a word, only nod. "But, you wouldn't have thrown the chisel."

"No," I say. "Not with this pitching arm. I suppose not."

"You know that's not what I meant."

Dalt smoothes down the butterfly's tape, plucks the wrapper from my fingers without a word about them. "Mad," he says. He crumples the paper into a wad, rolls it tight between his fingers, something that will never flutter again. "This thing, prepping for whatever might come. It's not looking on the dark side. I, it's, it's about you. That's all. It's not not fighting it. It's getting the tools ready. We'll fight it till, till . . ."

He's tongue tied himself. How do you end that? Till the bitter end? Not so good. Till it kills you? Worse. And, MS, it doesn't kill you. Just fucks you up more and more. There've already been days, like when Atty was tiny, those hormones gone—maybe, I admit, the same kind of stretch I'm heading into now—when it not killing me seemed like the nastiest part of the whole affair. "We'll fight it until I'm shoveling the dirt over you," I say.

He smiles. Nods. "Then you'll keep on going on your own," he says, which is just about the most desolate thing I've ever heard, but he adds, "I so would not want to be MS then. When the gloves come off. Kick its sorry ass."

I say, "You got that," and then, from the hallway, comes this tiny, lost voice. "How long, Daddy?"

Dalt shakes his head, still smiling. "How long what, sweet pea?"

"Do I hold the railing?"

"Oh god," Dalt says. He shoves back, and I take his stabbed hand in mine, bring it up to my lips, kiss it, say, "All better."

"Thanks," he says, and he lifts my bad hand to his lips, but can't quite bring himself to say anything as useless and forlorn as "All better." Then he's gone, and I listen to him tell Atty what a great job he's done, how he's got guys on his crew who couldn't hold a railing like that, guys who'd forget that's even what they were doing, just walk off, let the railing fall, breaking everything, ruining the whole job.

Atty answers all that with, "Is your hand okay?"

And Dalt just says, "It's fine. Sometimes, if you forget to pay attention, you'll give yourself a little reminder. See this here?"

I listen as he points out scars I know as well as my own, showing Atty every time he got too close, too absent minded, too rushed. Atty says, "Did you cry?"

"Not that time. But there's others I have."

There's a long pause, and even from here I can feel Atty's doubt.

"I have," Dalt says. "When Mom told me you were in her tummy. I cried that night, camped out in the middle of nowhere."

"Why?"

"Because I was so happy."

"Being happy doesn't make you cry."

"It does sometimes. If it's just like the best thing you ever knew. If you can't even believe your own luck. Come to think of it, I should be crying all the time, huh?"

"Why?"

"Because I'm the luckiest. I got you, and Mom, and now Iz."

I turn Izzy's car seat just enough to see her face. Taking crazy chances, I brush her cheek with my fingertip.

In the hallway, Atty says, "What about when you're sad?"

"What do I possibly have to be sad about?" Dalt answers, and his dodge pulls me toward them like a string, straining to hear At's answer.

"When Mommy gets sick."

Dalt taps something, something hard against something wood. The flat of the chisel, I guess, against the bottom of the rail. "Yes," he says. "Sometimes that makes me cry."

"Do you throw things then, too?"

"No," Dalt says. How he keeps from cracking up, or, hell, breaking down, I don't know. "That was because I got mad. At myself. I knew I was going to cut myself, but I didn't take the time to stop."

"You weren't careful."

"No. I wasn't."

There's a break in Atty's questions, and Dalt, stilling his tapping, says, "What say we finish getting this railing up?"

"Okay."

"Do you want to put some of the screws in? Use the screw gun?"

Atty thinks it over before saying, "I can do that." Then he reconsiders, says, "Do you think Mommy's going to need these, so she can walk?"

I hear a scrape of clothing, maybe Dalt just moving to the next bracket he's going to attach, maybe him reaching out, pulling Atty into his lap. "I hope not," he says. "She might though, so, just in case, we're putting them up."

"You better do it then," Atty says.

I keep brushing Izzy's cheek, shaking my head. "You," I say. "Good god, you've no idea the luck you've fallen into."

Izzy sleeps on, and I brace myself for the bad times I know lie just ahead, the roar of the whitewater you hear before you see the drop, when I'll cling to those railings like the tourons cling to the lifeline. Like a little bit of rope will save them from the waves and the drops and the holes, the whole world rushing them straight into the heart of it. Dalt's railings, Atty's, they'll hold me up forever.

Trying

"TRYING?" DALT SAYS, his eyebrow lifting in a way I know. One thing I haven't forgotten. He's just crept out of the kid's room, At-ty's new one still nothing more than studs and insulation, the wires bored through and hanging from the boxes, the way they've been all summer. Dalt swears he'll get to it, finish it, but right now my question stops him cold.

"It's been bugging me for days," I tell him. "*Trying.* I know it means something. Something more than just, you know, dictionary."

Dalt shakes his head, comes sits beside me on the couch. I pinch my hand between my knees and reach across with my good one, touch his fingers.

"What was it?" I ask.

"Trying? I don't know, Mad. Doesn't ring any bells. Really."

It's the "really," that does it. He can no more lie to me than fly. "Tell me, Dalt. It's not a bad thing, I remember that much."

It's only eight o'clock. Some kind of record. Dalt had At and Iz at the river all day. Wore them straight out. They shouted their good nights to me even before he started reading. "We love you, Mom!" I'm not really at my best—maybe, hopefully, midway through this latest bout—but, still, Dalt and I've got a whole night ahead of us. Two hours, easy. I can barely remember what to do with such a thing. And it starts out with my kids yelling their good nights, knowing I can't lean in for a kiss, have had me stagger and fall over them once too often. No where to go now but up. "Dalt?"

"It wasn't a bad thing," he says. "You're right about that."

"What?" I say. "Come on, the suspense is killing me."

But he looks at the floor, picks at another sliver in his poor hands. "Honest?" he says. "You can't remember the trying?"

The trying. Shit. It was an object then, or an activity. Just the way he looks, I know I need to get it right.

He glances sideways at me, pushes himself straight. "Sex," he says, face flat as a pane of glass. "It started out meaning trying to get pregnant, trying for Atty." He shrugs. "Then it just got to mean trying, the whole deal. I said 'The fun's in the trying,' and you'd say, 'Well, let's try all over my effing place.'"

I bite my lips, then say, "Oh," but it sounds more startled than I meant. "I knew that, Dalt. I knew it was something good. I wouldn't have asked otherwise."

He takes my wrist, easing my clawed, quaking hand from between my legs. He holds it steady in my lap. It's his way of showing he's not freaked, that he'll take me any old way, but, really, I'd be fine with him leaving it alone. I can barely stand to look at it myself. "It's okay, Mad," he says.

But it's not okay, it's way past not okay. How could I have ever forgotten *trying?* "I'm sorry, Dalt," I say, but he just sits there holding my useless hand, letting me know that in the greater scheme of things, this is pretty much nothing at all.

Sex. I mean, what could be easier to forget? "Maybe," I say, "well, I mean, At, Iz, they're both asleep. At once. Maybe you could help me remember." It's not something we've done in quite, in, I mean, for too long a time. I can't remember when, if you want the truth. "Could we?" I ask.

Dalton eyes me, finally saying, "If you think you're up to it?"

"Oh, I see. Me. What about you? How *up* for it are you?"

He actually laughs, and I do remember that sound, close my eyes to hear it better. How long since I've heard that? Another thing that doesn't bear much thinking.

Dalt, though he's sitting right next to me, practically already on top of me, makes this big show out of swooping in for a kiss, planting one on me, kind of slow and teasing, his tongue tracing my lips before diving in. I respond every way I know how, make all the moves that after all our years feel more like rote than actual true memory, and I think, if that's all I have left maybe it will be good enough. Maybe it'll have to be.

But, really, while I'm trying to do everything the right way, I can't help but wonder if any of it's something I should have to think about. And, concentrating, I don't notice Dalt's arms, how he's wrapped them around me, under my shoulders, around my bum. When he lifts me off the couch, I'm not ready for it. I start to laugh, but my head feels left behind, and I say, "Whoa there," and before the words are out of my mouth he's stopped dead, is already asking, "Are you okay? Maddy?"

"God, yes, would you quit already? You're not going to break me." I hit him with my heel again, say, "Giddiyup. Okay? I mean, we've got business to attend to."

"Business?"

Shit. It's already gone. The word. But then, just as easy, it's back, and I say, "Trying."

"The fun's all . . ."

". . . in the trying."

He sets me down on the bed like I might do a cartoon crack and crumble. "Dalton," I say, but he covers my mouth with his, which is something I totally remember. We used to have wars this way, me trying to tell him something, him not letting me. Or vice versa, me all about the no talking. I start to smile, and he backs off just far enough to whisper, "What?" so I reach up after him and don't let him speak.

After that, he only pulls away long enough to tug his T-shirt over his head. He hasn't rowed for money since the year Atty was born, that one trip to Mongolia he still tells me stories about. But, even pounding nails for the last five years, me too big a mess to do a goddamn thing to help, he's still ripped, and I run my hands over his smooth chest, the ripple lines of his ribs, the standing waves of his six-pack. You'd think that alone would do it for me, that a guy like this would want anything to do with me at all. But, down under, I feel nothing. No tingles, or clenches, or lubing. Nothing.

He reaches down and unzips my pile sweater. Buttons are kind of a thing of my past. Gone soft as a sack of dough, I close my eyes, like that will keep him from seeing. I think, if things had gone all right, if we'd still been running rivers, the whole baby fat shit would have disappeared like spring runoff. But my body, twitching and tremoring like some horror movie blob, looks exactly like the train wreck it is. Now and then my head even snaps to the side, no warning, chin banging shoulder. Once, twice, sometimes three times, all in a second or two. I mean, we're not exactly talking scorching hot.

I want to apologize, but he kills me for that.

He lifts my hips, slips my pants down, and, the slick bastard, my panties in the same swoop. I reach up myself, some of this coming back to me, and grab his belt. If I'm holding onto something, can watch what my fingers are doing, I can still almost use my right hand, and without too much work, I get the buckle open, tug the leather to the sides. The two of us go at the buttons together.

It's like a dam breaks, and for a second, I see us how we used to be, our hands only straying from each other long enough to perform tasks vital for survival, rushing straight back as soon as possible, like, really, it was only the other we needed as much as air. But, like the rush out of any burst dam, it's gone, the tidal wave rushed downstream, and the past gets murky and washed out, a few scraps popping up above the eddies for a second, sinking back down.

Dalt lies beside me on the bed, and all I think is, when was the last time the two of us, since Izzy was born, have been totally naked together this way? The worst sleeper in the history of babies, like he was already dreaming of sweeping out of the steppes, setting civilization back a few centuries, Atty made sleep a thing of our past. Izzy was such a shock I used to send Dalt to her crib a couple of times a night just to make sure she was okay. He'd come back, marvel, "I think she's *sleeping*," like it was some unnatural wonder of the world, which to us, it was.

Dalt avoids my stomach, but only because I told him it embarrasses me, every time I look at it. Remodeling the bathroom, without saying a word, he built in these shelves. They're cute, and useful, and a bitch to keep the dust from carpeting, but mostly what they do is cut down the available mirror space. I only see my face there now, which, except for the occasional flip to the side, is still pretty much the old me. Seriously, Dalt is like the only guy on the planet who would have stuck around for this.

But, while I'm thinking about this, the lucky side of everything, Dalt's trying, his hand zeroed in, and, without getting all graphic, he knows what to do with his fingers. Still, while I can feel him down there, I can't really feel what it is he's doing. I mean, I know, but I can't feel it. It's kind of like only various pressures. I reach down with my good hand and take hold of him, find him pretty close to ready.

They told us this could happen, we even read about it, which makes it no easier at all. I remember reading it to him. "A loss in libido often occurs, a lessening in sensation and desire." I snorted. "Yeah, right," I'd said. "Like maybe if enough of that goes on we could dull down enough to be like normal people?"

The only thing I can feel for sure now is that I'm dry as dust. That's one thing I do remember. Being sopping. We called it priming. All I had to say was, "Um, Dalt, got a little priming issue going on here," and it'd be all over.

Dalt says, "Maddy, you okay?"

I want to punch him, strangle him until he promises never ever again to ask me that. I am so far from okay, it makes me want to scream.

But, I take a breath, and, in a second, say, "Remember what we read? The loss of all that stuff?" I swallow. "It's happening, Dalt. Happened. I don't know. I hate this."

His hand stops like it's been detached from his body.

"No," I say. "I don't hate *that*. Hello? It's me I'm so sick of."

"Mad."

"No. Not me. I don't mean that. Just, you know, my stupid body."

"I love your—"

"You know what I mean."

Dalt doesn't move or speak.

"Ah, shit," I say. "Nothing is . . . I mean, nothing works like . . . It's just, nothing works anymore, Dalt. Nothing. I can't even feel what you're doing."

This isn't exactly something that's caught me off guard. I mean, it is my body. Watching it fall apart has become a kind of hobby. Our faces only six inches apart, we stare at each other. "It's okay," I say. "I come bearing gifts."

I twist around to the nightstand. We used to, I think, way back in the beginning, keep condoms in there. Now I pull out a tube of KY. I'd seen an ad for it on TV. Even then, I remembered thinking, who'd ever need that? God, like bringing sand to the beach. But only a month ago, I pulled a tube off the shelf, tossed it into the cart like I couldn't care less, hoping it'd just get mixed up in the shuffle of produce, milk, diapers. I felt like a kid again, buying those condoms.

As soon as Dalt sees it, he says, "Ah, Mad, no."

"Shh," I say. "Just give me a second. Or, do you want to do this for me? It might be kind of hot."

"Mad, I don't want . . . If you can't feel anything, it's—"

I bump his hand away, slather it on, which is, well, not hot. As a matter of fact, it's cold. It's not like the nerve endings have all gone extinct.

"Okay," I say. "Totally primed." I take his hip in my hand, try to tip him over onto me. It's like trying to move a boulder.

"I can't, Mad."

"Dalton."

He shakes his head. "We don't have to do this, Mad," he says. "That's no place I want to go without you."

"I—"

"No. It's okay. I'm all right. Really. You don't have to do this."

"*You're* all right? You? God. That is so like you. Always all about you. Jesus."

"Mad."

I keep pulling on his hip, but it's not my good hand, my good arm, and it's just weaker than shit. I slap at him, say, "That is so not fair."

He lets me tip him onto me, but that's all. There's no, um, well, anything else. He just lies there.

"Dalt," I say. "Really. This is for me. You have to." Goddamn it. "I, I can't remember, Dalt. Do you get that? Those days. When."

He's got my good arm pinned, so I reach down and take him in my twitching hand and can hardly feel him. I mean, I can hardly even feel him. In my hand. I try to guide him into me, can feel him bump against me, somewhere close, I think, but maybe only against my leg, and I clamp my eyes shut before they do anything really stupid, and whisper, "You are going to have to help here."

I keep them closed, feeling him shift, lift, an arm leaving my side. There's some pressure, and he says, "Are you sure?" and, biting my lips, I shake my head, like don't you dare even ask, and somehow, thank god, he gets it, doesn't take it for a no. There's more pressure, insistent, and just as I wonder if this is it, if that's all, if he's even inside me yet, I hear the sharp exhale of my own breath, that old gasp, the air literally pushed from my lungs, making that much more room for him.

When he says, "Jesus, Maddy," I can't help a smile. Pure relief.

Then he says, "Are you okay?" and I shake my head again, making just as much sense, and put both my hands on his rear, help him to start rocking back and forth. I can sort of sense him inside. We used to call it "my place." Like in, trying all over my effing place. I used to say *effing* every other word. I used to do so much. So much stupid, stupid stuff.

I blink, get my good hand up to my eyes, wipe them clear. We are going to make this work.

I pull on him, trying to hold him to me, my one hand slipping, the other cupping the dish in the side of his rear, just holding him so much closer than we've been in ages. My hand, not used to the work, begins to tap, my whole arm following, forearm, elbow, biceps. I pull tighter, trying to get it to calm the hell down, at least quit tapping endlessly the way Atty can, begging for that last ounce of attention you try to hold for yourself, and Dalt slides forward, not really back and forth, just up, tight against me, and I remember that move, that pressure, and I blink for real, and he says, "Good, god," and I say, "Dalt," and he closes his lips over mine.

Then I see him clearly enough to see that his own flood gates have cracked too.

"Shit, Dalt," I say. "No way. Stop it. Please?"

I try pushing him away, pulling him back, getting us into a rhythm that will override everything else. I mean, some of this stuff you just don't forget, hell, never even really had to learn. There's a word for that, but damned if I can come up with it.

"Please," I say, and, finally, Dalt moves again. Even not really feeling it, well, it's still like coming up for air after you thought the river had claimed you.

He's trying, working up the pace, holding on to me, but he has his head tipped down, so I can't see his face. It couldn't be more obvious what he's hiding. Which only makes it worse for me. Trying is not supposed to be this way. There are still enough unscarred connections for me to know that much.

"*Please?*" I say. "I don't remember that. Having to beg you? Is that how it used to go?"

"No," he says, like I'm serious. "You never had to beg."

He gets up on his elbows, straddling me with his arms, pinching mine to my sides, trying, without being too obvious, to hold the tremors still for me. I watch his chest, his stomach, see it flex and clench as he starts moving in me like he means it.

"Mad," he says, "there wasn't any begging." His words come in rhythm with his breathing, which is in the same rhythm as us, the two of us, moving together. "And," he says, "there wasn't ever any crying."

"I remember," I say. "Howling at the moon, but no crying."

We both laugh. The two of us, laughing.

"That," Dalt says. "That's it. That's what we were doing. Always." He pinches me tighter with his arms, his hands grasping my shoulders, squeezing so tight I might complain if I'd completely lost my mind.

My head snaps to the side, but I lift it as soon as I can, touch my forehead to his. I can barely feel a thing, but, really, I don't have to.

"Remember laughing," he says. "The two of us laughing."

"If you don't get serious about this job, there's not going to be much else for me to do."

"It's not *job*, it's not *business*, it's *trying*."

"Whatever," I say, but he leans in, like he's going to shut me up with his lips, and I do a preemptive strike, and when I pull away, I say, "Don't ever let me forget, okay? Promise? That's just not something I can live through. All this other shit? Child's play. But not us."

"Promise," he says. "I promise."

He shifts, cups my rear in his hands, lifts me, and I look up at him, smile, no tears, and he's moving slow, and I so remember this, and then, right on cue, Atty.

"Daddy? Daddy!" All urgent as hell.

Dalton doesn't stop, just turns his head to the door, which is open, always open, and says, "I'm right here, Atty. Right here with Mommy."

"I had a dream. A bad one."

"You're okay. We're right here. Just put your heady down. Go back to sleep."

Dalton moves in me slow and quiet, something I need like a heartbeat. There's silence from down the hall, and he turns back to me, smiling like a miracle worker, and then, just when we think it's safe, Atty says, "Dad? Can you come in with me?"

He knows I can't. Has long since given up asking for his mom. Why won't this shit just kill me? Is that all I have left to beg for?

Dalt closes his eyes. There are tears on his cheeks, caught in the stubble of his beard. I wipe them away with my bad hand, the tremor sweeping my fingers like a broom. "Go," I whisper.

He pinches the bridge of his nose, and I'm almost sure I can feel the moment he slides out of me. "I'll be back," he says, grabbing up his shorts from the floor, stepping into them.

"I'm not going anywhere," I answer, and I watch him as he steps away, down the hall, to Atty and Izzy, our lives, the best things ever, the best we have left.

Touron

I'VE DONE EVERYTHING I can. Dusted as high as I could before the dizzies soared in, Atty staggering me even more, volunteering to finish for me, my nervousness that apparent. He climbed his stool again and again, sweeping the mantel, the tops of lamps. He knocked down this huge cobweb in the corner, though he admitted it was kind of his favorite. "It blows when the door's open. Like waves." I've never been a Martha Stewart, and looking up, a sure way to bring on the dizzies, is something I avoid whenever possible, but good god, favorite cobwebs? I had no idea how far things had deteriorated. You could have farmed what he knocked off the back of Taimen boy.

In on it too, in her own way, Iz unbraids her hair for the first time in who knows when, brushes it out till it glows. She's, well, stunning. Four years old and already scary beautiful. I'd say that even if she weren't mine.

So then, the house sparkling, we wait, Atty perched on the back of the couch like a Mongol lookout on his peak, gazing up the street, down, Izzy asking again about Allie. "Is she like Janice?" she says.

I'm hollowed by just the name. It's a moment before I can get out, "Yes." I wasn't sure Izzy would remember Jan. Gone a year and a half now, the hole of her absence yawns like something I need to skirt to get down the street. I can still get jittery with the shock of her telling me they were leaving, that it was always their plan. "As soon as Seabring finished high school."

"But," I said. "People come here to stay. This is not a step on the ladder, it's the top, the step that says, *This Is Not A Step.* What could be better?"

"I'm not saying better, Maddy. But, we'll be close to Jared's parents. We have to. It's that time."

All our beautiful terraces in full bloom around us, At and Iz down in the brambles, tearing back up the railroad tie steps with their prize blackberries, offering them to us, their hands black with them, their mouths, it was all I could do to breathe. "Who will I...," I started, but could not say a word more, just sat there, alone, hardly aware Jan was holding my hand.

"Is Allie your best friend?" Izzy asks.

"She was," I manage. "But I haven't seen her in years. Years and years." Seven, I think, though that kind of cataloguing is no longer easy. Eight? She came out the once with, with, who? Some guy, another guy. Even with myelin slick as Teflon, that parade would be tough to keep in order. We still had Half Moon, I remember that. She's never met At or Iz. We floated, camped out at, at ... Goddamn, a night on a river? I never thought I'd lose one of those. But, though the name escapes, I feel the heat of the sand under my feet, dig my toes into that like a massage. There was a kind of cave, a big limestone overhang the fire played off of. Dalt will know. He'll remember. I'll have to ask. He promised he'd be home as soon as humanly possible. I made him promise. God. Like seeing Allie again is something I need back up for.

But the dancing firelight, the soot stains on the amphitheater of the cave roof, they're right here. I smile, remembering watching Allie and the man of the hour, whatever the hell his name was, playing grab ass around the fire. How when Dalton and I walked upstream to fish, give them a little time, Dalt said it was a shame, he kind of liked this one, that it was too bad the odds of seeing him again were so slim. When we got back they'd already pitched their pads and bags way back against the rock, so Dalt and I made our bed out at the mouth, the swimming hole eddy swirling only feet away. Dalt glanced up at the sky, saying, "Let's pray it doesn't rain upstream." Later, but not later enough for any considerations of modesty, the fire light dying, but still aglow, glimmering on the cave roof over our heads, Allie started into it with nameless boy. The amphitheater, Dalt and I discovered, as did the Romans or Greeks or whoever, acted like a giant ear, treating me and Dalt to every whisper, every moan and gasp, every single slurp and suck. We died trying to hold it in. Dalt whispered, "Sounds like hogs at the trough," and I nearly peed myself, said, "Oh, it is." We fought so hard not to spoil it for them, not to blow the mood with our gales of laughter, that I was sore the next morning, my ribs bruised with hugging it all in. But, even so, listening to that, well, it caused issues, priming, and Dalt and I, we were stealth itself, and I fall back into that, the two of us going all slow and silent, stretching it out and out until long after Allie and her guy had fallen away, long after we thought we could, and then, at the end, every nerve frazzled and frayed to snap point, I had to fight not to scream, not to bellow, "We win!" Instead, our breaths barely caught, without a word of planning, even a question, a request, Dalt and I slipped the few feet into the river, slick as otters with each others sweat, came up cold together, each wiping the hair, the water out of the others face. We went round and round the eddy, watery kisses, kicking only enough not to cross the line, get swept downstream, the cave black now, the fire out, the moon bright behind the hill, the tops of the pines etched out like battlements against it, holding everything at bay, the world, the future, all that's marred under the harsh light of tomorrow.

Izzy says, "Aren't best friends forever?"

I run my hand over her hair. Like silk. "Of course. It's just that we moved so far away."

"She's here," Atty says.

I jump, having watched Izzy play with her hair instead of even looking at mine. I'm wearing a sweatshirt for Christ's sake, knowing Allie would be on me like stink if she thought I dressed up for this. But the big belly handwarmer pocket, besides covering a multitude of sins around my waistline, is a pretty good spot to bury a claw. I actually, and I'm not proud of this, dug out an old rescue kit, the triangle bandages, and dusting off long dormant first aid skills, rigged myself a sling, took another triangle and tied my arm against my body, tight enough to stop the shaking, tight enough I could barely breathe. In the end though, there was my hand, hanging out of the creamy, tattered cloth, curled and twitching. I tugged it all off. Had to get Iz to help me untie the knots, re-roll the bandages. I wondered about calling any one of my docs, begging for a cast, amputation, anything. And I wind up with a sweatshirt. But it's got "We ♡ Mom" blazed across the chest, and that kind of says it all, too. Who I am now. And corny enough it'll give us something to laugh over. I shake my head, think, *Fabulous, you're wearing an icebreaker.* She's my best friend, and even four-year-olds know what that's all about. Where have I gone, I wonder. I miss me.

But I hear a car door slam, and burrow my bad hand as far as it will reach into the pocket, finger comb my feral hair, and instead of heading for the door, or even the window, I ask Atty, "Is she still beautiful?"

He twists around with a look on his face that so says, *How the hell would I know?* it gives me the smile I need to open the door.

Allie is not still beautiful, she is more so. Izzy could be hers. Her hair's a cascade of blonde, highlights that, goddamn her, are completely natural, her legs miles long, still sheathed in Levi's, a sleeveless shirt showing off her tanned guns, a fleece vest I'm sure got plucked out of some seconds bin, but on her looks tailored, hugging in, swelling out, in places that on normal people would have to be airbrushed.

We stop a second, both of us doing the check out, and she grins, says, "Holy effing shit. We *all* heart Mom. Duh." And then she grabs me, flattens me all over her, my lame arm pinched between us, something I wonder if she feels pattering there against her belly, the heartbeat of something alien between us.

She leans back to look at At in the doorway, whispers, "You did it! Just like you said you would." She bends low, says, "Hello," and Atty comes out and shakes her hand. Poor guy looks like an ambassador delivering the surrender documents.

Allie sucks in a breath when Iz steps out, says, "Oh my god, Mad, she's gorgeous."

"I know. Who'd've figured."

"Well, there's Dalton. She's got *some* genes on her side."

"Bitch."

Atty's eyes widen.

"Girl talk," Allie says. "You'll get used to it. You and your dad had Mom outnumbered too long. I'm the reinforcements. We've got the odds now." She dips her head to the side, shrugs an apology, says, "Sucks for you."

"My dad will be back soon," Atty promises, which absolutely slays Allie, and poor At, he doesn't get it, can't, and he retreats to the house with his sense of dignity in shambles, and I know Allie will never win him back. Good eye, I want to say to him, you steer clear of every Allie you ever meet. I mean, if I was a guy, I'd wait years for my turn, decades. But my son? No way. Not ever.

I can't help a glance to her car, the empty passenger seat. I can't remember the last time I saw her alone. She only said she was going to be out this way, that she'd love to see me, how'd we ever let it get this long to begin with?

I really don't know. Well, yes I do. I know exactly when my calls began tapering off, my emails. To everyone. Can you say dizzies? Nasties? Tremors? Sure you can. It's easy. M fucking S. Who the hell would I want to tell about that? Why? Who would want to hear? If I had to make a list of those people, Jan's the only outsider who'd make the cut, and, I'd have to say, though I love her to death, Allie would not even make the finals. But really, not many have. Even my parents. Every time they came out, I played Mad the Invincible, sapping myself of energy I didn't have to spare, collapsing for weeks the moment they left.

No, that news has wrapped only around us, me and Dalt, At and Iz, not much I'm able to hide from them, all of us cocooned within it together. Really, leaving the valley, all our old friends, made at least that easier. Not having people watch me decline. I just couldn't stand that.

"So," Allie says, "gorgeous kids, darling house." She looks around. "Where's the hot husband?"

"Working," I say. "He really will be back soon. Atty wasn't kidding."

"Atty?" She gives me a question look I remember squirming under before, the same one she used to skewer me with when she'd pass on a message from Troy, when I thought I was hiding Dalt. She was outraged that I'd go behind Troy's back, or maybe just hers—her with the turnstile on her bed. "What's Atty short for? Some old boyfriend?"

"An old boyfriend? Allie, even you. Not that twisted. And you know exactly how many boyfriends I've had."

"Not enough," she says.

"What was it I called you before?"

Allie rolls her fingers, out with it. "The name?"

"Bitch, that was it."

"Atty." She takes a stab in the dark. "Atticus?"

"Attila."

Allie eyes me long and hard, says, "Honey, what have you got to drink?"

And that's how Dalt finds us, out back on the deck he made, away from the prying eyes of any neighbors. We've fallen into first one six pack, then another.

Izzy is swinging in her tire, and even Atty has loosened up some, standing on top of the tire above Iz, hanging on to the rope. When they see Dalt they launch off, come running, hit him just as he's cracking open a beer. He sets it down, foam cascading over the rim, puddling around its base while he rolls around in the grass with the kids. He's avoided the hug with Allie this way, which she sees as plainly as I do. She fixes me with a look. "Are you guys always this disgusting?"

"Pretty much," I say.

Dalt grills, burgers for the kids, and then, glancing at us, tallying our empties, burgers for us too. The scallops, marinating in the fridge, I can see him think, might be better saved for tomorrow.

Later, Dalt puts the kids to bed, and they both hug me goodnight, kiss me, then go and hug Allie, too, tell her goodnight. She's surprised, I catch her flinch, then she hugs back, tells them to sleep tight, watches them tail Dalt into the house until they're all gone, and it's just me and Allie and the dusk. Maybe that's all she's been waiting for. I think she might say something about the kids, Dalt, my luck, but she wags the neck of her beer bottle towards my bad arm and says, "So, what's up with that?"

It's the beer, I suppose, that made me think I was going to skate through the whole visit. An absolute pipe dream, but I'm caught off guard. I stammer, say, "What?" and she says, "Your arm," not delayed a second by any dodge, then, "Come on, Mad. What's going on?"

I look around the yard, wish we had fireflies here, like we did in Ohio, something I haven't thought of in years. The kids would just love them. We could catch them in jars.

"Maddy?" Allie says, but she's not her usual insistent self. She's concerned, and I hate that.

"It's nothing," I say. "Just banged up."

"My ass," she says.

"That's banged up, too?"

She slaps her rear, says, "No junk in this trunk," and for that second I think I'm off the hook, but she follows immediately with,

"What is it, Mad? Parkinson's or something?" She's almost kidding, coming up with the worst she can think of so the truth will be easier.

I look down the neck of my empty bottle, that little black hole, and shake my head. "No. Not Parkinson's." I give her the lowdown.

Allie doesn't say anything, not for a long time, and I sit with my bottle, peel the label off, flatten it against my thigh, which, thank god, is not doing any of its twitches. The label, which I read for the first time, is a Rogue, and I say, "We were thinking, if Dalt can get away, we might do the Rogue while you're here. The Wild and Scenic stretch. You up for it?"

"MS?" Allie says. "You're sure? Not PMS?"

I shake my head. "They're kind of different."

"Fuck, Mad."

I take a pull on my empty bottle and Allie says, "There's nothing in that," and before I know it she's waiting on me. See what I mean? She presses a fresh bottle into my hand, takes a knee in front of my Adirondack chair, and I say, "Dalt made these chairs," and she puts her arms around me, and doesn't say a word.

It's nice and all, but, to tell the truth, I'd rather have fire ants crawling over me. I mean, I'd take a hug from Al any day of the week, any time there wasn't some guy there already, hogging all the space. But not for this. Not for pity. Not because I can no longer hide my arm, my self.

"Come on, Al," I say. "It's okay."

But she doesn't let go, just looks up at me, her hair clinging to my sweatshirt, same way Izzy's does. It's almost dark, but her eyes sparkle. They always do, but I'm terrified they're misting up, that this could tip into horrible in the next instant.

"Allie," I say. "Get up. Dalt'll come out and think I switched teams."

She lowers her head to my chest, so much like Iz now it's all I can do not to wrap her up, promise her we'll always be okay. "He'll want to shoot videos," she says.

I try a chuckle, but it's dust dry. I swig from the beer Allie brought. "Get up," I say. "Please."

She does, pats my leg, takes the step back, sags down into her chair. "I can't believe you didn't let me know," she says.

"*Oh, hi, Allie, I'm fucked up. Just thought I'd let you know.* It's stupid."

"Not telling me is stupid."

"Why? There's nothing you can do."

"Do? You called both times you were pregnant, didn't you? There was nothing I could do about that."

"You could be happy."

"And what, I can't be sad?"

"No. There's no point. It just turns into pity, and that's, I don't know. I hate that."

"*I hate that?* Holy shit, Mad. You need to get out some, talk to adults now and then."

I tilt my head back, daring the dizzies, and look up at the stars. "I'm fine, Allie. Really, I am."

"How bad is it?"

I smile. Those are exactly the words she used when she finally asked me straight out about Dalt. *How bad is it?* Only Allie. Like the real deal is this kind of affliction. Man, if only she could know.

"Maddy?" she presses.

"It depends on the day," I say, blow a breath up to the sky. "There can be bad ones, but, mostly, it's no big deal."

"No big deal how?"

"God, Allie, would you? It just wears me down sometimes. Makes me tired. That's all."

"And just the one arm's tired now?"

"Oh, for fuck's sake." I yank my hand out of my pocket, hold it waving between us, my thumb clicking against my curled fingers like some Spanish dancer's. I stuff it back in its pocket.

I look away from Allie's face, her eyes. Just what I expected. Stricken. I take a swig of beer, and say, "It's okay, Allie. Really. It is."

Allie nods, and I see her struggle, the way she works up a smile, if a shaky one, awfully brittle. She clears her throat. "I suppose a girl could do a wicked handjob with that," she says, and the beer shoots straight up into my sinuses, and I splutter, "Ass!" and she says, "Well?" and we laugh and Dalt slides open the back door, takes one look and says, "I don't have a chance back here, do I?" and I say, "You never did," and Allie snorts, says, "We should have both done you that night in the moonlight," and Dalt says, "Um, right. Well, I'm going to call it then. I got Friday. The weekend. We can do the Rogue if you want."

"Check him out," Allie says, "still hoping."

But I only smile at that, the hilarity gone as fast as it came, because I don't really like watching Allie see that there is one guy on the planet who isn't lusting for her, don't like seeing the cracks it exposes in her. I mean, if that's all you've got, and you know it can't last long, shit, give me MS. And since she's been all relentless about my arm, I finally ask what I've been meaning to since she stepped out of that car alone. "So, where's your guy?"

"Which one?" she shoots back.

"Any. Alissa solo. Don't know if I've seen that before."

She plucks a beer from the cooler beside her, swooping it up and twisting off the cap in a move that could be on a commercial. "Rebounding a little bit," she says.

"*You?*"

"A little."

"Allie, that's like me having a little MS."

"Being a little pregnant."

It's an old joke, and I almost miss that she doesn't say it quite right. It's a beat or two before I say, "Are you?"

"A slip up."

"With who?"

"You don't know him."

"Well." I lean forward. "Tell me. Where is he?" I hadn't expected this kind of juice.

"Fuck if I know," she says, and, even with all her men, this is the very first time I've ever seen her the way I've always imagined them, stunned and staggered as she lowers the boom, flips the switch, lets them know she's moving on.

"What?"

"He wasn't in it for that," she says.

"And?" I'm so shocked I give a wave toward her tummy, and I use my bad hand, don't realize till then that it's found its way out of my pocket.

"Taken care of," she says. She's studying the deck boards, Dalt's spacing between them so regular it looks fake.

I try to take a sip, but only clink the bottle rim against my teeth. This with my good hand. *Taken care of.* It's not the first time, I know that. I drove her to the clinic in Corvallis, back when we were first in school. I hardly knew her then. She hadn't even asked me to summer in Wyoming with her yet, learn the river trade. It's kind of, I realize, what we bonded over.

"Allie," I say. "I'm sorry."

She shrugs. "I, it's . . ." She traces the neck of her bottle across her lower lip. "It's harder when you're older," she says. "I wasn't expecting that."

I don't know what to say. I've never expected anything about it. Those scary years with Dalt, wondering if it was ever going to happen, I would have never been anything but overjoyed by the news. I never, ever, would have gone the other way. But then I think, Troy. If something had happened there, despite his claims to be firing nothing but blanks. No. That would not have worked.

"You get wondering how many chances you're going to get," Allie says, and I look up, see that night is full on around us, Allie just a shadow beside me.

"You, you're thinking about having kids?"

"Maddy," she says, "sitting here, watching you, how could you even ask? You guys are like the Cosbys or something."

"But I've been wanting this my whole life. You, Allie, not exactly your style."

"Styles can change, can't they? Is that against some rule?"

"Sure, Al, sure they can."

We sit in the dark. I hear Allie picking at her label now, the tear of paper.

"So," I say, after we've been quiet long enough. "This guy."

"Dad?"

I close my eyes. "Yeah. Him."

"I told you about him. Last year, when you called on my birthday."

I rack my brain, but these are the kind of things that are the hardest for me to bring up, all birthday calls I've ever made sifting down into one lump—The birthday call. Nothing at all about a guy Allie talked about. There are a lot more of them than birthday calls. But a year ago. That's a long haul for her.

"The married one," Allie says into the darkness.

Now that detail should stand out, but still I draw a blank. "Married, Al? That's kind of off limits, isn't it?"

"Was supposed to be. But, it wasn't ever a plan," she says, then, "You don't remember talking about this?"

"I'm sorry, Al. It's just, this shit plays hell with my memory."

She's silent, and I say, "It's not just some lame excuse."

"When I went in to pee," she says. "I . . . You've got railings in your hall. I thought maybe there was something wrong with one of your kids, something I missed. Or maybe that they just came with the house."

"Dalt put them there," I say.

"Figures," she says. "Mr. Fricking Perfect."

I smile.

"You have trouble walking?"

"We're talking about you here, Allie. Hello? Married guy. What the hell?"

"But, walking, Mad. That's like pretty basic stuff."

"It's only when it's really bad. I get off balance. Dalt overreacted."

"Off balance," Allie says. "Overreacted. Lot of that going around."

"Al."

"It wasn't a plan, Mad. It could have been. But it wasn't. And the getting pregnant. That was a terrible plan."

"You planned it?"

"Sarcasm, Mad. No. No way in hell I would have planned that."

"So. That was the end of it?"

"There never should have been a start." Allie lets out a breath. "But it could have been great, Mad. It really, really could have been. So great. But, um, somebody'd beaten me to the punch."

I wish it wasn't so dark, that Dalt had remembered to turn on the light. I need to see her face to believe this is Alissa talking, Allie, the master spinner, caught in her own web. It's more than I can fathom. "But, he's running around on his wife," I say. "It couldn't be that great. He couldn't be."

"Like I said, you don't know him."

"Allie?" I say. "Is this really you?"

She laughs then, a little, and says, "I know. And, no, I'm not sure this is me. Not sure who me is anymore."

"Allie," I say. "What happened?"

She clinks her bottle against the arm of her chair. It sounds empty. "I don't know. I just, I don't know, got stupid or something. It just happened. Then we were so far over our heads so fast. It was like boiling down the canyon in a canoe."

"Is he still, married?"

I hear movement, a nod or a shake, I can't tell. "He couldn't leave his kids. Do that to them."

"So, you do know where he is."

"Yes." It's only a whisper.

"Are you still . . ."

"No. I can't. We can't."

"Did he know? About—"

"Yes. Like I said, it wasn't something we could do."

There's a tiny part of me that wants to ask, Well, what part of it *was* something you could do? I mean, she totally dragged me over the coals about Tony. I stop. Tony? No, Tyron. Byron. I collect my breath, my thoughts. Jesus.

Troy. Troy. She was brutal about Troy, when I finally fessed up about what was going on with Dalt. She was merciless. *That kid*, she kept calling him, making me wonder if Troy had called her, signed her up to play for his side.

Allie says something, but that brain hiccup—Troy's name dodging away—that kind of shit throws me every time. "What?" I say.

"It wasn't like the clichés," Allie says. "Nothing like that at all. It wasn't all sordid."

"Okay," I answer. I'm getting better at this, feeling my way back into conversations I've slipped away from. But, a pregnant mistress, the guy fleeing back to the wife and kids? What's not sordid?

"You think I'm full of shit, don't you?"

"Allie. No. I don't know anything about it."

"Maddy. It's me, Allie. Remember? You can tell me the truth."

I reach out into the darkness, clink my empty against hers. "You're talking to a woman who shared a room with you," I say. "I wouldn't lie to you."

"No, you just wouldn't tell me," she says, then quick, "I'm talking to a woman who saw Mr. Right and grabbed on for dear life. A woman smart enough to do that."

"Well. But. That's not normal. It just happened, Allie. We both just knew. There wasn't any wondering."

"Well, I've done a lot of wondering. With a lot of guys. And this time, we both just knew, too. We had it, Mad. God. Right in the palms of our fucking hands."

"Except . . ."

"Exactly."

"Well, it's not like he's the only—"

"Tell me, Maddy, how many times has it happened for you? Where you just knew?"

"But, Al . . ."

"Yep. And I've been out in the field a whole lot longer, doing a whole lot more research."

I don't know what to say.

"And so I come here, to see my old wild child pal, cheer myself up, only to find a mild child, all cozy in paradise, everything you've ever wanted all tucked in around you."

"With railings on the walls," I say.

You can nearly see the sudden pall of frost in the air between us. I hold my breath, don't want to see the ice queen cloud it would leave before me.

It's Allie who exhales first. "But he doesn't give a shit, does he, Mad?" she says, like one long sigh. "About how you get. Only tries to help. Happy to take you any way you come."

"I try not to let him see." I can only whisper. "When it gets bad." I have never even admitted this to myself.

"Keep it secret?" She tilts her head back to the night. "God, Maddy, you two."

She runs a hand up through her hair, the golden fall of it. "I caught a glimpse of something that good myself, but couldn't have it, had to turn away."

Now I want to get down on my knees, wrap my arms around her, cry all night. "Allie," I say.

"Yeah, I know. Sucks for me." She waits, but I can't answer, can't muster so much as one forlorn chuckle. "Are we out of beer here?" she asks. I've seen this before, Allie slumped on her stool in the corner, gearing up for the next round. Come out swinging.

"There's more inside," I tell her.

"Perfect," she says, pulling herself up out of her chair. "I've got to pee anyway."

I say, "Me too," and get up to follow her in, use the chance to slip in behind her, instead of having her behind me studying my lurching gait, my trampoline walk, grabbing at everything in sight. Actually a beer usually helps, but four, five, six? Doubtful, at best.

But as soon as she hears me trying to rise, Allie steps back, takes my elbow, walks beside me. "I saw you before," she whispers into my ear. "You really did almost hide it."

I'm so grateful for her presence, more than her arm, I lean into her, tip my head against hers. "The Rogue," I say. "You never answered. You'll stick around long enough for that, won't you?"

I feel her shrug. "I don't know, Mad. Not sure I could take seeing all of you so perfect. Or listening to you and Mr. Wonderful going at it all long and slow. So right. You go skinny dipping again afterwards, it might just break what's left of my heart."

I stagger, and she holds me up. "You knew?" I say.

She puts her arm around my shoulder, no stupid Boy Scout elbow touch, but the real deal, and she says, "That's when I knew. That I wanted that. What you had. First time ever. I mean, how stupid could I have been?"

"God," I say, nearly giggling. "Dalt'd just die."

She squeezes hard, really hugging me. I don't need to be held up, but it's all right now, this way. "Hiding stuff is stupid, Mad," she says. "Believe me. It doesn't work. People get hurt. Nobody ends up happy. It's a bad plan. A very bad plan."

We get inside and she leaves me in the kitchen, starts off for the bathroom. "Use the railing," I shout after her.

"I may need to," she says, and she laughs, and I remember that sound with no trouble at all, something immune to sheath scarring, to poor planning, to all things ever hidden.

Pirates

AFTER DALT'S USUAL rush to get all his places closed in before the rains, Indian Summer wraps around us like a quilt, and we take a breath, even Dalt coming close to relaxing. He even, and I can hardly believe it, says he can skip a few days of work. We don't let the kids know straight off, instead trundling them off to school like any day, and then we come straight back here, linger over coffee the way we used to in the river days, between trips, a cancelled group, all those winter mornings. It's like heaven, time I could steep in forever. I'm exhausted, but we talk about busting the kids out, taking a trip, a float even, maybe a couple of nights on the Klamath, all sorts of plans spooling out before us.

Dalt doesn't go fidgety for at least the first hour. I'll give him that. But when he does push away from the table, already gathering dishes, I can't quite keep myself from saying, "Stay, Dalt," like I'm talking to a dog. "We'll get all that later."

He acts like he doesn't hear, just clears the dishes, loads the washer, wipes the counters, reshelves the cereal, me planted like a fern at my spot at the table. The way he darts around leaves me feeling nauseous and I know I'm headed for the abyss. But the whole time he's still just talking with me, not making any of his plans, which part of which house today, laying out his schedules, and I don't tell him a thing about any abyss. As soon as he starts the whirlwind routine, I know I won't hold him long, and if I let him know I'm starting a bad round, he'll just go into the *You Okays?* which will only make it worse. But if his taking a day off is shocking, he nearly stops my heart when he wipes his hands on the dish towel and says, "How about a nap? Feels like I haven't slept in years."

I hardly know what to say, so I just nod, and we steal back to our room, go so far as to slip out of our clothes, all of them, and lay down, skin to skin. I kind of look for signs, gear myself up for that, but he just stretches out flat on his back, and we nap together at nine in the morning. As his breathing eases, I lie there, my head on his shoulder, and stare out at nothing, too stunned to even think about closing my eyes. Actually sleeping at a time like this is the last thing we'd have done back in the day, but, still, this is as fabulous as it is unbelievable. Dalt relaxing, letting down, taking five. I brush his wispy chest hair with my good hand, kiss the side of his pec, that wide, flat slab of overworked muscle, and let myself drift off with him.

But I've hardly sunk below the surface before I feel him easing my head onto nothing but a pillow, catch him slipping away. He naps like a cat. Ten minutes. Fifteen tops. I hate that. I watch him step into his pants, not his stay-at-home sweats, but work clothes, the tattered Carhartts. I whisper, "No. Not really."

He shakes his head, says, "I just thought of something," which might as well be, "See you for dinner maybe. I'll do my best."

I stay in bed, listen to the door close, the truck start up, drop my fist down on the mattress, watch it bounce. If there's one thing I could change . . . But I know better than to start that list. No end in sight there. Still, he was not this way when we worked the rivers. Wasn't always charging off to work even back when it was something he loved, never let it consume his life. I wished we did live in a tree, under a rock, somewhere without payments, medical bills.

With the nap, though I know I'm teetering at the edge, my body is practically at ease, my hand still, my head just sitting there on my neck like a normal person's, the bed not adrift, no tilting, no whirlpools. I slow-roll onto my back, and pick out the familiar patterns in the ceiling's old plaster slap coat, until I find the falls, the reversal beneath it, a boat-eater for sure. Our Class V ceiling. Cataloging all the things my body is not doing, my things to be proud of today list, I think I'll try to add cutting Dalt some slack. If he was not this way back in the river days, well, I wasn't quite this way either. I mean, really, what am I to come back home to?

Not that I think he's slipping off anywhere ugly, to some chick who can still feel him, still want him, who can pump up a boat without tipping over, hell, just put on a display with the pump. I caught him ogling once as I pistoned up and down on the barrel pump, the girls, well, all but racing each other to be first out of my top. I glanced down, said, "Oh, hello," and his stupid, sloppy grin just slew me. Maybe he would like some chick who could still crash through the gnarlies with him, muscles all ripped and tanned and functioning, twitch-free. But, I really don't think that. Not Dalt.

Mired in my last bad spell, the revolting quagmire of self-pity that comes with it, clinging and sucking like quicksand, I told him that if I ever got this helpless all the time, he should find somebody else, an affair like, something on the side. Well, actually, I didn't quite get to "on the side." He glared at me, his face like it might boil. I tried to go on, but he slashed his hand through the air between us and shouted. It wasn't even a word. Just this bellow, this roar of decibels blurting out anything I might say. Never before had he ever tried to shush me. Only in a game, with kisses.

I tried once more, and he did it again, the shout maybe a word that time. Maybe, "Never!" I couldn't quite be sure. To tell the truth, it wasn't the worse thing I could've heard.

But now, as I shrink into the smaller and smaller space of my working brain, I think, Really, who *would* rush back to this? Why not build one more wall, hang one more piece of rock, work out one more bid? If he wasn't taking over most of the cooking, I wonder if we'd see him for dinner.

I drift off into that hideous, snag-filled reversal until, not an hour after he left, I wake to Dalt backing up the drive, reverse slipping like it does. I sit up, weather a momentary spin, and don't bother pulling up the sheet. Fighting this round of the nasties' quicksand, I say, "Time to pump up the boat," to the girls, just as I hear him tiptoe to the hallway, see his head poke around.

He looks me up, and down, a total check out, and he grins, which I could hug him for. I say, "Saved you a place."

He steps forward, drops one knee onto the bed, plants a kiss on me. "Been a lot of traffic, huh?"

"The usual crush."

His hand cups one of the girls, a perfect fit. "Poor bastards," he says, "getting sent away from this."

"Sucks for them," I say, and he smiles, but before I can lift back the sheet for him, he leans away, starts down the hallway. "Just wanted to make sure I didn't wake you out of your beauty rest," he says, "we wouldn't want that," and he's out the door, not coming back until he's got his arms full of boards, knocking a little paint off the hallway casing as he makes the turn for Atty's room, the project I had all but labeled abandoned.

I stare at the chip of white lying on the oak floor boards, listen to the boards clatter down, the crinkle of the craft paper that's been taped down since spring.

Just the sound, that discordant banging, sets my head sparking. "What are you doing?" I call.

He comes out on his way for more material, and winks at me. "I have an idea."

I swallow, open my eyes. "Well, look at me," I say. "This doesn't give you ideas?"

"Only one," he says. "But it's a good one. A brilliant one." And with that he's gone again, back in seconds with more boards. The next load is this wafer thin plywood, thinnest stuff I've ever seen.

"What in the world?"

"I got an idea," he says again, cutting himself off when he shuts the door between us.

I ease back into the pillow, careful not to set off any waves. I look down at my boobs, not too bad yet, even after the kids, and say, "Well, girls, you know how he is once he gets an idea."

I'm nearly dozing when the saw winds out, screeching and screaming, cutting some way it's not meant to, Dalt ad-libbing. My eyes water, my breath comes in gasps. The resinous sting of scorched pine seeps down the hallway. The saw kicks in again and again, breaks only long enough for him to pick up the next piece. Then the hammering begins. He doesn't let up for anything, no coffee breaks, no slipping out to bring his lovely wife a bit of breakfast in bed, nothing but banging and buzzing, sharp teeth searing soft pine, steel and muscle driving spikes into the yielding wood, straight through the hailed-out fibers of my brain.

Finally, though it's kind of the last thing I feel like, I sit and swing my legs over the side of the bed, take a moment there, let my head catch up. I'm only going to tell him he's killing me, but I catch a glimpse of myself in the mirror, this harpy coming to stop his latest project.

I sag, drag the sheet up over my shoulders. No matter what's coming on, I've got to try. It's all that'll keep the quicksand from sliding over my head, not a trace of me left but a few bursting bubbles of woe is Mad. Yanking the sheet with me, I stand up, waver, and seriously check myself out in the mirror. I put out an arm, my good one, which I'll need on the rail, and drape the sheet around me. That shoulder stays bare, looking nice, if I do say so, and I nudge the sheet lower over that boob, hike it up over the other collar bone. My hair's a mess from the pillow, but, I tell myself, in a good way. I put a few curls where they belong, one almost hiding an eye, falling across my cheek.

I take a breath, whisper, "Aphrodite, you hag," and try out a smile, going for seduction, settling for maybe brave, then set off, my feet searching for the floor with every step. I concentrate on how I'll ease open the door, sneak up behind him, let him see me, let the sheet slip a little, let him know this day of work is going to be put on hold. God, I just hope I can get through it without my legs cramping up. Last time it was like a seizure, fiery pokers grating down my femurs as we tried, knotting muscles wrenching apart my very bones until finally I couldn't even pretend, had to stop him, have him massage my legs, pretend it was just the touch of his hands bringing tears to my eyes. We do not need that again.

I make it down the hall, everything in its place, the floor staying vaguely beneath me, and work my thumb into my thighs for a minute before barely touching the knob, turning it slowly, stealth incarnate. Until I realize it's locked. I had no idea these old locks worked. I turn it this way and that, rattle it. It really is locked.

"Dalt?" I say. But his saw's running. As soon as it goes quiet I say, "Dalt. You locked the door." Like it could have been an accident.

"It's going to be a surprise."

"What is?" How can you make a surprise out of a room?

His saw goes again, whining high, not just chopping through a stud. My teeth grate. He's ripping that thin-ass ply. It takes more than a second.

When he's done, I say, "Dalt? The door's locked."

"Just to keep out prying eyes," he says.

"They're at school, Dalt." This is Dalt relaxing. Taking a day. Locking himself into a room with his saws and hammers, his all but naked wife locked out in the hallway. I bang the door with my fist. Lights flash behind my eyes. "Dalt."

The paper crinkles beneath his feet as he turns. I hit the door again, hard. Even with my marionette wrist, it feels good.

I hear his steps sweep across the paper, the clunk of the bolt drawn home. The door cracks open, maybe two inches. His eye's there. A narrow slash of cheek. "Maddy?" I see him glance down over my stupid sheet. He's not blind. The door opens wider, maybe a gaping half foot. He smiles, says, "Oh, Helena."

"What is wrong with you?" I say.

His hand is half way up to me, to my chest, the side that's almost bare. But it stops, wavers, and he says, "What?"

"What are you doing in there?"

"Doing? I'm making At's room. It's a surprise."

"I could help you know. I can still do things."

He laughs. He fucking laughs. He says, "Oh. Yeah. I see you're wearing your Carhartt toga." He goes for my waist, settles his hand on the top of my hip, moves it around back. "Can't seem to find your belt."

I brush my hair out of my face. "I'll get changed."

"Why on earth would you do that?"

I fix him with a stare that stops his hand dead. He says, "I just thought, since I've finally got some time, I could do this. I've got the perfect plan."

"And how do you think Atty'll feel being locked out here, listening to you pounding away?"

"Excited," he says. "Kind of like I thought you'd be."

I drop my hand from his railing. Stand there on my own two legs. Check me out. "Dalt, we have a day off. When was the last time that happened?"

He eyes me. "You know, Mad," he says. "It's not like I work for fun. The thrill of lifting another wall."

"I know that. But, today, you don't have to saw and, and," the word skates away. "By yourself. I really can help, you know. I know what I'm doing."

He looks around his room, his Sawzall and wall bore, Skil saw and hammer, and pulls in this sigh I'd love to ram straight down his throat. I know what he's going to say. "Maddy. I'd love that, I would, but, honestly, it'd be, I don't know, dangerous, it wouldn't—"

"I don't have to run power tools to help, ass. God, I—"

He holds up his hand. "How many days have you asked me when this would be done? How many times?"

"Great. Now you're all about it. And you won't even show me what you're doing, won't even let me try—"

"Fine," he says, quick as a fist, flinging the door open wide. It bangs into his sawhorses. A piece of ply slithers to the floor, a little splintering, a corner he's not going to be able to use now.

He waves me into the room like he's leading a tour, a real estate snake hard-selling the fixer-upper. But I catch the hitch in the sweep of his arm when I turn away, my sheet falling when I reach for the wall. I could maybe catch it if I was fast enough, but I'd probably go down with it. Quick moves are no longer my forte. But now he's got the set wings of my shoulder blades to look at, my bare ass, doubtfully my best asset anymore. I leave him in his dust-filled room with his clutter of tools and scraps and cords.

"You're not missing anything, Mad. I'm making a room. That's all."

"'That's all.' You said it."

"It's going to be—"

"Never mind, keep your secret," I start, but the last of the sheet tangles around my ankle, my foot, and I'm already on my last legs. I stumble, have to grab the goddamn doorway with both hands. My claw hand, startled out of dormancy, jumps right into its lunatic's beat against the trim, which so pisses me off. I take the last step to the bed as behind me he says, "Maddy, come on."

I shake my head, say, "I don't want to know. I might spoil it for everybody." I kick the door shut between us, collapse on my bed like a pouting teenager. The bounce on the bed. I could puke. If I was watching this from above, I'd bitch slap me into next week.

The door opens quietly and he's standing there, his Skil saw still dangling from his hand. "Is it so wrong to try to surprise a kid?" he says.

"Is it so right to pretend I'm part of the fricking furniture, just something to be moved around, gotten out of the way? 'Don't want poor Maddy hurting herself.' You think saws are the only things that cut?"

He sits on the edge of the bed. He reaches for me, finally realizes his hand is not empty. The heavy worm-drive hits the floor with a solid bang, a slither of cord. He covers me with the bedspread, which was nothing but a crumple on the floor. I've got laundry to do.

Why does he cover me up? Why that, first thing? I always thought it was because I complained, told him how I embarrassed myself, would rather not be looked at, but now, when I'm trying, I'm maybe not so sure. I mean, hell, I put on a fricking toga.

"What do you want to do today, Maddy? Can you tell me that much?"

"Jack shit."

I hear him suck in a long, slow breath, can practically hear the ratcheting of his brain as he searches through his books, tries to remember the bullet-points for dealing with mood swings. How to be helpful and supportive for your partner with MS. "Go finish your stupid room," I say.

"Do you want to take a drive?" he asks.

I don't say anything.

"A walk? I can get your stick."

I walk with a stick now. Isn't that just fab? Like some kind of fairy tale creature. Some wizened goddamned wizard. Yeah, Dalt, that's exactly what I want to do, go out on one of my fucking Gandalf patrols. Shit, that's why I donned my sheet, close as I could get to a cloak. "Go away," I say, and it occurs to me that those are two words I've never before said to him.

He's silent, and I don't know if he's pondering his next suggestion, or trying not to get mad, doing some ten-breath thing. Then the bed shifts, he stands up. Very quietly—so it's the pissed off route after all—he says, "You have asked me, over and over again, to please finish Atty's room, that they're getting bigger, that this place isn't big enough to leave a room empty, that it's time for Atty, that he'd love it, that looking at that closed door day after day is driving you nuts." He pauses just long enough for a breath. "You know who

I'm working for today, Mad? For you." When I don't answer, he can't keep himself from saying, "Same as every other fucking day."

Then I hear him stoop down, jerk up his saw, clanking it against the bed frame, its steel edge nicking into the cherry he cut and polished for our bed. He walks down the hall, calls out, "I'm closing the door, but only to keep the dust down. You can come and look any time you feel like it."

The door shuts, and I'm left alone, stark naked under a tangle of bedspread, my sheet in the hall, on the floor. I think it through, realize it's not the thing to do, and shout, "Just lock the damn thing!"

The door smacks like he was waiting, the bolt snapping shut. His saw roars, too fast to possibly be cutting anything, just Dalt in there pulling a trigger, being a man, a dope. I hope he doesn't saw off his leg.

And then my head, though I'm lying on my face, does it's side flip, grinding my nose, my cheek, across the mattress, and I pound my temple with my fist, say, "Stop it," every time it jerks down. "Stop it. Stop it. Stop it." I see stars. When it does stop, I peek over at the clock. It's a while before I can focus, then put the numbers in order, and then I only see I've got an hour before I'll have to grab my stick and crab-crawl down to kindergarten for Izzy. There's no way Dalt's coming out of that room now. I should trade my stick for a broom.

ૠ ૠ ૠ

DALT, AS A matter of fact, barely emerges for the rest of the week, never again mentions floats or camp-outs or, really, anything. Just some trips to the store, shipping in more lumber, drywall, mud, paint. Even once, these two huge coils of rope. I have to admit, I get curious, and only more so when I catch him going past, after an afternoon in the shop, with an armload of what look like swords. But there is no way I'm going to peek. Going to ask. I do, though, begin to wonder if he's okay. I wonder who is running his business, if his pager is filling with calls from home owners wondering why no work is being done after that glorious rush of seeing their walls go up, their roofs down, windows in.

He comes out for dinners, only smiles and shrugs at Atty's desperate interrogations, even Izzy dying to see, to know. They plead with me when Dalt goes back in, when I settle into the couch with them for the nighttime reading. The words on the pages, lately, have started rearranging themselves before my eyes, making no sense, and I thank god I know the stories by heart, can fake my way through with no one guessing, unless I hit a run of slurring, that *moose juice not goose juice is juices for mooses*. Having to give this up, too, is not something I'm sure my heart can take.

But they're not listening anyway. Toasty in their flannels, snug against me, they're begging for secrets, what *might* be in the room, and I do my best not to sound angry when I tell them I don't know, that if someone wants to hide something from me, I'm fine with never knowing. "I don't like secrets," I say, and Izzy tilts her head and says, "Surprises?"

I bite my lip. "You're right, honey. That's all Daddy's doing. Making a surprise. We don't want to spoil it for him."

"I do," Atty says, and by the end of the week he can hardly sleep. Instead of "I love you," at night, he only says, "Please tell me."

Personally, I don't think this is doing him much good. No matter the payoff. Any of us any good.

After bedtime, when Dalt finally reappears, we lie next to each other in bed like statues. Over a room. Something we've all wanted done. But not like it's just the next job, the next item on the punch list. Not Dalt all by himself, the rest of us only circling the edge of the whirlpool, watching him go under. At one point, midsummer, we'd talked about all of us painting it, At picking the colors. A kid's room, you know, them helping way more important than how it looks. Nobody's talking that way now.

And then, that Friday, after I stagger down to school on my own one more time, a walk I know I'm going to have to wean them off of, have them get used to the idea of making it themselves, before they start sneaking away to keep any of their friends from seeing their mom, the hobbling, swaying crone, stumbling down the blocks behind them, we come up the drive to find Dalt standing there. The kids are startled, Atty's hand tightening in mine, and I see that Dalt's wearing an eye patch, and I think, oh god, no, not his eye, not his perfect, blandly blue eye. My mind, still gloriously quick, showing off, gives me splinters knifing away from planks, nails ricocheting from hammer blows, a lone carbide tip cracking off a blade tooth, a white hot arc burning into iris. When he says, "Ahoy," and I finally get it, the relief makes my knees rubbery, my breath short, only my stick holding me up.

"Ahoy, Cap'n!" Atty shouts, and lets go of me to charge into Dalt, hand curved into a hook I don't like the look of one bit. My own is in my pocket, its semi-permanent home, rocking quietly.

Dalt, I see, is holding out a handful of eye patches. Atty gets his on in a second. Dalt helps Iz with hers, the elastic string catching in her long hair.

Finally, down on his knee, he looks up at me, in the eye for the first time in a week, and holds out the last patch. "Mom?" he says.

"You don't have a lantern you want to lock me in?" I ask. But that's just being a bitch, and I take my patch, adjust it over my eye, and the world goes flat, two-dimensional, which, really, I'm not at all sure I can do.

I reach out, and Dalt has my hand that fast. He says, "You don't have to wear it."

I say, "No, it's all right. I can," and I'm kind of loving holding his hand, even as Atty jumps around, keeps saying, "Why are we pirates? Why are we pirates?"

But he's been a pirate for years, and Dalt only looks at me, my one eye, squeezing my fingers. He's taken my stick, what I use to hold myself up with, and whips it down to his side, hikes one foot up to his rear, pegs around, goes all hunchback, sings low and growly, "Fifteen men on a dead man's chest," and Atty bellows, "Yo ho ho, and a bottle of rum!"

Sometimes At greets us in the morning with nothing more than a deadly serious "Avast."

Pulling me along behind him, tapping my stick like a wooden leg, Dalt leads us into the house, and it's only then that any of us tip, that I realize he's not locked into the room, that Atty shrieks, "My room!"

He tears off down the hallway, flings in the door, and stops dead in his tracks. We can hear him breathe, big, gulping, stunned gasps, his head, for just a moment, stock still—I can all but see the bulge of his eyes, the drop of his mouth—then he starts to look this way, that, trying to take it all in. Izzy darts past him, and he grabs her, says, "No! It's mine!" and Dalt says, "Don't even think about it," in the voice that gives no quarter. Only then do they step forward, the two of them together, and only then do I look beyond them, into the vast secret, Dalt's surprise.

Dalt has not made a room. He's made a ship. The walls don't drop straight and plumb to the floor, they curve in beside giant curved braces, flying buttresses or whatever, no, that's cathedrals, architecture. I lose the word, though I can see it, and then it's back, ribs, just like our bones, the one Eve took from Adam, put to so much better use. Atty's at a trio of big wooden casks in the corner, discovers the pulls, whips open the drawers, cries, "Iz, they're dressers!"

Izzy, and I am not making this up, is clambering up rigging, lifeline thick rope spliced and splined together into real live rigging, a rope ladder tapering up to the top bunk. The Jolly Roger flies just off to the side. As she leaps off, bouncing onto the mattress, I remember Dalt in Wyoming, back-splicing all his lines, sneering at the duct tape wrapped free ends of most boaters' ropes. It takes forever. I wonder if after I fell asleep every night, he snuck back in here and wove rope through till dawn, like that spooky guy in the fairy tale, spinning straw into gold, just waiting to steal the first born. I can't remember his name, though I bring up *Today I bake, tomorrow I brew, Today for one, tomorrow for two* without even trying.

Izzy screams, "At!" and whips open a window above the bunk, which is really a porthole. She peers out, shouts, "Ahoy!"

Atty is at a cannon, a monstrous black cylinder poked into the wall, complete with a fuse sticking out the top. "Chain-shot for the masts!" he yells. "Bring 'em down!" But then he leaps across to a rack on the wall, half a dozen wooden cutlasses hanging there, waiting to repel boarders. He grabs one, wields it left and right, pulls down another and throws it to Izzy, who, climbing down the rigging, can't possibly catch it, who says, "At!" full of indignation, but Atty has just shrieked, spotting, at last, before the one window Dalt's left wide open, gazing out onto the bounding main, the captain's wheel, which I hope to god Dalt found somewhere, didn't spend days making on his own, squirreled away in his shop alone, lathe whirring, clamps grabbing, tightening, holding everything together.

"It's a ship, it's a ship, it's a ship!" Atty cries, and Izzy takes it up too. My eyes water. They grab the turned knobs, and together wheel the ship left, then right, then back again, tacking us up against the winds, crossing the T, what the hell ever else it is you do with a pirate ship in a mountain town, and I feel the sway of the deck beneath my feet and have to lift the patch off my eye to stop it, so I can see, really see, Dalton beside me, Dalton who has never once come close to spoiling these kids.

"My god, Dalt," I say.

He's got a grin I'm not sure I've seen on him before. "I started with a Mongol tent scheme, you know, Attila's nomadic base camp on the steppes, but," he laughs, "well, it kind of just looked like the fish camp yurt. He's always been more into pirates anyway."

The kids are calling each other scurvy dogs, landlubbers, bloody barnacles, wherever that came from, and there's the telltale crack of wooden swords, each one sending a jolt down my spine, and Dalt's watching it all while I watch him.

"It's," I say, "It's . . . How long do you think it'll last? Before he grows up, thinks this is embarrassing?"

Dalt looks at me like I may have gone mad. "Does it matter?" he says. "Look at them."

And I realize he's right, that it doesn't matter. That none of it has. That it's not about me anymore, even us, and, though I don't think Dalt has a clue about this yet himself, maybe he's sawed and nailed the idea onto me, an idea I'd just as soon not have clamped to my soul. Not yet. I say, "What on earth are you possibly going to do for Izzy?"

He groans. "Don't know yet. Sheena of the jungle? Xena? Some Amazon theme?"

"Our tree house," I say.

He turns to me, his face aglow. "That's it," he says.

And I don't say, *My lantern. Some place you can hang me up, us up, keep us out of the way.*

Atty crashes into Dalton's legs, saying thank you, it's the best, all that, and Izzy hugs me, asking if I see, if I want to climb the rigging with her to the crow's nest. I touch the top of her head, and I keep a secret myself, that this is not the kind of thrill we've ever had here, that this is trip to Disneyland stuff, something else we never considered doing. I don't say, *Dalt, you took a week off. You could have taken us on a real boat, taken us down real rivers, built fires in the sand, tucked them into sleeping bags around the leaping flames, under the scorching stars, and made up whole lifetimes of pi-rateering for them, tales they would never forget, the dashing Atty, the remorseless Iz, scourges of the seven seas, stories they would tell their own children around their own campfires, and they around theirs. But instead you locked yourself away from all of us and gave them a room, built them a trick.*

Oh, Dalt, I want to say, *it's so beautiful and so empty when all they need is you, not rigging you didn't even let them watch you make, show them how you weave your beautiful splices.*

When he puts his arm around me, I stop myself on beautiful, because, really, what might be behind all this is the nasties, my stupid stick, my wondering how long I can walk them to school, pick them up. Read to them. How long I have left to run those rivers, to do any of this with them. What I say is, "It's beautiful, Dalt. It is," and I let Atty take my hand, lead me into his ship, sit me down on his bunk, put a sword into my good hand, and I try to join in as they all sing about the bottle of rum, the dead man's chest.

Divorce

THE LIGHT ABOVE the kitchen table gives me a headache. I hate it. Why did we end up sitting here for this? Is there some kind of ominous, cold hard light scrutiny thing going on? I swear you could do surgery on this table, dissect anything, but Dalt just sits there spinning the empty salt shaker around and around, getting no closer to any answer. If I could reach it, I'd slap it across the room. "Tell me it's something you haven't thought about," I say again, then hold my hand in my lap, waiting.

Dalt looks up from his thumbs, gives the shaker a rest. It slows and slows, spin-the-bottle, a game I actually played once, in college I think. Though maybe high school. I hope not high school. I wait to see which one of us it will point to. Dalt says, "Thought about?"

"Yes," I say. The shaker points at me. I can't remember who was there when we spun the bottle, only that we did at least start to remove clothes. That breathless waiting hangs with me, the tantalization, the bated breath, the tingle and dread and elation.

"Have I thought about it?" He waves his hand around the kitchen, Iz's unfinished homework a scrabble of paper and colored pencils shoved toward a corner, something we'll have to rush her through in the morning, Atty's science fair volcano a vivid purple lump on the counter, baking soda splashed around it, the vinegar bottle tipped on its side, miraculously capped. Whether he means to or not, Dalt's wave ends up on my wheelchair, just a hospital loaner, nothing permanent. "Walk away from all this?" he says. "How could you even ask?"

"I'm serious, Dalt. And I'm asking. Now." As soon as the words are out of my mouth, I know I've heard them before, and, like another sort of miracle, it comes to me right away, waltzing down my sheathing—Troy, on the banks of the Snake, the night after my first night with Dalt. Troy asking if I loved him, demanding to know. *I'm asking now.* Jesus. The way my brain works anymore. It's like living with a cobra, no idea when it will strike next, where.

So softly it doesn't really bring me back, Dalt says, "Of course I've thought about it."

"What?" Spin-the-bottle, Troy, cobras. I'm lost.

"Of course I have," he says. "Thought about it."

"You have?" If my voice rose any closer to a squeak, I'd be taking out hair by the handfuls.

"I've thought about everything, Mad. Who hasn't?" He takes this huge breath. "I've thought about running rivers again, too. Man, I've driven across the Rogue and thought about swerving off the bridge just to be on the water, even for just that instant." He looks down at the table, readjusts the salt and pepper shakers. "Just to end this upstream slog."

I run my hand over the rock hard rubber of my chair tires, feel the spokes click against my knuckles, brushing my fingers away. On the Snake sometimes, the Buffalo Fork, exploring, we'd end up in dead-ends, channels that petered out, grew choked with ancient jams. Dalt'd hop out, do his African Queen, bulling back upstream, the stern line taut over his shoulder, until we could set off again on the main channel. "Upstream slog?" I say. "That's what we're doing?"

"Whatever you want to call it."

"Jesus, Dalt."

"Well, for Christ's sake, Mad. You say, 'I think it might be best if we split up.' Say it's something you've been thinking about. You hold me under until I confess." He takes a breath, shakes his head. "What the hell did you expect me to say?"

"I don't know," I say. "Something different."

"Okay," he says, dropping his hands onto the table. "I'll tell you this, that this right here . . . If there's one thing that makes me think about it, it's this on the nail head."

"What?" I say. It feels like my wheelchair's grown in the last seconds, like I'm tiny within it, being swallowed whole.

"This whole Maddy the Martyr act."

Every nerve cell I have left blasts off at once. "What?" I blurt, way bigger now than any fricking wheelchair. I lean so far over I'm on the table, the chair almost squirting away from me. "What the fuck?"

He glares straight back. "Your whole, 'Oh, I'm not worthy, go, be free, find someone else, someone healthy, true happiness, all you deserve. Don't worry about poor old Mad.'"

I do a cartoon jaw drop and bobble. It's honestly all I can manage. I can't think of the first thing to say.

"The whole act," he says, "makes me sick."

"Act?" I say, totally failing in any attempt to sound calm. "Act my ass! I am thinking about you here, Dalt. Maybe you should try it sometime. Thinking about somebody else for a change."

"You're thinking about me? 'Jeez, honey, let's get divorced. Just for your sake, okay?' Do me a favor, think a little less about me."

"I couldn't think less of you right now if I tried."

He narrows his eyes. "Nice to see there are some synapses left unscarred."

"You," I say, but ass is so puny, and I've never tipped over to fucker or bastard. Not and meant it. I stand up, kick that lame-ass chair into the wall, stutter for a moment, "B, b, b," which so pisses me off I could strangle. I'm not even sure if I'm trying to get out bastard or believe, but it's believe that finally lurches out, so I go on. "Believe me," I say, "if our positions were flipped, I sure wouldn't be sticking around for these jollies."

"But they aren't flipped. For fuck's sake, they won't ever be flipped. So you can spout on all you want about *if this*, and *if that*, and *if only*, and it's all just crap."

"So, if it makes you so sick, why are you still here?"

"I didn't say that. I said this, this right here, right now, is what makes me sick." He stares, waiting. Then runs his hand up through his hair. "God. I love you. Do you still not get even that?"

"Oh, yeah. You're making that pretty obvious. Dalt, my missing-in-action husband. Tell me, does everyone else on your crew work your kind of hours? Or are you the only one who acts like home is some foreign country?"

"Work? What?"

"God, I hate that. *What?* Like what I'm saying is so completely incomprehensible."

"Well, if it's so comprehensible, why don't you explain it to me?"

"What, are you blind now, too? How about we start with Saturdays? I mean, there are actually places in the world where they're considered part of what's known as the weekend. Weekend, Dalt. Days off. To rest. To spend time with your family."

"So, this is about me working, not about you as my hideously diseased ball and chain?"

"Tell me right this instant that divorce sounds like a bad idea."

"Right this instant? Nope. Not bad at all. It's the next instant, though. I'm not so blind I don't see that."

That stops me. Long enough Dalt gets in, "You know what I hate most about this, your whole deal? Not the twitches, the leg cramps, even the dizzies, the exhaustion." His voice cracks, and he pinches the bridge of his nose. "Not your poor failed hand." He shakes his head. "It's this. The way it leaves you feeling like you're something less than you used to be. That is just such utter bullshit, Mad."

I look away. Bite my lip.

"You really have no idea, do you? As fucked as this is, Mad, it doesn't make you less. Good god. It makes you more. Me, if the roles *were* flipped, I'm not even sure I'd still be around, wouldn't have pushed myself into Lava without a jacket or boat, tied to an anvil. But you," he stops a second, wondering how to get it out right, then makes his qualification. "Except for these bouts, which are just another part of the fucking disease, not a part of you, you just keep cruising. We laughed about the twitching, Mad. For Christ's sake. You told At your hand was a pirate hook. You used to chase him with it, calling him a scurvy dog." He comes close to smiling. "You think there are other people on the planet who do that? Who would even think about it?"

He stares at me, like he could still spin around and bolt out the door forever, and says, "You've no idea who you are, do you? How I look at you going through what you do, and think, *If only it could be me, I'd take it on in a second for her*, but knowing for real I never could, that I don't have a trace of your strength."

"That is so not fair," I say. I can't even begin to look at him.

He doesn't answer.

"You ass," I say. "Can't you see I'm trying to kick you out? And then you say something like that. Can't you ever, just once, make things easy for me? It's always hurdles with you, isn't it?"

He sort of laughs. More just a rush out of pent up air. Pent up something.

"Dalt," I say. "You've really thought about driving off the bridge?"

I glance up just in time to catch his nod. "And I haven't done that either," he says.

"I'd kill you if you did."

"Of course you would," he says.

I smile, more at us, than from any drop dead humor. Only us, making jokes out of the end. "Seriously, Dalt," I say. "I just wanted to know if you thought about it."

"I have," he says. "But seriously?" He shakes his head. "Not even once. Just daydreaming. Something to do while pounding nails—

wondering how dead-ass empty and horrible it would be possible to make my life."

"Really?"

"Leave you, Mad? For what possible reason?"

I wave my hand down at my twitching arm, the rest of my thrashed body, my whole eddied-out life. My legs are trembling. I haven't been on my feet this long in a week. "For what *reason?* Boy. Let me see. That's a stumper."

"Mad, you need reassurance like you need a hole in the head. I do, you know that, always have, ever since you attacked me at that boat party."

"You," I say, "attacked me."

He shakes his head. "Standing there minding my own business, when the keg girls moved in for the kill."

I stare at him. "Whatever."

"You think a few twitches are going to steer me away from that?"

"A few twitches." I point back toward the wheelchair. "A few twitches?"

"Shit, Mad. You pull it off. I mean, you make even that look work for you."

I roll my eyes. I can't help it. "Would you, please? Just once. This is serious stuff, Dalt. Way serious."

"Divorcing? Us? I can't think of anything less serious."

I stagger over to retrieve my chair. Collapse into it. I'm dying. "It's no fucking act, Dalt. God. I could kill you for that. You know what *I* hate most about this? Watching what it does to you. You know how much I want you to do all the things we always talked about? You never signed on for any of this. I know you didn't. Remember? We couldn't even say 'I do,' because it was too stupid, not knowing what might come at us."

"That was the stupid part."

I shrug. "Maybe. But neither of us ever saw this shit coming." I hold up my curled right hand, let it do its maraca thing there between us.

"It's an arm, Mad. It's not you."

I hide it away between my legs. I really can't stand looking at it. "It's part of me," I say.

Dalt nods, no slick way around that one. "And you're part of me," he says.

Goddamn it. The guy can be slick at the worst of times.

He knows he's scored. "Maddy. No matter where your arm goes, have you ever really wanted it gone, amputated?"

"No," I admit. "But, I've thought about it."

He thumps his hand against the table. "Exactly."

Shit. I can't believe I walked into that one. My brain used to really work. I swear it.

"No matter where you go, Mad, where this goddamned, son of a bitching, mother fucking MS takes you, I'm going too. I'd no sooner think losing you was a solution than you would cutting off your arm." He makes a fist on the table, trying to hammer the deal down. "I mean, you? Lose you? Way worse than an arm. Somewhere in the world there are probably one-armed carpenters, but you can't live without your heart, Mad. Nobody can. Not even you."

We sit there with the table between us, our crowded, messy, kitchen. "'It is my strongest desire,'" I say, our lame-ass wedding vow. "You know what you just did, Dalt?"

He shakes his head.

"You called yourself a carpenter. That's what I'm talking about. You don't even think of yourself as a boatman anymore."

"We were kids, Mad," he says, but he taps his chest. "And that's all still in here anyway, always will be, you and me, boatmen extraordinaire. Remember Lava? Caldera? Dragon's Tooth? Ranie Falls?" He snorts. "Hell, the whole fricking Selway."

All those rapids we've run, names like words you don't even read, all the names in those fat-ass Russian novels, the tangled polyglots of syllables and consonants you don't wind through every time, let alone try to pronounce, but that still bring that person straight to mind. Each name he ticks off puts me on that exact spot, on that exact river. Colorado, Upper Klamath, Lower, Rogue. I feel the huge pillow to my right surge, the house boulder it pushes me toward, the hole below it that will never let you go if you get too far left. Do *not* get too far left. My broken oar through the Rockslide on the Rio Grande, what Dalt called my floating leaf line. His pinball through, well, the entire Lochsa.

Dalt reaches across the table, taps my hand, brings me back. "See?" he says.

I purse my lips, shake my head. "I hate it when you're right."

"Not something you have to get used to."

I say, "God, right again."

He smiles. "So, can we put this one to rest? The two of us ever not being the two of us? It just doesn't work. Doesn't even sound right."

"But you have thought about it?"

Dalt pulls at his hair, groans something that does not sound good.

"Kidding, Dalt. Just kidding."

He eyes me. Then says, "Good," and stands up, comes around the table. He walks behind me, pushes me onto the porch, leaves me there for a second, alone, then comes back out with a single bottle of beer. The night's syringe. He pops the cap with his keychain, holds it out to me, says, "First sip."

We've been doing this forever. And though we know our neighbors now, even like some of them, we don't invite them over in the quiet end of the nights, when we just sit and watch the day close down, the sky purple and darken, the first pin pricks of stars leaking through. I pass the beer to him, and just like always, he brushes his fingers against mine as he takes the bottle, then passes it to his other hand, keeps hold of my fingers. I listen to him drink, just a swallow, nothing hoggish, we're good sharers, and I can picture the bob of his Adam's apple, nearly every hair and crease, knot and scar of his body.

I close my eyes when I hear him stand, squat beside me, whisper, "Left tonight?"

I nod, and as he pinches up the loose flesh at the back of my arm, slips in the needle, I picture again that hideous run through Rockslide, my right oar just a splintered stick, the blade only flotsam. He never made a move to help, just stayed hunched in front of me, arms braced out to the sides, holding onto the frame, whooping as my line disintegrated. Trust incarnate. He had to have heard that awful snap, felt the shudder and shatter, had to have seen the spare swing up as I wheeled it into the lock, felt those moments of freefall.

But it wasn't until we were in the tail-out, the canyon walls tight beside us, vertical, the whole rest of the world only that thin, winding band of washed out desert sky, like looking up at a river from underneath, from Hades, say, that Dalt turned to me, that perfectly crooked holy shit grin stuck across his face, his eyes wide and pale as the sky. And it wasn't until that very instant that I realized that if that's what awaits us, in Hades, that perfect view of all our rivers together, I'll hang on to Dalt through everything anyone or anything can throw at us to reach that place with him. I mean, if that's the underworld, bring it on.

I hear him set down the syringe, ease back into his chair. He settles the bottle between my fingers, doesn't let go until he's sure I've got it. "To us," he says.

"Come hell or high water," I answer. It's just this thing we say, something that started at the head of all those rapids. If I'd thought of it, it's definitely what we would have said at the wedding. *My strongest desire.* God, we were asses.

Slap

IT'S NOTHING. OR maybe something new only to Dalt's ears. He's gotten me into the front seat and is wrestling with the wheelchair, the damn sticky collapse lever, holding up the kids from their tumble into the back of the van. Atty, and we're just talking hormones here, grumbles, "God, we'd be there already if Mom could just walk."

He's cut off from whatever else he might say by the slap. I've never heard one before, not beyond TV, the movies, but there is no mistaking it. Dalton's hands, back when we'd been rowing, were already half concrete block, but now, swinging a hammer for a dozen years? They're like hammer heads themselves, annealed with calluses, bristling with splinters he no longer even notices. Days he has to help me get dressed, undressed, his very skin catches on my clothes, snares in the finery of my undies. The crack of that hand on my child's flesh leaves a gaping silence in its wake, framed by the quick suck of Izzy's breath, then her whispered, "Well, it's true."

Which is followed instantly by another crack, his hand, Dalton's hand—my Dalt—cutting across Izzy's rear. I see it in the mirror, where things are supposed to be reversed, not turned on their head; closer than they appear, but not completely impossible. Izzy's mouth, barely visible through the wild tangle of her sun-bleached hair, drops into the same stunned O as mine. Atty's already nothing but a blur streaking up the ramp into the house.

It takes me a second to catch my own breath, to shout, "Dalton!"

Still in the mirror, I watch him bend low to Iz, say, "Get in the house!" a voice I would never recognize if I hadn't overheard it nights he reads to them, his villain's voice, a rasping hiss so full of menace I'd asked him to quit, said, "No wonder Atty has nightmares."

I try to meet his eye in the mirror, see who this doppelganger of my husband is. I want to shake it, demand, "What have you done with Dalton?" I mean, he still reads to them, almost every night, though Atty's in middle school, Izzy right behind.

Instead, as I watch him storm up the ramp after them, I call, "Dalt?" and when he doesn't answer, I shout it. "Dalton!"

He stops almost at the top, turns half around to look at me. His chest heaves, the way it used to when he leapt up stairs, four at a time, like he might miss something great if he ever once slowed down.

"Dalton," I say again.

"No," he says, that voice barely under control. "Not ever."

"Dalton," I say. "They're kids. You think it's not frustrating? For them too?"

"Not that much. Never that much."

"Dalt. It's okay. I'm a big girl. I can handle some adolescent grousing."

"Maybe from some stranger, some asshole staring in a store. But not from my kids."

"Yours?" I say.

His lips move, but he doesn't say anything, his anger, something I've hardly ever seen, already flaming out.

"Dalt," I say. "What are you going to do? Inside? Do you have some plan to fix this?"

"I'm going to sit down and talk to them."

"After that? You hit them, Dalt. Our kids."

"You think Attila the Hun never got a . . . ," but he can't continue. There's no way to joke around this. I see he's trembling. He starts down the ramp to me.

"Go in and tell them you're sorry. See if you can get them to come back out."

"Like they'll have to be talked into it now? A movie?"

"It's not about a movie anymore."

He takes that like a challenge, which is not at all what I meant. He turns at the bottom of the ramp, before ever reaching me, and marches back up like he's heading to his own execution. If he comes back out the door with the two of them it will only be because he's ordered them to obey. I don't know what he'll say to them, can't imagine even how he'll begin, but I know he'll come back out alone, to retrieve me.

I mean, my chair is lying tipped over by the side door, half collapsed. Or is it half open? Just how optimistic am I about this day? I lower my head to my hand and wait, because there's nothing else I can do.

I jerk up straight when I think I hear the screen door creak, but there's no one there. I've moved fast enough I've pulled my bad hand out from between my legs, and I stare at it a moment, rocking uselessly in my lap, the wretched, foreign fingers twisted into their permanent curl, as if they're first into the fetal position, just waiting for the rest of my body to get a clue, catch up. I know they can't uncurl, that they're locked there, ten years of therapy and anti-spasticity drugs flushed straight down the toilet, but I reach down anyway and tug at them, try to straighten them out one more time. Just to see that.

It can't work, but I pull, and pull, forcing this one part of me to be normal again. Even just for a second. I close my eyes and keep up the pressure, like bringing in a steelhead, never letting him feel in charge. I don't let up until I hear the first bone snap, a sound so much smaller than Dalt's hand on Atty's cheek. My finger, pointer, sticks out at a ninety to the back of my hand, but still curls toward the others, helpless in its draw back down toward the flock. It doesn't hurt. I haven't felt much there in a long time, but it's as wrong as that slap, and when Dalt does come out alone, comes to my door and apologizes, says we'll go to the movie tonight, that Atty's going to take some time, he's almost through his third string of apologies before he stops dead, touches the side of my thin, quaking wrist, the unbroken bones there. He says, "I'll grab the cell, let the kids know."

It's a mission they're accustomed to, orders they've obeyed so many times before. The time on their own, without their parents, unlimited computer time, is something I think they've grown to wait for.

Dalt ducks away, almost trips over the wheelchair, whips it up into the air as if it weighs nothing, and now that it doesn't matter, it folds so fast it nearly catches his fingers. He slides it in behind my seat, whips the door shut and heads inside to pass the news to the kids, taking Mom to the hospital. He's up the ramp in his old charge, a man with a mission again, finally.

He's out in a second, and as he backs down the drive, I see Izzy standing shadowy behind the screen, her hand up in a kind of wave or salute or something. I reach across with my good hand, and wave back. As a baby she was a waver and a half. We used to sit on the porch for hours, her in my lap, gazing down the street, quiet, waiting for the mailman, the chance to wave at this nice man.

Dalt says, "Hurt?"

"Nope. Pain-free. The magic of MS."

He doesn't say anything. Just drives, paying way more attention to the road, other drivers, than he usually does. I mean, he's careful and all, but like sixth sense stuff. Today he's driving like he's eighty.

"You do know," I say, "don't you, that this whole hand strangulation is very rare for MS? Usually, to get this kind of joy, you have to have Parkinson's or something. There's even a name for it, if you get it all by itself. Dupuytren's contracture. Some Frog, had it, cured it, well, no, not cured, there's no cure. Man, leave it to the French, you know? Get a disease named after them just for giving up. That is so like them. Can you say World War? It's—"

"Maddy," he says.

"I mean, you can get just that one thing all by itself. Just the hand. How half-assed and pathetic is that? Not have your arm twitching all over the place, your fucking legs knotting up if you try to do something as stupid as have sex with your husband, just a couple of fingers curling for no good reason at all, just—"

"Maddy. Stop."

"I mean, your husband starts beating his kids, who he loves more than his own life times ten, and you, sitting there with your measly two curled fingers, would have no fricking clue as to why. This MS, though," I start banging my good fist against the dash with every word, "it, just, explains, absolutely, every, fucking, thing."

Dalton's trying to pull over, but some asshole has got him blocked off, and Dalton looks like he could kill. And, despite what's just happened with At and Iz, there's a part of me, no doubt twisted by myelin sheath scarring, that would love to watch that. Watch Dalton finally able to unleash every ounce of raw power that's been locked away and helpless in him all these years.

"Ram the fucker," I say.

"Maddy," he says, "are you okay?"

"Don't," I say, back to fist pounding, "Ever. Ask. Me. That. Again. Not. Ever."

"Maddy."

"It makes you sound retarded. Asking me that."

"Jesus, Maddy. You just broke your own finger."

"You just slapped Atty across his face. Iz across her tiny bum. I saw you."

He looks back to the road. We're almost there.

"I'd say we're handling the psychological stresses like pros, wouldn't you?"

"Today," he says, "was not a good day."

"And we take it one day at a time, don't we. One glorious, miserable-assed day at a time."

He parks. Jumps out. Gets my chair, unfolds it, locks it open, pops my door. I bat his arm away. "I can get it myself," I say. "I'm not a cripple."

"That a girl," he says.

I glare at him. "I am *so* winning that spirit award."

They have to X-ray it, though, even without my superhero powers at full flow, my X-ray vision tells me the same thing as their big, expensive machine. My finger's broken. They splint it up after a consultation about what position: up, or curled. Curled wins. It's all the muscles will allow once they set the bone. They ask few questions, though, once it's again properly clawed, I show it off, volunteer that I was using it to open beer bottles. That raises a few eyebrows and I add, "Well, pop for the kids. What kind of a mother do you take me for?"

As he's loading me back into the van, Dalt has the balls to ask if I'm on any new meds he wasn't aware of, if there are side effects that could be blindsiding me.

"Nope," I say. "Totally eyes wide open." Then, "How about you, Dalt? Some new drug regimen for you? Steroid cocktails?"

"I snapped," he says, so low anybody could have missed it. But I've been tuned into him forever. "I'm sorrier than you could know."

"No," I say. "I know exactly. You'll beat yourself up about this until the day I shovel the dirt over you."

He nods. "I never thought . . ."

"The sad thing?" I say. "They'll understand. They'll be over it before we will."

"All they wanted was to go to the movie."

"All I wanted was to go with them. To be able to do anything with them. Even just sit in the dark."

He backs up, the asphalt behind us shimmering. I watch the mirages in my mirror.

"We'll go tonight," he says. "After dinner."

"Start over. Anew. Afresh. Whatever. Tonight is the first black hole of the rest of your life."

"I'll make it a light dinner."

"Don't want to spoil their appetite for the popcorn."

"Exactly. Extra butter."

I close my eyes as the acceleration leaves my head in spin cycle. We're back to what we're good at, teasing, making light, and we'll continue straight down this road until it smoothes out, till we find ourselves home again, where At and Iz will step out onto the porch, not quite meeting our eyes, anxious and afraid, not sure they want to see what version of me Dad's brought home this time, what's next to get used to. And this time they've got Dad to worry about, too. Dad, their rock.

"What'll we tell them?" I say, turning to look at Dalt as he drives. I reach across, my good hand handily nearby, and take his big, club of a hand in mine.

"I already told them I'm sorry, that I didn't know what happened, that it will never happen again. I could hardly get it out, them apologizing at the same time, that they didn't mean anything about you, only the time, the rush to get tickets."

I thump his hand up and down on the carseat. "No," I say. "About me. My finger."

"Four to six weeks," he says.

"Not the splint time, you dope. About how I managed to break my finger sitting alone in a car."

Dalt turns onto our street, starts up it. "Nose picking mishap?"

"You," I say, "are such an ass."

Then, as he pulls up toward the drive, so quiet I know only he'll hear me, not that there's someone else who could, but just to show that he's still so tuned in to me, I say, "I'm serious, Dalt. About the not asking. If I'm okay."

He's checking his mirrors, backing in today for some reason. All ready for action, pointing out at the world.

"We know we'll be okay, right, Dalt? We've always known that. No matter what. Right?"

"Oh, golden," he says, but he's not looking at me when he says it, and that is something new. Something for me to gnaw on all through the movie, along with the greasy popcorn, the watery pop, my kids, my husband, lined out in the theater seats besides my gap in the row, empty of any seats until Dalt rolls my wheelchair in, backs me up, sets the brake. A family at the movies. Totally golden.

Around the World

FACING ME, GRINNING, Izzy takes a backward step down the wild decline of Nutley toward the park, the creek, arms out to her side ready for any emergency, as if I might actually fly loose down this hill. Behind me Atty holds tight to the chair handles. "Are you sure about this?" I say.

"I do it all the time, Mom," he says. "It rocks."

"All the time? When?"

"Sometimes if Dad takes you out, without the chair. And at night sometimes."

"At night?"

"After you're in bed."

"But, after I'm in bed, you're in bed too, you're . . ."

"Not always," he says, just above a whisper.

Great. Fabulous. Now he's sneaking out at night. Telling me about it. But it is in my wheelchair. There is that. I wonder how much easier this is for him standing behind me, where I can't see his face.

"Please tell me you don't drag your sister along on these expeditions."

"Not usually. Sometimes Brian shows up."

Good lord. The Johnsons. Owners of the tightest asses in the city. They'd seize up and keel over at the first hint of this rumor.

"And you never bothered telling me you were using my chair for thrill rides. Why do you suppose that would be?"

"Hello? Would you have let us?"

I peer around Iz. A jogger chugs past, way, way down there. "You really just let go?"

"Yep. It's a gas, Mom. Really."

"You don't have to, Mom," Izzy says.

"Well, nice to know I still have a choice."

"Would it kill you?" At asks, serious now.

"This looks like it could kill Evel Knievel."

"I mean, like, your head."

I look at the cracked pavement, the drop bigger than any white-water chute I've ever lined up in. "Could be puking a blue streak before I get half way down."

"Blue?" Izzy says.

"That'd be kind of cool," Atty says.

"It's," I say, "good god, it's an expression. Were you two raised by wolves?"

"Close enough," Atty says.

Iz says, "Ass," at the exact second I do. We high-five each other.

"We got raised by superheroes," Atty says. "How much different is that?"

"Nice try," I say.

"So," At says, drawing it out, rolling me back and forth at the lip of the hill. "You ready to ride the Silver Comet?"

I grip the arms of the chair as if I'm already being hurled free, look once more down the hill, those unsuspecting innocent by-standers down there. I *am* ready, just to show them Mom has some juice left, ever had any at all. All they've ever seen is the picture in the bathroom, wrinkled and warped with years of shower steam, my boat tipped up beyond 45, dropping into Ranie Falls, hands on the sticks, my line perf, a boat load of clients open-mouthed in mid scream. I'm wearing a grin like, I don't know, like I just got a clean bill of health or something.

But just Atty's rocking is making the world blur around its edges, forcing my eyes shut. My stomach does a little roll, testing the waters. "At," I say, and hold up a hand. He stops dead, the signal far too well known, and I come up against the chair's back. "I really want to," I say.

"You don't have to, Mom," Iz says, and I open my eyes to hers narrowed down on Atty like vice-grips. I pity the man who crosses her. Love her for that.

"No," I say. "I'd love to. Really. Back in my day, I'd be the one sneaking out with you At. You'd have had to have fought me for the chair. You'd have lost."

"But," he says.

He sounds so broken, I say, "If you clean up the street, take me to the hospital, explain it all to Dalt, I'll do it."

He says, "Mom."

"Let's just show her," Izzy says. "Like I said all along."

"Like she'll let us."

"You think she won't let *us*, but you're asking *her* to do it? How did you ever get to be my brother? That is so not fair."

"Um," I say. "Did I vanish or something? Is there a reason you're talking like I have?"

Iz smiles, says, "Let's just watch Attila, Mom. Since he's so all about this."

"I just thought that if she—"

"You're doing it again. *She* is right here."

Izzy takes the two steps back to me, reaches out, takes my good hand. "Come on, Mom. Here, between me and the No Parking sign, we'll be golden."

I let her pull me up out of my chair. It's not like my legs are completely worthless. Just unreliable, all the stamina and stoutness of pasta gone considerably past al dente. I take the steps to the sign, get a grip on its perforated steel post, Iz there on the other arm, the twitcher.

Atty climbs into my chair like he's gained the cockpit of some fighter.

"Should there be helmets involved?" I ask.

He looks over his shoulder, rolls his eyes. All he needs is a silk scarf, a thumbs up. He is, and there's no other word for it, dashing. In a wheelchair. What on earth is wrong with me? How did I miss how hugely wrong and horrible this picture is?

"Atty," I say. "I don't really like seeing you in there."

"In the Comet?" he asks, as if nothing I've ever said to him has been harder to comprehend.

"Ready?" he says.

Izzy, right beside me, lifts her wrist, says, "You want me to time this one?"

"Of course."

"Time?"

"For the land speed record," Atty says. "Come on, Mom. Try to keep up."

"I'll keep you up, Buster." I shake a fist at him, stand for that second on my own two feet, unsupported.

"Okay," Atty says. "Five, four, three, two,"

Izzy's got her finger on the start button of her watch. Together they say, "One!" drowning out my quick, "Atty?"

It's not like he's catapulted into space. It takes time to get up to speed. But half way down the hill his progress is well beyond terrifying, the chair chattering across the cracks, hopping, bouncing, At, a ragdoll clinging to the seat. There are no seat belts.

I have no idea how they've done this before, but the curb at the end of the street isn't like some new hazard. Atty hits it just as he's cracking the sound barrier. The wreck makes me long for Class Vs, water to fall into rather than bounce off of, skid along.

Izzy and I take off before, I think, he actually touches down. It's not something we could have considered if we'd tried. But, within two steps she's out ahead of me, and the pull of the slope is already more gravity than I can challenge. I have to take a knee to keep from going down just like Atty, a lot more hill to tumble down before me.

I sprawl there on the sidewalk, watching my daughter run for my son, nearly as out of control as he had been. They blur a bit, swirl, but I close my eyes, fighting, and for that instant I see Atty at three, in this same park, Iz in the stroller, a fall day, maple leaves the size of dinner plates clotting the paths, clogging the creek, damming the riffles with their piled bodies. Atty picked up a giant one, big enough for an umbrella, and put it on his head. Stringing together three more, their stems as thread and awl both, I made him a hat. He swung his stick round, threatening all comers, invincible in his leaf helmet. In the stroller, Izzy balked and bawled until she too had a leaf on her head. Soon I wore one of my own, like the old first communion pictures, all the girls with the white doilies pinned to their hair, praying, at that age, for who could imagine what.

When I open my eyes, she's just reaching him, but At's already sitting up, and I focus long enough to see his grin, hear his words climb the hill as Izzy pulls him to his feet, a breathless, "Well, fuck me!" a word I have never heard come from his mouth, but, given that he was raised by wolves, was only inevitable. I smile so wide it hurts, and whisper his own words back at him. "Well, fuck me." How did we ever find ourselves here?

Izzy says, "Nice job, Ace."

Atty studies his elbow, says, "Hey, I'm bleeding."

"Is it red?" Izzy says. "Like human blood?"

I can't stop smiling, don't ever want them to do exactly what they do next, which is stop, in unison, and turn back toward me, Izzy's hand going up to her mouth, Atty saying, "Mom?" all trace of fun and thrill scorched clear of their world.

I shake my head, hold myself up with my good arm, wave away their worries with my bad, say, "I'm fine," then, "That was some ride."

Izzy's already darting up the hill to me, like she can fly, so it's Atty who goes into the brambles and brush to retrieve the chair.

He's a long time coming back out, though he's not thrashing around much, more as if he's just disappeared.

Izzy's puffing a little when she says, "Really, Mom? You're okay?"

"Golden," I say. I'm still smiling.

Then Atty steps backward, pulling the chair out of the thicket. Even from up here I can see the one wheel canted way out on top, folding in under the seat. "Atty!" Iz cries.

He climbs the hill with the chair like Christ with his cross, as if the same end awaits.

"The Silver Comet," I say.

"Mom, it, I," he looks everywhere but at me, fiddles with the wheel, like it might be something he could fix with his Swiss army knife. "It never broke before."

"True for everything that's ever broken," I say.

He nods. "I am so sorry."

It's Izzy who says, "Well, really, Mom."

I glance at her as she sits beside me on the curb.

"You really are kind of overdue for an upgrade."

"What?"

"The Comet, Mom, it's kind of—"

"It's a used hospital loaner," Atty finishes. "A mom like you—"

"Could flash a little more bling in the chair department," Izzy says.

I've refused Dalt's every offer, the chair itself, barely holding up, proof that it is not something I will need for long. My kids are so much smarter than me.

"You want it?" I ask Atty. "Hotrod it?"

"Mom," he says. "How are you going to get home?"

"It's what, three blocks? I think I'll make that."

But, truth is, I don't make it one. Atty, holding on to my good arm, hauling the chair after him with his other hand, says, "Iz, stop." We lurch to a halt just before my toes start dragging. I'm breathing like it's all been up Everest.

"Take the chair," he tells Iz, and before either of us have any clue what he has in mind, he's dropped the chair and in some super stealth ninja move has flipped me up onto his back piggy back style. I squeak. Literally squeak, "At!"

But he's already walking, my own child, who could not possibly have gotten big enough to do this, not before my very eyes. I say, "At?" again, but I see he's taller than I am, that my feet do not scuff along the ground, and I feel the thick balls of his shoulders beneath my fingers, hook my chin over, and drop my head against the side of his. His hair's too long, brushes against my face, and I close my eyes to better feel it.

He's going to be as big as Dalt, but, with my genes, even more beautiful. Superheroes raised by wolves. It just doesn't figure, stand up to any kind of logic. I open my eyes, his face right there beside mine, and I ask if he's going to be okay, if he'll make it all right.

"Around the world, Mom. Around the fu—" He catches himself in the nick, says, "around the whole wide world."

I don't know if it's something they're all saying now, "'How's it going, dude?' 'Oh, around the world, man,'" but, if it is, I pretend it isn't. With these two? I am so ready for the trip.

Peas

DALT'S WORKED LATE again, but he knows the kids are hungry and he pulls out stuff for dinner, dragging around the kitchen like he's wearing shackles. I turn my chair towards the fridge, ask if he wants a beer, but he shakes his head, says they framed all day, that even one would put him right out. Race framing, he calls it, trying to get two more houses closed in before winter.

He slices mushrooms and onions, his shirt hazed with sawdust, flaked with the odd wood chip, the Carhartt bibs stained and frayed. The knife's a blur, and I fear for his scarred knuckles, but he slides everything into the sizzling butter without drawing blood. Not, I guess, that he'd notice if he had.

I draw in a breath, like the smell's something I can savor.

"Still one of your faves?" he asks.

"Duh," I say.

The loss of taste is something I've kept to myself. Maybe it's a privacy issue, that being another thing I don't have much left of, but, really, what good would it do him to know I can't taste a thing he cooks for me? The kids gave him a chef's hammer a few father's days ago, and he wields it now like he's still driving nails, flattening entire chicken breasts in four or five blows.

He breads the chicken—a little flour now to go with the sawdust—slips it in after the mushrooms, then the wine, and soon he's got plates out, the pasta drained. He's started wearing glasses in the last few years, and the steam fogs them at the sink. There's some gray at the temples now too, and with the glasses, he looks good, which I tell him.

He smiles, shakes his head. "You're going gray and out of focus. That's hot."

He calls At and Iz, slides the plates onto the table, snags the parmesan, yesterday's salad, not too wilted, a few bottles of dressing, and pours milk for the kids, which makes them groan, which he answers with the single word, "Bones."

I'm still learning the controls on the electric chair—Atty's term, not mine—and when Dalt asks if I want help, I say, "No," but then, "Oh, sure, just up to the table." It's the fine tuning that gives me the biggest trouble. Like learning to parallel park all over again.

The kids watch in silence. I don't know if that's what puts them into their funk—the electric chair a lot harder to pretend I'll ever leave—but dinner settles around us like an ice fog. Dalt's just done in, his shoulders slumped forward, Atty's hormonal sullenness driving him to the edge. But Iz, too, just picks at her chicken. I look at mine only a second before Dalt says, "Oh, sorry," and lifts my plate, pushes his aside and slices my chicken for me. With my right arm, hand, cutting on my own goes beyond comedy. But I say, "Dalt, I can cut it with a fork."

He gives a single shoulder shrug and sets my plate back in front of me, no bite bigger than any one of the peas. We've had a few incidents this year—sometimes swallowing can get to be a bitch—and one night I rolled in to find him going over the Heimlich with At and Iz, talking about airway obstructions and all. It made me think for the millionth time how lucky I am, but, at the same time, Jesus, your kids, barely teenagers, having to go through that?

So, we sit and chew. A few silverware clinks, the scrape of Iz inching her milk farther and farther from her plate.

I'm a total left-hander by now—a cockroach could learn, given the years—but, just to liven things up, I work my fork under the clawed fingers of my right. It's maybe not my best idea ever, but I lift up my arm, my hand, the fork waving like a snake's head, and leaning forward, I swoop down to my plate, manage to lift a good dose of peas into the air.

My hand's shaking, the fork worse, peas flinging off every which way. "The jackhammer operator home for dinner," I say. It's a gag I haven't dusted off in years, since the kids were tiny, when the MS wasn't something I could keep hiding. I have to admit, though, that back in the day, I could hold the peas on a lot longer, make it look like I actually had a chance.

I'm concentrating on getting the few surviving peas toward my mouth—the last thing I need is a fork in the eye—but I don't hear anybody laughing. Dalt says just, "Mad."

I lose the last pea, bend down for another load, and, new peas bounding across the table like hail, I say, "The starving man in the earthquake."

"Maddy," Dalt says. "Stop."

I stab down at a pea near my plate with the tines of the fork, miss by inches. "The blind trash collector," I say, one of the all time favorites.

The crash is so stunning, at first I think the house has been hit by a runaway truck, a meteor maybe. Silverware rattles, plates jump, milk spills. On the bounce from Dalton's fists, the table knocks the fork right out of my hand. He roars, "Stop it!"

I sit holding my quaking, empty hand in the air. The kid's are stunned speechless, pushed back from the table. "Dalt?"

"It is not funny," he says, his voice shaking harder than my hand ever has.

"They loved that game."

He almost strangles. "They didn't know any better."

"Well, come on—"

"I'm done laughing, Mad," Dalt says. "I've been done laughing for a long time."

"I'll, I'll get new material."

He stands up so fast his chair crashes into the wall, slides to the floor.

"You're not funny," he says, balling his napkin into a wad he chucks across the table. "Nothing about this has ever been funny."

Shit, he's got tears in his eyes, and the kids are just flabbergasted. Like watching him unravel in mid air, the best magic trick ever suddenly ending in tragedy, their father vanishing in a cloud of dirty smoke.

"Dalton," I say, "it's okay."

"This?" he says, waving his hand at the table, the dripping milk, my peas. "This is your idea of okay?"

"It's not her fault," Atty says.

We all turn. If the table itself had spoken it would have been no more a surprise.

"Always worrying when you'll go off?" he says, looking right at Dalt. "It makes us all crazy."

"What?" Dalt says.

"'What?'" Atty parrots. "So you don't think it's funny. Big deal. I think it's hysterical. Ha. Ha."

All poor Dalton can do is stare. Their whole lives the two of them have been thick as thieves, peas in a pod.

"You don't talk for a year," Dalton says, and just his tone makes me want to interrupt before he can go on, but I can find no words. "You don't talk for a year, and that's all you can come up with?"

Atty glares. "Why would I bother talking to you?" he says.

Dalton shakes his head, blindsided. He wipes at his face. His fingers scrape across his cheeks like sandpaper.

Before I can come up with a word, he's out of the room, and before I can think of anything I would have actually said, Atty pushes his chair back, stacks plates to clear away. Nobody's finished. He sweeps up the peas from around my plate.

Iz says, "Mom, he was crying," same way you'd say, *The sky has fallen.*

Atty says, "Don't worry about him. He'll be fine."

He'll be fine. Now there's a switch.

I work the controls to face Atty, see who has taken over, and, with its ever perfect timing, my head picks that instant to launch down to my shoulder. Only a double, and it comes back to center, instead of sticking there.

I try a smile. "We forget about him," I say, my voice as shaky as Dalt's, but quieter. "We all think it's hardest on us, me on me, you on you, but . . ." I have to pause, keep it together until I can get someplace private, the bathroom, the closet, shit, just my chair crunched face-in to a corner, I don't care. "But, your dad, he, he," I really have no idea what I'm going to say, and finally end up offering the only truth I know. "He cares about me. Too much. He always has."

"But, he—" Izzy starts.

"He won't accept that this is hard for anybody but me," I say. "Won't even hear of it."

Atty picks up the stack of four plates and starts for the kitchen.

"Wait," I say, and Atty falters, turns. "Of course you've seen that?" I say, stunned now, searching their faces, that apparently they haven't. "I mean, what else do you think explains him?"

"Explains him?" Atty asks, and I wonder what, beyond hormones, has driven his withdrawal. Not Dalt. Surely not Dalt.

He gapes. "Explains *him*?" he says again. "What? You mean you?"

"Well, of course," I say, but I see with one of my rare flashes, that it will be years and years, decades maybe, before they ever get this, before they see us as real people, not just the fucked up mom, the quiet, working dad. I so want to tell them about our rivers, the moonlight floats, Jesus, about tearing into each other under the stars, about the way Dalt screamed down that river valley when he heard that you were coming, Atty. I want to say, Yes, Atty, you, as long as you live there will never be another person so excited about your life as your dad was before it had even begun. I want to remind them about their own river trips with us, then with him alone, fishing, hiking, the stories they'd bring home to me, how each breathless tale they told tore huge strips off his broad rower's back, because they were only telling me because I couldn't be there. How, goddamn you, couldn't you see he used his own tattered hide to build this world for us, this boat, how he never tired at the oars, just kept digging in, though it was an impossible distance for anyone, ever, to row. How he did it, every single stroke, for you and me, how he never once, until this very night, thought to complain, to ask for one single thing in return. And then it's only for me to quit with the jokes. Jesus, Dalton, I'll do anything for you, you dope, don't you know that?

The kids, I see, are staring at me, big-eyed, scared. I wonder how long I've been away. "Are you all right, Mom?" Atty asks. He's not holding the plates anymore. I see them stacked on the edge of the table, close to crashing down. "Mom?" Iz echoes, like maybe I've already taken the final plunge. "Can you breathe?"

I can't answer, just stare at them, seeing no way to ever let them know us, and I start to shake my head, which turns into a tremor, and then the snaps, and Atty, his voice a breaking tremor all it's own, cries, "Dad?!" all the fear in his young life in that one word, and I manage, "No," and then, "I'm fine," and of all things, in a total MS leap, I say, "Do your homework," which almost cracks me up.

I don't know where Dalton ran off to, what wall he's torn down, pounded to rubble to keep us safe from every demon he keeps bottled up, but he flies around the corner before Atty's cry dies out, already calling, "Maddy?" and there is so much more fear in his voice than Atty could ever put into his, so many more years of it built up, I just hold up my good arm and let him dive into me, grip him as hard and rough as I can, like I used to, in the throes of all that was good, and he's surprised, I can still feel that much, still know him that well, and he says, "What, Maddy? What? Are you okay?"

And I bury my head against him, smell the sawdust, and say, "Of course I am."

We could have a total Hallmark moment if Atty and Iz would just crowd around my chair, touch us, tell us that we'll all be all right, but, my god, they're only kids, and what we're doing, really, is scaring the shit out of them. They see no power here, none of what has made us us. All they see is the fear, and the tears, which, hell, are just building blocks, and, not for the first time, I get swept over with regret that they, neither of them, will ever know anything so great. Because, really, me and Dalt? There's no way anything this huge could ever happen again, not in this universe. We've used it up. All the luck. Which, well, sucks for them.

And thinking that, I laugh, which really sets the kids off. Great, now she's crazy, too. But I hug Dalt tighter, say, "Don't worry, no jokes." I have to pause, which makes me so pissed I could scream. "I'm not laughing," I get out. "At you. I'm just, I don't know, I'm just, I guess, I'm so . . ." I have to swallow. "Happy," I say, though happy is not what I mean. Lucky maybe, but the words are so hard to sort. Loved. That might be closest yet. But to get that over the tortured pathways of broken and scarred synapses, all the way out to my tongue, make that work right, and still remember the word? Not likely. And, really, happy is close enough. Dalt knows me. He'll know what I mean.

And Dalt, his head pressed into my withered chest, nods. I mean, we could never get more perfect, or happy, or loved. Whatever it is. And the kids just stand there gaping, not seeing that at all. Atty picks up his plates, and in the set of his back as he starts away, I can see him casting me off to my fate. A fate I'd do whatever it took to have all over again.

∿ ∿ ∿

WE'RE QUIET THE rest of the night, worn out or in shock, and At and Iz slip off to their rooms without announcements. After giving me my shot, checking the doors, the thermostat, Dalt comes into our room and helps me undress, getting his arm under mine and guiding me into the bed, shifting my legs over for me, tucking me in. I'm not usually this helpless, but a night like this could splinter oak. I only sigh, rather than start anything, but Dalt says, "He's right you know."

I raise an eyebrow.

"Atty. My temper. Never had that before."

"You don't. Now."

Dalt glances at me. "Denial," he says. "Which of your rules does that break?"

"Schmules," I get out, half better than nothing.

He looks away, then goes into the bathroom, leaving me there with that, his temper naked and waiting.

When he comes back, his teeth brushed, the toilet flush roaring down the pipes, he turns off the lights first thing. I sink a bit toward him when he sits on the bed, lifts the covers, lies down and scooches over until we're side by side, touching knee to shoulder. Sleeping together? Just the lying down part? We're still experts.

The quiet settles around us before he says, "I'm not very happy with who I've become."

"Whom," I say—I can't stop myself—but I go off wondering if it's even correct. Nights, even ordinary ones, are not my time. I probably have a rule about this, too, conversations in bed. One word responses can get to seem as laborious as a speech. I build up the energy, the courage, like going off the high dive as a kid, teetering there forever on the edge, before I say, "He's not . . . ," I breathe, ". . . right. He's, fourteen."

He doesn't answer and I reach over and pat him on the point of his hip, just where my hand lands. "I do," I say, which is what it's been reduced to over the years, though how *I love you* became *I do*, I can't say. Hell, we never even said that at our wedding. Then I get a memory flash, one of the bolts from who knows where that seem to have replaced most cogent thought for me. Like cogent. Where the ef did that come from? Or ef? How many years have passed since I said that? But what I hear now is Izzy, a tiny girl, consonants still a Class V run for her, reducing I love you to Lu-lu. I say that now, but just from my hand on his hip, the conductivity between us, I know he doesn't remember. So I wonder if I really do, or if my myelin sheathing is twisting itself in such a way that it will give me whole new lives to replace this golden one it's stealing away.

"How do I make this up to him?" Dalt says, still in his world, not mine. He's staring at the ceiling in the darkness, forearm across his forehead. I don't have to see to know that's exactly how he's lying. Don't even have to open my eyes.

"He quits speaking to me, and when he finally opens his mouth I ram my fist into it."

I pat him again, which is stupid. He probably thinks my good hand is tremoring now. I'm tempted to reach just a little bit farther, grab his, his, the word we've used for it all our lives dances away. His what? His . . . "Shit," I say, though I don't know it's out loud until Dalt says, "What?" and his voice, just that one word, is so weary, so worn out, so sick of wondering what now, what next, which piece of his wife, his life, is caving in this time, that I do reach over, take his whatever we called it in my hand, and say, "How about," totally minor word struggle, "a twitch sesh?"

It just came to me, one of his lines, early on, when he still tried to laugh through the unexplained tremorings, saying if he could catch it from me he would, so we could lie on each other and twitch together. "Might be kind of hot," he said, which was sick, of course, but easier than wondering.

Nothing happens to him down there now though, and he makes no move toward me, and I realize I've just done what we've never done, using that, one of our greatest, our original superpower, for nothing more than changing the subject. And Dalt doesn't like who *he's* become?

But I don't know how to answer his question, how he and Atty will reconnect. I want to explain again about hormones, pulling away, the crystalline world view of the young, how he's been Atty's world, and now, just to survive as his own person, At's got to tear that world down. I want to say *You know all this yourself, Dalt*, but I high-center on the word that means all this, not teen-aged, but something like that, that begins with an *A*, and even, I think, has four syllables. So I don't say anything, just keep running my fingers along him, looking for that word as well, and I say the most common thing I know, "Tomorrow," our night time mantra, a gentle reminder about not bringing up anything serious at bedtime, when asking me my own name can tax synapses to snap point.

He's drifting off, and I'm fondling his member, which is definitely *not* the word, but member whisks me, with no preparation at all, to Wilson, Wyoming, into my horseshoer's ramshackle place, tack covering the walls—a shrine to his line of work even in his bedroom—him just home, stripping out of his horse reeking jeans, eyeing me, never even wondering about a shower first. He's telling me about a stallion he had to shoe that day, how "its member was full on, full out," how he worried about his own safety. Holding up his hands too far apart, he said, "There's only so much a guy should have to put up with," and I said, "Why don't you show me how much I have to put up with?" and I have not thought about this, or him, in god knows how long, and I do not want him here with us now, and I think, god, I am so glad I didn't go that route, and in the same instant, thoughts tripping over each other in their own ramshackle clusters, I think how glad I am he can't see me now, like this, because, to him, I will always be nineteen, twenty, perfect, a virgin for god's sake, and look at me now. God I was beautiful, and he's the only one I will always be that way for, and oh my sweet Jesus, even in my mind—these unasked for, unwanted flashes—I've called him the horseshoer, and I realize I can't come close to remembering his name, not a syllable, not a letter, and I'm desperate to, lying in bed with my husband, holding his—goddamn it, how can I not know that word?—and all I want to do is ask him my old lover's name, have him save that for me before it's gone forever, but all that comes out is, "Lu-lu," which, well, is the truth, but not for the horseshoer, no, for Dalt, and Atty, and Iz, but, good lord, for the rest of me too, even as it fades away, leaving only shadows of who I am, and is there any way, in the clear light of day sometime when I can get Dalt to say his name, to salvage that for me before it sinks beneath the waves?

So desperate am I, so throat-catching, sinking myself, scared senseless, that it's minutes before I realize what I'm hearing: Dalt's breathing, open-mouthed, exhausted, sunk beneath his own waves, swamped by work, by family, by life, given over to sleep now, at last, and I'm still holding onto his nameless thing in the dark, and I realize Dalt knows me too, from the age of my perfection, and that no matter what I've become that's still in him too, that what I will ask him in that sunlit moment will not be for Troy's name, but just to tell me about us back then, and maybe we'll have the kids listen in, no matter the NC-17 rating we'd get, just so they can maybe begin to see us as living, breathing people, not just their life support systems, and—

Troy. That's him, his name. I drift off with him holding his hands apart, talking about a stallion, work, me holding his stallion part, talking about the work it looks like I've got ahead of me. I fall asleep beside my husband, smiling with that, like someone they invented Gomorrah for, hating myself for Dalt's sake, but unable to hide how relieved I am. Troy, I say to myself, Troy, trying to invent some mnemonic to always remember that name, tie it somehow to horseshoe in perpetuity. I mean, if I can come up with mnemonic and perpetuity, how hard can Troy be? And, without asking, a joke springs straight up out of *How hard can Troy be?* and I have to keep from giggling. How in the world would I explain that moment of levity to Dalt?

"Lu-lu," I say again, barely a whisper, but I mean it this time, it's not some random MS blurting, and I let myself go, another day behind us, and ahead, already looming, tomorrow. Always that, like some endlessly repeated punch line. Tomorrow. Even when it's the last thing you want, to see what now, what next. Tomorrow.

Osprey

FOR YEARS BEFORE fledging, Atty tested the waters, our patience, but still, the gaping hole he bored out of us was something I had to remind myself was only in my heart, not a splintered-oak/shattered-joist abyss I needed to edge my wheelchair around, as if I might plunge in, never be heard from again. It just felt so possible I couldn't help it, even as I watched Dalt and Iz skirt around me, not recognizing this new, wild-eyed version of their old Mad, their old mom. All I've left now is Iz, who, though free of Atty's rebellion, his lightning flares from sullen to flaming, is always just Iz herself, our model child, going to the dances, shooting through driver's-ed straight to the wheel of the busted down pick-up Dalt swears she picked out herself, is still creeping to the edge of the nest, looking down, flexing her wings. Summers she works the rivers for Glory, and she comes home brown and tough and happy and I cower into my chair, knowing I'm losing her too. That I'm bound to. Caught in this hideous keeper hole of time. Going round and round, knowing there's no throw bag that will reach me, no rogue wave that will ever push me clear.

Where Izzy glides by all the pitfalls, Atty gripped and clawed, like an osprey first learning to fly, landing back at the nest always the toughest part. On the Snake I've watched them overshoot their nest of sticks, reaching out and grasping the last possible branch at the last possible instant, going too fast, too far, turning from this magnificent winged creature to a flipping ragtag of feathers, smacking upside down into the side of the nest, tumbling, catching, with luck, just enough air beneath their crooked wings to crash land on the gravel bars without damaging anything more than their pride. Atty always managed just that, just barely surviving, Dalt taking most of the hits himself, absorbing them, usually, with something approaching grace.

But maybe they took their toll after all, for now I watch Dalt stand back from Iz, keep his eye on her, but his distance too, as if he's not going to let himself get burned that way again, putting every ounce of himself into someone who is only going to hurt him in the end. He eyes her dates not with loathing, exactly, but some distant cousin of it. Suspicion maybe, some lurking fear that this one, this one here, will be the one who steals her away.

But, Izzy, she's magic. These boys come and go, so hopeful, so breathlessly daring to believe. And she brings out the best of them, takes the best from them—she has yet to bring home anyone scary, anyone with the loser's "L" branded across his pimpled forehead—and then they part, pain free as far as I can tell, though there must be the occasional sliver. I watch with admiration as she uses the break of the river, summer after summer, like a surgeon wields a scalpel, excising another hapless boy from her life, none daring to follow her down those wild waters. She is not one bit like Allie in this. More as if she just holds too much joy, has to, at times, share some, slough it off on some lucky guy, just to keep herself from overflowing.

I wheel out onto the porch every afternoon, wait to see her coming home from school—she still rides her bike most days, for crying out loud—and these are the kind of things I think about, get completely lost in. Arm fallen unnoticed from the padded armrest, hand chattering against the spokes of my chair, I peer down the street, thinking angels could take lessons from her, that maybe, actually, she has wings hidden beneath her fleece, that the spray of sunlight off her summer bleached hair is actually a halo. If I told anyone about any of this, they'd start talking treatments, therapy, or just hurl right there on the spot. Dalt would roll his eyes, then, very quietly, whisper, "You okay, Mad? There anything you need? Want? Anything I can do?" I'd shake my head, say, "Can't you see I'm in love here, have this huge crush thing?" Then he'd smile, puff out his chest a little, flex his forearm in that pitch back to my mom once saying he had arms like steel, and say, "Still?" and I'd wallop him and say, "Ass."

There are days, sitting out here in the spring of her senior year, the last of her days falling through my fingers like sand, our house empty and forlorn and fully handicap accessible behind me—I hate it, I hate it, I hate it, no one in there but me—and on my lap the afghan that she, and I hate to even have to add this to the stack, crocheted for me last Christmas, when I want to beg her, "Take me with you!" as if I'm a prisoner here in my life. A job would help, I know. Something, anything. Not exactly by my own choosing, I've spent every second of their lives here in this house with them. I've grown into them, woven my roots among theirs, have loved that I have, don't, despite all the bad jokes people make about sending their angry adolescents to schools as far away as airplanes can fly, ever want it to end. I doubt, really, that there's any hobby, or job, or career that could ever distract me from that. I mean, what could ever possibly mean more?

Back in the day, holing myself up here, hiding out seemed like this heaven sent chance to avoid the pity, the looks, the horror. And, really, beyond Dalt, Atty, Iz, what more was there I'd ever need? I missed the rivers, of course, god, like a piece of me, the people I worked with there, most of them, but that was over and done, not much in the way of any decisions to be made about it.

But, now, Jesus, what a fool. Cut the ties that way? Janice still calls, but I haven't heard from Allie since her second divorce, years and years ago. My parents have been gone even longer. I've no ties at all anymore to anywhere else, anyone. Hell, I'm an orphan. Atty's gone. Dalt, too often, seems hardly more than a visitor. And Izzy's on her way. I have never been good at alone, and I'm no better at it now. All those awkward looks, the pity and horror? How long would they have lasted? They only had to get used to me. Like At and Iz, it'd be the way they always knew me. *Oh, yeah, Mad, she's that hot, twitchy chick in the chair.* The wives all, *Oh yeah, she's the one with THE husband.* But I never gave them a chance.

I catch myself, only sometimes, wondering why I let myself dwell on all this, let myself drift into these dark, lonely waters. I mean, I think I could stop, if I wanted to badly enough. But I've no desire for that. Even though it makes me so sad, surprises me with tears trickling down my face that I never feel, never know are there. I mean, it's just all so pedestrian. So boringly normal. It's cliché, something every parent must go through. More woe is Mad, look at me, I'm like every parent losing their children to their own lives. Boo hoo hoo.

But, maybe that's the key to it right there. Wrapped in only those few words. *Every. Normal. Parent.* Do I tie myself up this way only to be that normal parent? Not someone who, for laughs, tried to eat peas with her spastic's fork. Who once broke her own finger because she was left alone in a van, trying to be, for a second anyway, and here's that word again, normal. Who their whole lives has told them we were the luckiest people on the planet. I mean, what on earth was I trying to bury with that?

I'm lost in all I've fucked up in this hideously wonderful, instructionless game, sweating over every mistake and misstep, what it's cost them, when there's a touch on my wrist out of nowhere, one I try to startle away from, then look up to see only Izzy, clearing my fingers out of the spokes, resetting my arm on the chair's rest. She says, "Oh, I thought you were asleep," then, without any sort of look that would embarrass me, or put me on the defensive, nothing but a smile at finding me awake, she shrugs her sleeve down over her hand and wipes my cheeks with it. I've been crying again, the mysterious tears, and I say, "No, I was only dreaming," and her face lights up and she says, "I had the *weirdest* dream last night."

I wag my bad hand at the porch swing, one of Dalt's worst ideas for me ever, and say, "Tell me," but she only laughs, says, "You hate people blabbing about dreams." She imitates me. "'Starts in the middle of nowhere, makes no sense whatsoever, then ends in the same place. It's not a story, it's a nightmare.'"

I keep waving at the swing, say, "Sit," take a breath, and say, "Tell me," and, "I want to hear."

So she sits, knows enough, and thinks enough, not to start swinging, and I hold out my hand to her, my bad one, because she's on that side, and she takes it like it is nothing, just a part of her mom, which, of course, to her, it is. She has never known me any other way. And solely for that, I want to stay that way, but I can't feel her, at all, not in that hand, nothing but a slight tug at my shoulder, so I say, "Just a second," and I touch the control knob and wheel myself around, my back now toward the school, like she'll never come down that road a last time, and I hold out my good hand, which she takes without a trace of self-consciousness, and begins to tell me her dream. When she's done I ask for another, and when she's done with that, I want more. I can't believe I ever hushed a single one of their dreams. I so want them all.

Bride

Two nights out in a row is more, frankly, than I can handle, and Izzy tells us Tom thinks his father and his father's wife will enjoy the dinner at our house, that his mother would always prefer a night out. So that's the schedule we tackle, taking on dad first, Dalt tearing around all day to have everything set and nice when they show up, the first time we'll meet this man, the father of this boy taking Izzy away, see if genetics might offer more hope than meets the eye in the son.

At first glance, there isn't. While he shakes Dalt's hand, introduces his young wife, I study him like a specimen in an aging experiment. Same kind of horse face as the son—Atty has taken to calling Tom, Seabiscuit—just older, more worn, more jowly. Izzy is just so the opposite of everything we can make out in Tom I could cry. A customer on one of her whitewater trips. A fricking *touron*. *Iz* I wanted to scream from the very first, *Throw him back! This one is not a keeper!* And now, even before the father looks down at me, I want to tug her aside, hiss, "This is what you're getting. Do you really want to live with *this* for the rest of your life?"

Dalton tells me I'm taking his job, that he's supposed to be the one who thinks no one is good enough for his daughter, but, really, who could possibly deserve our Iz? And it's Dalton I can feel stiffen now when Tom's father—Leonard, I have to remember—first glances down at me, taking an actual step backward before summoning the courage to step up again, into the abyss, and say, "And you must be Maddy."

Like I'm three, like he might next ruffle my hair, marvel over how much I've grown. I reach up with my left hand, and squeeze his extended right with everything that's left of my rower's grip, smiling when I hear knuckles crack. What does that mean anyway, *You must be Maddy?* That he'd been warned there'd be a troll under a bridge? Fighting back a grimace, he looks at his hand trapped in mine, like he's wondering when I'll be rolled back to my cage. He must be thinking, *Tom, this is what you're getting. Do you really want to live with this for the rest of your life?* He says, "Izzy has told us so much about you."

"Really? We've hardly heard a thing about you."

"Which is why," Dalt says, touching my shoulder, "we're so glad you could make it tonight."

The wife, I cannot for the life of me remember her name, though she's way younger, one of those replacements men love to parade about, foregoes my claw-of-death handshake, the cowardly bitch, and just says, "Something smells wonderful. What is that?"

"Garlic," Dalt says, and I crack up, inside only. I mean, I've got manners up the ass. But Dalt, that was perfect.

He's all about not making eye contact with me. We've had a shot or two in preparation, acting like we're the ones getting married, meeting the Ps, and we've been rude little snots until the moment the bell rang, when we swore we'd stop, behave. Atty's been in on it all along, making fun of every single thing they've planned. The whole church rigamarole. He said, "Why not just shove off on some river, right? Separate boats though. Iz just below the Falls of Doom, him just above."

Now Dalt relents. "And lemon, and dill. It's salmon, really. Nothing special."

Leonard looks toward the mantel, nods at the shattered taimen there, who I would have dusted if I could reach that high. "So, you're a fisherman?" he says.

"We used to be," Dalt says.

That *we*. I could jump his bones right here and now. What is it about weddings? I feel like I'm twenty again.

"That's a helluva salmon."

"Taimen," I say, like the easiest thing in the world. That word's been AWOL for months, and now it just pops back up. Taimen. I say it again. Check me out.

"It's the largest living salmonid," Dalt explains. "Native to Russia, Mongolia."

"You've . . . ," Leonard starts.

"Maddy and I started a business once, guiding fishermen there. It was a long time ago."

Leonard takes a step closer, examines the broken jaw, the popped eye. "I hope this damage isn't from some tempter tantrum of Izzy's."

Oh my god. It jokes. I clench both arms of my chair. I have got to stop. "Nope," I say. "Atty."

Atty says, "What?"

"Even as a zygote," I say. "Kid, pack a punch."

Leonard and wife glance at each other. "Where are they?" the wife asks. "The kids?"

Kids? *Like what, honey, four, five years younger than you?* Ten at the very outside.

"They were setting the table out back," Dalt says. "I'll let them know you're here."

"On it, Dad," At says. Chicken shit. But all he does is turn toward the open back door and bellow, "Iz!"

I do crack up then. Wifey about jumps out of her skin. "They, always done that," I say, and Dalt says, "No matter how we beat them."

First thing Tom says, before any greeting or anything, is, "Dad, you have got to see Atty's room."

I mean, honestly.

Atty says, "*Old* room." But even Dalt can hear the pride in his voice. A blind man could. Oh. Blind. Blind man could hear. Good one, Maddy.

They all troop off, leaving me and Dalt a second alone, which really allows the first bit of good will I've ever felt toward Tom. But I can't help watch them go. Izzy kept working the rivers for Glory all through college, and her bare shoulders are broad and muscled and bronzed. Shoulders like I used to have. The sexiest thing on the planet, Dalt used to say, then touch me someplace else, anywhere else, say, "Except for here. Here. Here." She's as tall as Tom, her shoulders wider. She could break him without thinking.

"Well," Dalton says, "they seem . . ."

I have to struggle to remember the parents. "Nice," I say.

He grins. "You're in bad-Mad form, aren't you."

"Her boobs," I say. "Total manmade."

"Nice job, though," he says.

"I'll," stutter, stutter, stutter, "nice job you." The shots beforehand were a horrible idea, which I knew—and then they're back, marveling over the pirate ship room, something Atty never did want changed. As a teenager he even, someplace, found an old Navy hammock, pounds of stiff as a board canvas, and, without asking Dalt—reveling in not asking Dalt—sank huge eyebolts into the wall, only missing one of the studs, and then only once, calling the resulting hole musket damage, and slept that way until he graduated, *to feel the sway of the ship.* The Flying Taimen he christened it.

I once caught him in there with one of his girlfriends, the electric chair as silent as any sneak thief could hope for. Door wide open. I don't know where he thought I could have waltzed off to, with Dalt at work. Maybe he thought Iz had swept me away somewhere, maybe they'd made arrangements, a plan. I never bothered to ask. To this day I'm not sure they were ever aware of my presence, but I can still see, with perfect clarity, his bare buns striving to do this thing he needed so badly to do, that they both needed so badly, in his hammock, in the good ship Taimen, and I scootered out to the farthest corner of the house, hoping they'd never find me. Hammock swinging as if possessed, her legs hooked over the edges, canvas sides curling around them, it hadn't look destined for success. It had looked perfect. I told Dalt about it later, asked if he thought he could get me up into the hammock as soon as they were off to school, and we laughed like kids ourselves. "We would so not have a problem," he said.

"Problem? We'd be in the record books. They'd have to rewrite the Suma Katra."

"Again?" he said, gliding right over my inversion.

I look at Wifey now. "Atty give you, ride in the hammock?"

She says, "Oh, no," but Dalt about spits out his beer, and Atty reddens, gives me an eye, and I raise up a brow, I think, and smile, almost controlling the head dip to my shoulder.

It's up to him how voluntary he wants to think that was, how much just spastic. He shakes his head, stares, like, *How on earth do you know everything?* and I keep smiling at him.

Izzy knows nothing of this, just keeps smiling away herself, walking the plank. Blindfolded.

"You're husband's quite a carpenter," Wifey says to me.

"He is," I answer, but I wanted, thought I was going to say, *He is quite everything*. I just got edited. I try again, but Leonard says, "And quite a fisherman."

"Maddy could always out fish me," Dalt says. "Though we were about equal on the sticks."

"Oars," I say, seeing their confusion. Hey, check me out again. Just the right word in just the right place.

"Maddy's a river runner of unparalleled abilities," he goes on. "It's what drew me to her in the first place."

"Liar," I say, and the room cools so suddenly you can only wonder what bones the two of them have rattling in their closets. *Run, Iz!* I want to scream. I say, "I was guarding the keg." I meant hoarding.

Dalt explains, leading straight into our wedding story, the dawn float off on the Buffalo, then the last big trip we took, the Canyon, and I catch Iz rolling her eyes at Atty, and Atty, coming to the rescue, says, "Dad, please, *please* tell us you'll let us all watch the video."

"Actually," Dalt says, "I got it transferred to DVD. Every member of the wedding party will get a copy in their gift baskets. Izzy insisted."

"I did no such—"

"Not in so many words, but it was perfectly clear in your gestures, Iz."

Izzy looks stunned, a breath away from mortified. "Dad, really—"

"Kidding," I manage. "Iz. God." I mean, where are you Iz, who has stolen you away?

Atty leaps into the void. "They took this huge trip. Three weeks down the Grand Canyon. Then, when everybody else roared back to their lives, their showers, they tore off for two more weeks down the Rio Grande, solo. They were, only, what, a thousand miles away? How could they not?"

Leonard and Wifey are trying mightily to follow. We're being asshole hosts. Dalt says, "It was a honeymoon."

Iz says, "You'd been married like three years, four."

"Still," I say. "Still." Nothing else comes. Maybe they can figure it out, but my hopes aren't high.

Leonard says, "Still married. Of course."

I smile my ice queen best. "Still," I say, then my word slips away, the first half, something sweet. "Mooning," I say.

Atty says, "Honeymooning. Still on their honeymoon. Still on it now, right, Dad?"

"Damn straight," Dalt says.

Iz rolls her eyes. Aliens have stolen her.

Atty says, "They're the honeymoon champs. It was so embarrassing when we were little. Always all over each other."

I start, but can't get past the S. Sound like some sort of snake.

Dalt finishes for me. "Still are."

I blurt, "Luck," but then get caught in a stammer, and Leonard smiles at me like he's finally understood I'm retarded, and says, "I'm sure it wasn't all luck, a good marriage takes a lot of work." He turns to Iz and Tom. "A lot of hard work."

Tom says, "Dad, do you mind?" and I get distracted wondering if Leonard was *working* on Wifey instead of his own marriage, but I'm not done, luck not all I meant to say, and I pound my good hand on the arm of my chair. People look at me.

Atty says, "It kind of pisses her off if she gets cut off." Then, and I'll always be proud of him for this, he says, "It kind of pisses us all off."

In the silence after that, I say, "Keys."

Leonard just looks away, giving up, but Iz smiles, resurfacing as her old self, and says, "Luck. Keys. Luckies. It's what they call themselves. Mom and Dad. The Luckies. Like superheroes."

Leonard and Wifey look like they wish some superhero would burst through the wall right now, whisk them the hell away from this night.

Dalt looks to Iz and her boy. "We just wish you two could be as happy, as lucky. That such a thing were possible."

"They've long let us know such heights are unattainable," Atty says. "That all we can hope for, try for, is something nearly as good, some pale imitation."

Dalt smiles. "We used up all the luck." He shrugs. "We never could understand moderation as a goal."

I smile beatifically, think, *Though it was nice of you two to save it all for the kids.*

Dalt raises his glass. "To Izzy and Tom. For as close as they can get." He leans down, puts one arm around my shoulder, squeezes, holds his glass to my lips, lets me drink first.

"The Luckies, phase two," Atty says, and I can't help wonder where he came from? Just me and Dalt? We did that?

But Iz. What if this Tom character has even a shred of his father's genes left, somehow, hideously, unmutated? Maybe, for a wedding present, we could get him a tanning booth. Set it on Danger, hope the radiation fries those double helixes, takes him as far from the source as he can get. Iz, so beautiful, so perfect, with this toad? It's a crime.

Then I remember my mother, hearing of our wedding plans, our first visit home to Dayton, introing poor Dalt to the parents. She gawked as if I'd brought the bull straight into the china shop, stood back to watch the destruction. He tucked his arms against his sides, and tacked about, shifting his shoulders, weaving through the knick-knacks and doilies and trinkets. Mom all but slowed down the way she spoke. We snuck out after the dinner, Dalton drawing his first breath of the night, and we hit the bars, showing him off to the few friends I still had from high school. The drinks stacked up all over the place, way too high, and when we finally crawled home, we were in a state, mauling each other on the walk, giggling over Mom and Dad putting us not only in separate bedrooms, but on separate floors, Dalt actually in the basement on Dad's old camping cot. Not exactly the welcome mat, the red carpet.

His hand was up my shirt, mine down his pants, and I was saying, "The cot," but, well, we never made it that far, just kind of slid down the dining room wall, got worked up on the floor. Between kisses, I told him how I used to make forts under the dining room table, castles, and it was all over, we were pushing chairs out of our way, clothing, and next thing we knew we were totally engaged under the dining room table, the princess finally bringing her Prince Charming back to the castle.

And then the hallway light flicks on, and we hear Dad's slippers padding down, turning, shushing on the carpet right past us. He has to move a chair out of his way, for crying out loud. Then the fridge opens, more light spilling out, a little more glow on us.

Dalt's frozen on top of me, whispering, "Maddy?" but I just hug him tighter, and whisper back, "Pie." Mom's cherry pie. Dad can't keep his hands off it. Lot of that going on here. We listen to Dad cut out his slice, a fork clink against a plate, all by the light of the open fridge. I hear the cooler motor kick in and I so want to scream, "Close the door!" the way he would, I almost strangle holding it in.

A stool scrapes across the linoleum in the kitchen, and my eyes widen. He's going to eat it right there, about eight feet away from us. We hardly dare to breathe. We'll suffocate.

Then he says, "I'll just be a minute. Couldn't sleep."

Dalton's eyes bulge straight out of his head. I nearly bite through my lips.

He rinses his plate—only Dad—then, as he pads back by us, he says, "Watch yourselves down there. Your mother got a nasty conk on the head doing that once."

I still don't breathe, but I'm not exactly laughing anymore. Him and Mom? Under here? Doing this? No way. No way in the world.

And Dalton? Well, it kind of kills the mood for him. Useless, he slips out of me, off of me, says, "I got to go."

"Go? Where?"

"Siberia. Tierra del Fuego."

"What?"

"I cannot face him tomorrow. No way in the world."

"You aren't going anywhere, Buster," I tell him.

"But, Mad."

"Don't you get it?" I say. "What he did? He gave himself up for us. We're golden."

"But still, him, tomorrow, knowing he knows I was—"

"You? What about me? I was here too, wasn't I?"

"Okay, okay, that we were—"

"*Were* is right. What happened there? What, exactly, are we going to have to do about that?"

We made it to the cot, a little more privacy. And, right afterward, both of us still panting like wolves, I made a vow to Dalt, told him that no matter what, our kids would never ever not be able to picture us going at it like stoats, not grow up the way I had, figuring Mom and Dad had accidentally, once in their lives, had sex, had me, or maybe gritted their teeth through it in some Catholic way, waited, and breathed a huge sigh of relief when I made my presence apparent—won't have to go through *that* again.

I barely got to my room the next morning before Mom came out to make the coffee, do her bed checks. I knew Dad never told her a thing. Knew it for certain until the night Dalton and I laughed our heads off, me spilling the beans about Atty in his hammock.

God, I miss them.

And now, as a kind of penance, a kind of hope for Izzy, I try to picture her and Tom that way. I almost can't, they just seem so awkward, so, so, I don't know, old or something, so serious, but then, I suddenly can, can see the way Izzy can light up, can see, actually, more than I really want to. I mean, even rodents know that game. But I hope it means as much to them as it always did for me and Dalt, that Tom never once thought he was just getting laid, never once thought anything other than that he was receiving the greatest gift any man was ever offered, that he thinks of himself as every fucking bit as lucky as I did with Dalt, as Dalt did with me. Even luckier.

Realizing I've put that all in past tense, me and Dalt, I look around for him, find we're all at the table, that people are eating, that Dalt's already cut my salmon for me, which is just ridiculous, nobody needs to cut salmon, but, instead of reaching for my fork, I reach for Dalt's hand, get his wrist. I can't see. My eyes all misted over. This shit happens. Another thing I can't control. I wonder how long I've been missing in action, if my head's lolled, if I've drooled, twitched, yipped. Jesus.

I glance around the table, stop on Iz and this kid of hers. I'm sorry for being such a bitch, I want to say. Sorry for that whole, *you'll never be as lucky as us* game we've played your whole lives. What kind of asshole would ever do that to their own kids? Of course you'll be as lucky. Luckier. Way luckier. Because, I mean, just look at you. You're perfect. Nothing will ever happen to you you don't foresee, don't want, aren't striving for. How could anything bad ever happen to the two of you? The very idea is preposterous.

I try. I lift my fork, but it only clinks on the edge of my plate. I don't want to be this way, but we had this perfect life and now this blundering dolt, this effing Seabiscuit, is stealing us away. Does he even realize what he's doing, what he's getting? I squeeze my fork tighter. If I try a single bite I know I'll choke, and I wonder if that would be a bad thing.

Dalt leans over me, searching my face. "Bath," I murmur, and he knows the rest. *Get me out of here before I explode.* I want to shout warnings at them, tell them it's all a job they'll never know how to do, that things will come rolling down the pike that, if they could see them now, would send them screaming for the exits, scrambling razors to their wrists.

But Dalt is already excusing us, pushing me down the hall to my bathroom, all my goddamn handicap shit, the fucking chrome bars, lipless shower stall, and when we get in, I clutch at his arm, draw him into as much a hug as I have left and say, "We have to warn them, Dalt. We have to, to, to, to tell them."

"What, Mad? Warn them about what?"

"I don't," I say. "Life."

"How great it is?"

"Yeah, exactly what, I was thinking."

He takes a knee in front of my chair, holds my chin in his hand, looks me in the eye. It's so something I can see him doing with the kids when they were little. Ordinarily, I'd bop him for something like that, but now?

"I'll go tell them," he says, "to watch out for happiness. Tell them how it can blindside you, take your breath away, leave you only hoping for more. Is that what you want?"

I smile, not something that comes easily this time, and say, "Exactly. It's something, they should, prepare for."

"Of course they should," he says. "We raised her, didn't we?"

I try grabbing his hand, get it on the first shot, hold it way more fiercely than I did Poppa Jackasses. "We did," I say.

"You need to pee?" he says, "or was that just some diversion?"

"I need you," I say.

"Here?" he says with a smile. "Now?"

And, if things had worked out differently, we'd be doing it right here and now, the guests wondering, our kids so knowing, so staring down at their plates, so aware that one glance at each other and it would be all over, all the wrong kinds of stories for polite dinner conversation tumbling out. I say, "No, dope." I shake my head, hope he understands. "The Taimen. Get up, in that hammock."

He says, "Aye, aye, cap'n," and then kisses me, a real one, right on the lips. And though that sense is long gone, I taste wine now, and salmon, lemon, garlic and dill, and as I close my eyes, taste all of him, I'm sure I find smoke from all our campfires, even a little grit from the sand of the Canyon, and there is Izzy and Atty, and every other golden thing we have ever done, and my fingers go through his hair as he tries to come up for breath, and I pull him back, whisper, "There'll, none of that." He's on his knees on the tiles he lay in here a decade ago, and I am half pulled out of my chair, and we're having a make-out sesh in my handicap bathroom, and why my eyes mist now I know exactly, and I have no plans of ever letting go.

Keeper Hole

"I'LL BE," I say, "shoveling dirt over you, long, ever before, you beat me, ever at this game." It's a veritable speech, and so close to totally intelligible, I grin across the table at him.

Dalt shrugs, likes he's not so sure, as close as he can get to a poker face. He would absolutely suck at poker. He has, I know, been lowering his cognitive test scores for years. He knows I know. I always go first, so he knows exactly how poorly he has to do. We never act this way, but it's just so, so transparent or something, so stupid for stupid's sake, that it's okay, and there's nothing else about this that is.

But, it's not easy watching him struggle to come up with only seven words that begin with C, and when the sixth is cemetery, I can't help a laugh. It's the shoveling dirt that took him there, but still, cemetery? "Not even C *sound*," I say.

"Still a C," he says. "Still counts."

The timer goes off, and he cries, "Cheater! You distracted me. The home team lodges an official protest."

"Home town?" I say, and he shrugs, looks for what's next on his list from the therapist. *Count* and *cheater*. Eight and nine. He doesn't mention them if he notices.

"Dalt," I say, and I must sound bad, the way he turns to look at me, that *You okay?* teetering on the edge of his lips. But cemetery's taken me to something I've wanted to bring up for a long time, just can't ever remember to. "Dropping dirt," I get out, swallow, think through the next syllables. "No."

He kind of smiles, raises an eyebrow.

"Crem," I say. "Cream, cre . . ." I thump myself on the forehead. "Fuck. Burn."

"Cremate?" he says, glancing for exits, a corner to back into.

I nod, hold up my hand, trying to tell him to calm down. "When. No burying."

"But I thought—"

I keep my hand up, waving it, slow down. I look like a cop at the Special Olympics. "Dalt," I say, then wait for my breath. "I am so. So sick this body. Bury me with, I'll kill you."

He nods, not like he wants to, but he gets it. Hell, a two-year-old would get this. But then he smiles, shakes his head, and I think I've missed the mark. He says, "Only you, Mad. Only you ever, would threaten to kill someone for burying you incorrectly."

I smile. My head flashes to the side. Shit. A bad one. Two, three, four times. "I'd," I start, five, six. "Do it," I finish.

"Okay," he says, "okay," and I know I've put too much stress on it, subtlety of tone and inflection one more thing of my past.

He resets the timer, says, "Thirteen animals, sixty seconds."

It's such a dodge, such an obvious change of subject, I say, "Ass," and he says, "One."

I laugh. "Horse's," I say, and he says, "Two."

We're good at this. But I get *cat*, a complete rip off from the C-word list, and one other zooms in from left field, *steelhead*, I think, because I can see him smile, though already I can't remember the word I just said. A fish, I know, and suddenly I'm off on fish, all the ones we used to chase. I see their spots aglow, their ruddy gill plates, their pale bellies, even the tiny flies they came up to, how one hooked into the very tip of a jaw could so alter their lives. But their names, every one, dance away on their currents. The one on the mantel, though, the only kind I've never actually seen alive, I know that one. "Tie," I say, "Tie."

"Tiger," Dalt finishes with a glance at the timer. "I'll give you that one."

I shake my head, pound at the table. "N, n, n, no!" Sometimes this game is less than fun, no matter how hard we try. "Tie!"

He bends down to look at me as I lower my head in concentration.

"Man," I say, lifting my face to beam at him.

He scratches out a mark, only my fourth, and the timer dings, and he says, "Figures you'd count man as an animal."

"Tie, man," I say, and he gets it at last.

"Extra credit," he says. "Endangered species." Which is a lie, I think, but he makes the diagonal. Five.

"Don't," I start, but though I see the word *patronize* clearly enough, the very idea of getting it routed all the way down to my tongue is too much to consider.

Dalt knows though, and erases the slash, says, "Four. More than I'll ever get anyway."

Watching him choke out sixty seconds and come up with nothing more than *Felis concolor*, *Castor canadensis*, and *Ursus horribilis*, is, well, just pathetic. I've married a moron. We're dying laughing though. Even my laugh scares me anymore, some weird screech seeping into it. Latin names? He can kiss my ass. Showoff.

We get through the day's regimen, an exercise I'm never quite sure about, if it's supposed to keep me sharp, or just catalogue my decline. Either way, if Dalt hadn't invented the game, I'd never do it again. Relentless as a river, this shit slows for nothing other than what it wants to, those sweet spots where the gradient levels out, those calm pools where you catch your breath between the rapids, can barely believe you're still breathing at all.

Dalt slips everything back into the folder, dodging it down onto what used to be Atty's chair. The house reeks of their absence. Will always. I have days when I just wheel my silent chair around in my old routines without knowing what I'm doing, days I roll out onto the porch at exactly 3:20, look down the block toward the high school for minutes before I realize they aren't coming. That they're gone. That they have been for years. And years. Izzy, being Iz, calls all the time, no schedule for me to hope for, just these random bursts I live for anyway, schedule or not. She claims to love Phoenix, the world's most water-starved city. Toad boy—I love that I can never remember his name—got the bank manager job there. Whoopee. "Fee-nucks?" I always say, going all guttural, like Hungarian is my native language, like I'm trying to scrape shit off my tongue, more lingual exercise. She sighs, say, "Yes, Mom, they haven't changed the name of the city yet, though they appreciate your letters." On good days, when the words pour free, I try to tell her about the bird, flying up out of the ashes. Sometimes I get through the whole story, and then have to rein myself in before I go all the way, tell her it's my hope for her that Toad boy will burst into flame, spontaneously combust, and she'll be able to fly free. If not back to us, at least back to water somewhere, way the hell away from anybody who lives in a bank, a bank in the fricking desert. Give us back our old Iz. Dalt's only comment is that Phoenix isn't that far from the Grand Canyon.

Atty, being At, goes long stretches without a word, a clue, as if Corvallis were light years away. Month to month, we're not even sure what he does.

Now Dalt says, "There's something else," and I swoop my head low, pretending huge annoyance, as he pulls out Izzy's chair, lifts another folder from where it's been hidden there. My annoyance grows real. If he's been in to the clinic on his own again, coming up with some new gambit, I'll scream. "No," I say. Regressing to childhood seems to be MS's new thing, *No,* my favorite word again.

Dalt gets it of course. Always tuned to me, he's become nothing short of miraculous during these bad stretches, where staggering speech gets to be an Olympic event, me the current gold medalist. "It's not more work," he says. Work. Like, after all these years, decades, I'm finally employable. I can just imagine the line of employers stretching down the sidewalk, begging for my services.

Dalt splays the folder's contents out before me like a deck of cards, like a magician asking me to pick one, any one. I glance down, my head rocking just enough to make the words hard to pick up. I rest my chin on my good hand, but it's still a moment before I sort out the letters, make them line up, can see what the words really and truly say. Union pension papers. Retirement fund figures. I look up.

"I've been talking to Tom," he says, like he's admitting keeping porno mags under the mattress.

"Tom?" I say.

"Izzy's Tom," he says, then, "Toad?"

I stare.

He points back to his papers. "We can do it. Pull it off."

"What?"

"Retirement."

"When?"

"Now."

We both sit there and breathe for a few seconds. I stick my bad hand between my thighs. "What would you do?"

"Do?" he says. "I'll do whatever the hell we want."

Straight from I to we. I love that.

He inches out another folder, but not a folder, more a brochure, glossy. I have to tip it up to get the glare off of it. A travel agent's sale pitch for the isles of Greece.

"It's not the Colorado," he says, "but there's water everywhere."

For Christ's sake, it takes me two tries just to get out, "Really?"

"I've been giving him some money. He's done pretty well with it."

"Toad?"

He nods and shakes his head about the name at the same time. "And this place," he waves his arm around. "If we ever want to move. We're sitting on a gold mine."

"Our house?" I say. "Give it, Toad. If he brings, brings . . . back. Izzy back."

Dalt smiles, and nods. "Put a crimp in our retirement."

"Ef," I say. "Retire. Mint."

We spend the rest of the afternoon making plans. Greece. All those white ruins. Marble guys with no arms, no noses. I could give them a run for their money. Turquoise water. Really, I'd rather go to Alaska. We used to talk about that all the time. The rivers there, the salmon, the bears, *Ursus horribilis*, but I don't tell Dalton that. I mean, after all, we used to plan so much. We'll save Alaska for next. Maybe a cruise up the inland passage.

Now Dalt says something about Corfu, one of the islands, and it's a word I latch onto, for no reason I could ever explain, just something that slides down the myelin sheath as if greased and polished. "Cor-foo," I say over and over, until Dalton begins to laugh. "Corfu it is then."

ॐ   ॐ   ॐ

IT'S ONLY A few weeks later when he comes in with the check. Everything he got selling Half Moon Construction. "No turning back now," he says as I blink at the computer printing. But the 0s are still there. All of them. "It's for real," he says. "We *can* give Iz the house."

"Only if she, leaves, Toad."

"Toad," he says, then corrects himself. "Tom, Maddy. Tom, has been very good to us. And he worships Iz."

"Who," I say, "wouldn't?"

He tells me I'm awful, which makes me smile. But, then, I bring up the thing we've stepped all around. "Greece," I say. "After. Really. You all day?" Not at my best, it's a second before I can add, "Do?"

He starts his usual, "Whatever you want, we want," spiel, but I say, sharp and clear, "Really!"

He blinks. "Really."

"You," I say, "Can't sit, still. Never. Could."

"I can work around here."

"What, is, left?"

He has to think on that one. "I could build that widow walk."

I stare.

"Redo Atty's room. If we sell, I'm not sure the pirate motif is really going to bring in any extra dollars."

"Touch it," I say, "you die."

"Walk the plank, eh?"

I nod my head, wave my hook, and am actually able to control it when I feel the head snap coming on. It makes me smile.

"We'll be okay, Maddy," he says to me. "Can you imagine, all that time together again? We can drink coffee for hours. Stay in bed. Nap."

Without knowing it, he's pretty much described my standard day. But with him here, if he doesn't go crazy, they'll be days I'll look forward to again.

He's excited enough he takes off to double check everything with the travel agent. He doesn't say so, but I know he's making sure every inch will be wheelchair accessible. He'd pave Greece for me if he could.

He's so excited, Greece paving or no, he forgets to leave anything for lunch. Stays out far longer than I'd thought. I could call, beep him, but, Jesus, I can still make a sandwich. In fact, all bluster and dare, I put lettuce on top of my ham. "Check you out," I say, all in one breath. "Chez Madeline."

I get so worked up about this resurgence of my superpowers I don't even think to cut it up into the tiny finger sandwich hors d'ouvres Dalt leaves me with. To tell the truth, I've kind of always hated that.

I don't make it past my first bite.

When the air stops, I first look around, like, I don't know, someone somewhere has pinched a hose or something, my watering interrupted, Atty's smile, his hair all down in his eyes. Then I drop my sandwich. Going, I guess, back to instinct, to some lizard part of my brain geared for nothing more than brute survival, I clutch at my throat with my bad hand, feel it tapping there, slapping.

Fireworks begin shooting off, red, stars, but I fight myself like I'm at the top of the gnarliest of the Class Vs I've ever seen, tamp back the fear, think, be all smooth moves and clean lines. I grab the control stick with my left hand, my good one, and gun it straight into full speed reverse, knowing the wall's back there.

But the crash dislodges nothing. I go forward, slapping at my chest with my bad hand while I work the controls like a fighter pilot with my good. I even manage a glance behind me, make sure I've got the wall lined up, touch my toes to the near wall, giving myself all the acceleration potential I've got. I slam into reverse and close my eyes, trying to hide the moment of impact, not brace against it, but let it bounce out this one single harmless bite.

I only hit the wall with one wheel, maybe. My guess. The chair spins, teeters, tips, spilling me across the floor. I open my eyes, but the redness is there now for good, the room swimming. I flipped under a boat once, I remember, from somewhere, came up under that unforgiving black rubber floor, the world nothing but white foam, water supersaturated with oxygen but unbreathable all the same. That same roar fills my ears now. I grab myself around the middle, try to remember Dalt's lessons to the kids, where to push, but even my good hand barely sags into my soft abdomen.

The kids, I think, and feel the sting, the heat, of my pee letting loose. It's become something of a problem for me.

And, Jesus, Dalt. Coming home to find me like this?

I thrash my useless fucking legs, ropes of saliva slinging up across my cheeks, an eye, like just enough lubrication will get that damn thing to slide down. I can still smell, the pee, and god, please tell me I haven't shit myself. Not again.

I feel my mouth gaping like some poor fish tossed on the bank, a whitefish doomed to die for no crime worse than being undesired, and as the room darkens, I see, up above the mantel, my old nemesis the taimen, his face still broken, looking off over me with his crazy eye.

Undesired, I think. No. Not me. Not ever. No matter how I have felt, that has never happened to me. I have been so loved. So lucky.

My body stills, calms, even the twitching, and I can't help thinking, *At last.* I lie on my side, gazing up at Dalton's fish. Ours. I wish I had something to write with, some vein to open, to scrawl not "I'm sorry," because Dalt would kill me for that, but something quick, "Lu-lu," maybe, something only Dalt would know, not the ambulance guys, not the coroner, only Dalt. Just his, in private. And he has known that. Does know that.

God, Dalt. I do.

Buffalo Fork

I DO NOT have a balance problem. Or never did before. So I'm not sure why Atty and Iz hover beside me as we work our way down the hill. Nor have I ever had any real memory dysfunction, no matter my scores on all those cognitive tests I lost to Mad. So, when Atty glances the way I point, up at the empty grassy hill where Mad and I answered our own lines with my ridiculous, "It is my strongest desire," and tells me, "Dad, we know, we've been here before. With Mom. Remember?" I say, "I know that. I know that. I'm just—" I have to wipe at my forehead, pinch the bridge of my nose. "I'm just remembering, At. That's all."

"You okay, Dad?" Izzy asks. She's at my other arm, the two of them insistent about helping me down this hill I've all but flown down before.

"Golden," I answer. "Totally golden."

Before we reach the bottom, I work my arm away from Iz. The other from Atty. Not that I can't use their touch. Good god, no. But, what would Maddy think, me tottering down this hill like an old man? And if I even think of crying, she is seriously going to kick my ass. She never could . . . Oh hell. I'm not really at all sure I can do this.

Atty says, "You want me to take it?"

He's reached out his hand, holds it open to me.

The urn, he means, the ashes. It. Isn't that just right? "All those bastards," I say. "The one's with their gods."

"What?" Izzy asks.

"They've got it so easy," I say.

"That's why they invented them," Atty says, only giving back what we taught them, what, really, I truly, truly believe, but, man oh man, I am envious right now, so envious of those ignorant masses. To see Maddy again? For an eternity? My heart nearly stops at the idea, and if I could, I'm not sure I wouldn't will it to go the rest of the way. Me back with Maddy, Maddy whole and healthy? But no god would ever do this to me, take her away. And Maddy? I nearly stagger. What savage kind of a god would have ever done what he did to her? I'd kill the fucker in a second if I could. My own two hands never better employed.

Atty still has his hand out. I say, "No. Don't be ridiculous. We've come so far together. You think I can't make the last yards?"

"I just thought," he starts, but lets it drift off on the river breeze. We're there.

"We," I say, then clear my throat. "We put the boat in right here. Maddy was still up on the hill. Hugging her parents. I climbed back up for her." I can't help a chuckle. "Wound up ferrying her mother down instead."

"You guys told us, Dad," Atty says. "When we came down here when we were in high school. I couldn't—"

"Atty," Iz says, and he takes it just like the kick in the shins it is.

"Years later she told me that while we drifted into the fog she was just sure one of our buddies would lob out a torch." I shake my head, clutch at the urn more than I'd like to let on. "I wish we could have done that for her. Set her afloat like some Viking queen. She'd have loved that."

"Light the whole park on fire," Atty says. "The ranger's would be all over that."

Izzy lets go with niceties and just rears back and wallops him one on the shoulder. "You," she says, "are such an ass," and if there's one point where I might just turn to dust, that's it, seeing Maddy in this perfect re-creation of her, one that would make her so proud. How many times she said that to me, laughing, shaking her head, punching me that same way. Once in a while really meaning it. I stare hard into the willows, pick out each spear point leaf, follow it back along its stem to the branch. Count them. Work on breathing. "Okay," I say. "Ready?"

Even Atty looks shaken then, but he nods, and Izzy says, "How do we do it?"

I laugh, just a short sad bark of a thing, but I picture Maddy watching us, thinking, *Now you think about it?*

I don't have the first idea what to do. This was never the plan, nothing I ever pictured. She was always shoveling the dirt over me. Always. It was the way it was supposed to be.

I know, if you look at it under the scope, this way is for the best. How would she keep going along alone? Not that I was ever indispensable. She once told me she could replace me with a fairly well trained dog. I can't even remember what I'd fucked up that time. We laughed so hard. It was the fairly that did it. So Mad. She called me Rover for a week.

But, microscopes, they always miss the truth. Show me one of those doctors who ever saw the real Mad. She could have done this. I am just not strong enough. This, here, this way, it's just all wrong. Completely.

Iz touches my back. My god, I almost think it's Maddy, that tuned to when I'm going to break. She says, "Dad?"

"Hell, Iz," I say, "I don't know. I don't know what to do. Hold out your hands?"

They both cup their hands together, like I'm going to pour in something liquid, something invaluable, and I uncap the urn and before I let myself think, I shake out the ashes, into Atty's hands first, then Izzy's, the same order she gave them their lives. "Save some for yourself," Iz says, and I say, "Oh, sweet pea, I'm saving her all."

"Do we count to three or something?" Atty asks, and I wonder that Izzy lets him live through it.

I say, "No, I don't think we need to synchronize watches or anything." I swallow. "Just whenever you're ready, just, I don't know, when you feel a breeze that will carry her, or just . . . Just when you're ready."

Izzy goes first, sifting the gray stuff down through her beautiful fingers, leaning so it lands on the river, takes off, sinks in. Atty kind of lofts her up, onto the wind, lets her settle where she will.

I pour the rest into my own hand, drop the urn as the worthless, empty vessel it is, and squeeze. I can't stop myself. I can't let go. I can't. "Ah, Mad," I breathe. At and Iz aren't looking at me, just watching their own little projects.

With my left hand I reach out and force back the fingers of my right, a move I watched Mad do how many times? "There you go," I say. "Full circle, or what?"

The ash doesn't drift out of my hand. It's gritty and sticks to my skin, lines the creases and cuts. I shake it a little, spread my fingers, say, one last time, "There you go, Mad. We'll be okay."

I want to tell them, At and Iz, her children, every detail of every day since the moment we pushed off this shore together. But, really, we already have, so many times they tease us about it. When I pulled in behind the Heart Six this morning, the DeGroots gone for decades, not even a flash of recognition across the new owner's face, I showed them where the Coop used to be, and Atty said, "You guys stayed in that luxury condo A-frame?" and Iz clocked him one, said, "No, ass, don't you even remember the Coop? The loft? The stars on the shingles?"

"What?" Atty said.

I stared at Izzy, who only glanced at me, then quickly away. "Girls tell each other things," she said.

"Of course you do," I said. "Maddy told me everything." *There are no secrets in this house.* How many times had I heard that? Her biggest lie ever. How she worked at keeping it all secret, all her pain, her frustration, her tears. Nothing but her love, no secret there. No effing secret at all. More than any of us could ever use in a lifetime.

"You okay?" Izzy asks, and I blink, look over at her.

"Sure, Iz, we're good, eh?"

She smiles, nods, whispers, "Golden," and reaches to take my hand as I turn away from the water, Atty's quiet, "Bye, Mom," cutting what little's left of my heart straight out of my chest. Behind me I see the braided streams flowing away from us, through their snags and jams, dropping into their falls and their eddies, always out toward the scent of the sea, a path I was once young enough to be sure I knew by heart, that I used to be able to float by starlight, Mad picking out the bad stuff for me, guiding me through.

Without trying to be obvious, I pretend I don't see Izzy's hand. I glance down at my own, hardened and work scarred, virtually useless now for anything but swinging a hammer, clutching a board, and I see the last gray traces of her clinging there, caught in the deep runs of my flesh, and I don't want anybody, not even Izzy, brushing those away just yet. No. Not just yet.

Pete Fromm is a four-time winner of the Pacific Northwest Booksellers Literary Award for the novels *As Cool As I Am* and *How All This Started*, a story collection, *Dry Rain*, and a memoir, *Indian Creek Chronicles*. The film version of *As Cool As I Am,* starring Claire Danes, James Marsden, and Sarah Bolger, was released in June of 2013. He is the author of four other short story collections and has published over two hundred stories in magazines. A core faculty member at Pacific University's Low Residency MFA Program, he has a degree in wildlife biology from the University of Montana and worked for years as a river ranger in Grand Teton National Park. He lives with his family in Montana, where he can often be seen walking underneath his canoe to the river.

You can visit his website at www.petefromm.com.